Romance in the Spotlight

With all the attention focused on celebrity hook-ups and break-ups these days, we thought it would be exciting to publish a series of novels about love and the pressures of Hollywood fame, which we call **Romance in the Spotlight.**

In this year's summer series, we asked some of romance's bestselling authors to pen stories of love, intrigue and sizzling romance set against the backdrop of tabloid media and Hollywood.

Last month we kicked off the summer series with *Just the Man She Needs,* by Gwynne Forster, which tells the story of two high-profile yet private people, who reluctantly find themselves the subjects of intense publicity. In *Celluloid Memories,* this month's title from Sandra Kitt, a savvy screenwriter finds herself on the brink of success as she tries to unravel a family secret. In August, *Love, Lies & Videotape,* by Kayla Perrin, tells the story of a young actress on the verge of big-time success, and who is plagued by an unseemly videotape from her past. We wrap up the series in September with Donna Hill's *Moments Like This,* a story about an established actress looking to make the ultimate comeback.

We hope you enjoy *Celluloid Memories,* and be sure to look for the other titles in the **Romance in the Spotlight** series. We welcome your comments and feedback, and invite you to send us an e-mail at www.kimanipress.com.

Enjoy,

Evette Porter
Editor, Arabesque

SANDRA Kitt

Celluloid Memories

CELLULOID MEMORIES

An Arabesque novel

ISBN-13: 978-0-373-83015-7
ISBN-10: 0-373-83015-2

www.kimanipress.com

Printed in U.S.A.

To all my L.A. crew, who believe in and encourage
The Impossible Dreams.

Acknowledgments

Many thanks to Katherine Richards for her wonderful friendship, and for giving me a place to stay; to CB for the studio tour *then,* and your friendship and wisdom *now;* to Dennis Considine, who was a true believer; Laurie Hutzler who shared the dreams; Donna Brown Guillaume for always saying hello; Donald Welsh for inspiration; and all the others who laid the foundation and a path for me to follow.

A special thanks to Steve Heimberg for making the Hawaiian adventure possible and providing a fitting end to my story. Mahalo.

Dear Reader,

There is a line in the song, "Happy Talk," from the stage play and movie *South Pacific* that goes "if you never have a dream, then you'll never have a dream come true." Hollywood has always been a place for dream making, and I've had my share of reaching for the stars there, meeting a lot of wonderful people along the way. I hope you'll enjoy the turn of events in *Celluloid Memories,* which will prove to you why you should *never* give up on what you believe in, and *never* take no for an answer. Life is filled with surprises; go out and find your own.

Remember also that as you give, so shall you receive. I have been blessed in realizing so many of my dreams, and now I take part in actively giving to help others. I have been involved for some time with St. Jude Children's Hospital in Memphis, and I'm working on a book project to benefit St. Jude that is scheduled for release in the summer of 2008. Visit my Web site for more details on this worthy project, and for suggestions as to how you can help, as well.

Happy reading,

Sandra Kitt
sandikitt@hotmail.com

Prologue

Through the open front door of the house, Savannah Shelton watched the first car of house hunters arrive. The real estate agent, a statuesque sistah in torturous high heels, bodacious attire, oversized sunglasses and an even bigger California smile, gave her a thumbs-up as she turned to greet the approaching buppie couple.

Savannah took a deep breath, feeling a combination of surprise and annoyance. It seemed to her that the couple had wasted no time in responding to the advertised open house. Real estate in any part of Los Angeles's vast counties was coveted, but the speed at which they'd arrived to view the property was unseemly, she thought.

She equated their presence to lawyers who were ambulance chasers.

Her father's agent, Simon Raskin, who'd known and had worked closely with him for more than thirty years, had not weighed in one way or another. He'd only expressed the opinion that Hollywood needed more men like Will Shelton, and he hoped that one day he'd get the recognition he deserved.

Savannah was a little surprised by how disagreeable she was feeling about the open house that she herself had requested. It had seemed a good idea at the time. She glanced around the small foyer, which opened onto a spacious but low-ceilinged living room, and couldn't find a thing out of place. It was neat and clean. The agent had suggested putting away anything personal, including all photographs that could be used to identify the house owner, Will Shelton. The rooms were comfortably furnished, but not expensive or extravagant. For the open house, the agent had added a few plants at the last minute that would make the property seem homey and less like a showroom or historic site.

She watched as the agent greeted the arriving couple, throwing open the entranceway even farther. Savannah decided to make herself scarce. She walked back through the hallway into the kitchen, then out the back door to the yard, where her father had managed to squeeze in a decent-sized inground pool. Savannah opened another door to the high wrought-iron fence, and found herself at the side of the house, about forty or fifty feet from the front door. The couple had already disappeared inside with the agent.

Savannah put on her sunglasses, until now worn across the top of her head of short and naturally coifed hair, and crossed the quiet street to the other side. She turned at the corner onto a main thoroughfare. It was Sunday but there was little traffic. She stopped outside a café where there were a half-dozen bistro tables, some occupied by local residents who were reading the papers while drinking their low-fat, double-decaf lattes. Savannah sat herself at a table that allowed her a reasonable view of her father's small Mediterranean-style house a block and a half away. Two more cars had arrived.

"What can I get you?"

She quickly glanced up at the interruption. "Lemonade will be fine, if you have it."

"We sure do. Anything else?"

Antacid tablets, Savannah considered. She grimaced at the disturbing roiling of her stomach. "A toasted English muffin. Thanks."

When the young black waiter left, she turned her attention once more to the view down the street to her father's house. She'd always been surprised that in this upscale black neighborhood where the average house seemed big enough to accommodate two or more families, her father's home was so modest. It was clearly an older structure, probably built in the 1950s, but beautifully detailed, which actually made it stand out from its more contemporary neighbors. There was definitely a sense of place and history about it. It looked very Californian. All the rooms were on one level, although there was a dormer, and the detached garage had a second story. It had been space enough for one man living alone. It had easily accommodated her when she'd moved in with her father, eighteen months before.

Savannah adjusted her sunglasses, dismissing old history and recent memories and more recent losses. She didn't feel so much sad as numbed by the passing of her father. Given the infrequency that he'd seen her or her brother over the years, it was a wonder she felt anything at all. Moving in to care for him, however, when he had become seriously ill had been the right thing to do. She knew that. Yet his passing had left her in a time warp, with the imprint of a once handsome and charismatic man brought low by disease and age, shrunk by hard times, ever-changing trends, and loneliness. He'd been for too long in her memory, less her father than Will Shelton the actor.

"Here you are," the waiter said, placing a small round tray in front of her with her order.

"Thanks," Savannah smiled vaguely. But, once alone again, she wasn't inclined to eat anything. She was suddenly afraid that if she did she'd throw up.

She became aware that a couple two tables away was casually discussing the open house, as they shared sections of the paper and talked about the party they'd been to the night before.

"What do you think it'll go for?" the woman asked,

smoothing her hair, enhanced with extensions, behind her ear.

It suddenly struck Savannah that the well-cared-for woman was like a brown version of Joan Collins.

"Probably more than it's really worth," the man said. His heels popped out of his Kenneth Cole sandals as he pressed on the balls of his feet. He sipped his coffee and suddenly chuckled silently to himself.

"What?" she smiled in curiosity, already anticipating a good story.

"Hank said it would make a good starter home for his daughter."

"Allison? She's still in school, isn't she?"

"She'll graduate Stanford in April. Hank was thinking graduation gift. She has to live somewhere."

"Let her move back home," the woman suggested. "It's not like Hank and Carla don't have the room."

"I know, but I think they like having an empty nest. Having one of the kids return home might cramp their new social life."

Savannah let the conversation drift away and began picking at the English muffin and sipping on the lemonade, when her mouth became dry. An odd thickness in the back of her throat felt as if the passageway to her breathing was closing.

More cars had arrived. Two young men pulled up on a motorcycle. No one seemed to be leaving the house, but soon those already there were coming out front to look back at the property, to take in the whole view and the way the house sat back a little from the sidewalk. There was no formal driveway, except for the one leading into the garage. The front door of the house was partially protected by trees and shrubbery, giving it a secluded, private feel. Savannah had liked that about the house. The landscaping didn't allow people to notice it right away.

Her cell phone rang and she dug it out from her purse.

"Hello?"

"Hey, Vann. How's it going?"

"Hi, Harris. I don't know. I had to leave."

"Leave? Where to?"

"Just a block or so away. There was nothing for me to do after people started arriving. I didn't want to stand around watching strangers go through the house. It made me uncomfortable. I'm at a nearby café."

"Aren't you at least curious about who's interested in the property?"

"I can pretty much see the front of the house. There are a lot of people stopping to go inside. There must be a dozen folks roaming about right now."

"That's a good sign. I told you there was no need to worry. You'll probably get more than one offer and the house will sell quickly."

"Harris? Are you sure you're okay with this? You haven't had any time to come out and look through Daddy's things."

"Not interested," her brother said firmly. "It's nothing

against our father, but L.A.'s too messed up. It's not a real world. I'm not interested in living there. And I already have a house."

"The weather's nice," Savannah coaxed with a half smile. Harris laughed. "Whatever it goes for, you know you get half."

"Don't worry about me. You're the one that gave up everything to go out there and take care of the old man. I wasn't angry with him, Vann, but I don't think I would have done that. Whatever the house goes for, maybe it will help you move back to New York if that's what you want."

"You say that now, but if it sells for a million or more…"

"If it sells for that much, you'll be hearing from me."

Savannah allowed herself a quiet laugh.

"I know this must be really hard for you," her brother said in a more sober tone. "First Trey, a few years ago, and now Dad."

She swallowed hard and cleared her throat. "Trey was different. His death was an accident."

"Sorry I wasn't there to help you out with Dad."

"I'm okay with it. You have your career and family to think about. I didn't think the state department was going to give you a leave of absence for almost two years just because your father was ill. At least you were able to make the service."

"I should thank you for being there through it all."

"It's not like I really had a choice," Savannah said.

"You could have ignored Dad's phone call. You could have hung up on him, contacted a nursing home or hospice for him."

"Think I've earned my place in heaven?" Savannah asked dryly.

"Have you forgiven him, Vann?"

She shifted in her chair. Her lemonade was watered down with the melting ice. The English muffin was also not as appetizing now that it was cold.

"I don't know."

Harris wished her luck with the selling of their father's house, but he certainly didn't sound sentimentally attached, or sad about the inevitable outcome. They'd both learned, growing up with mostly their mother to raise them, how to move on. Harris had learned in the military that sometimes things are what they are. Not a lot of explanation, so no point in getting torn up about what couldn't be changed. Savannah hung up from the call knowing that, for her, it was a different story.

She left some bills to pay for her food and reluctantly started back toward the house. The front looked as though a party was going on. There were people everywhere. Someone had brought their dog, and not the lap kind that fit neatly in a carrier. People were comparing notes, taking pictures of the property from different angles. She watched as a middle-aged woman covertly broke a small branch of blossoms from a bougainvillea and stuffed it deep into her tote bag. Another woman had the nerve to arrange herself on the small side lawn to have her photograph taken with the house in the background.

Savannah made her way through the group and up the walkway to the door. The agent was standing just inside.

"There you are," she said in whispered relief, grabbing Savannah's arm and pulling her to the side. "Can you believe this?" She waved an arm to take in the crowd. "The response has been over the top. We've already had two offers."

"Wow," Savannah said, for want of a better response.

"There's a bunch of other folks duking it out in the kitchen. If they all want the house bad enough the bidding could top the asking price. That's fabulous!" the agent nearly squealed, visions of dollar signs dancing in her head.

Savannah tried to speak, and couldn't. Something was still lodged in her throat. Something else sat heavily across her chest. "Could you excuse me for a minute?" She didn't wait for an answer. She rushed toward the back of the house.

The door to what had been her father's room was open, but no one was inside. She stopped in the doorway and looked in. It was a nice bedroom with good solid, California furnishings, decidedly masculine and spare. Savannah only saw it as the room where her father had spent much of his time toward the end. Across the hall was the room she'd used since coming to L.A. to take care of him. That's how she referred to it, the room she used. Not *my* room.

The afghan she used to spread over his knees when he complained of being cold was now carefully draped over the arm of the easy chair in the corner of the room. Although there was no sign of his bathrobe and slippers, his books or albums or daily regimen of industry trades, and none of the many prescription bottles, Savannah could still see it all, and him, filling the space with his life and memories.

"It's a trip, right? I can't believe I'm actually inside Will Shelton's house," someone said at her elbow, startling her.

Savannah turned to find a young man dressed in a black T-shirt and jeans, sandals, a baseball cap with the Dodgers logo on the front. Everything about him said graduate student, production assistant or film school.

"Who's Will Shelton?" she couldn't resist asking.

"Black actor from the seventies. He was kind of a cult star among some folks, especially black film buffs."

"How do you know this is his house?"

He looked at her as if she was an idiot. "'Cause if you're in the business you always check out the city records on who owned what, when," he said. "You always know especially where *we* live. This is a famous house."

"He wasn't famous," Savannah helpfully supplied.

"That depends on who you ask," the young man said. "Maybe Will Shelton wasn't like Denzel or even Sydney, but he was good. Never got his due, but the man could act." He started to walk away but stopped to look at her with curiosity. "You thinking of making an offer?"

"Why do you want to know?"

"Curious about my competition. I probably can't afford this place by myself, but some buddies and me are going in together. We're looking at it as an investment property. But, to actually live in the same house that Will Shelton lived in…"

Leaving the sentence open, he shook his head in wonder and walked away. The thought came to her that it sounded like he wanted to turn her father's home into a glorified frat house. Pensive, Savannah headed back to the front of the house.

People were still arriving. The open house had turned into a home invasion. One couple was arguing because she thought the house too small. Yet another complained that it didn't have enough curb appeal. And, as it turned out, quite a few who'd arrived were just tourists. They attended open houses the way some people visit museums. They were voyeurs on other people's lives and property with no intentions of buying. This was entertainment.

Savannah spotted the real estate agent in conversation with a man, and then two women, and then two men. They were all negotiating. She couldn't tell if any palms had been greased, but wouldn't have been surprised. Suddenly, she felt everything closing in on her, pushing her out of the house that she was trying to sell. If everything went according to plan she'd have very few opportunities to walk freely through the home she'd shared with her father until his death, not even two months gone. She still wasn't even sure where she'd go next.

Back to New York, as her brother Harris suggested? Or where?

She let the humming of conversation wash over her, and headed out the back again, to the yard and the pool. It was quiet. Someone had been sitting in one of the lounge chairs. Someone had been smoking and had put out their cigarette on the pathway. Someone had left an empty can of Diet Pepsi on a small table.

Savannah sat on the very edge of the pool, pulling up the legs of her print capri pants. She took off her shoes and let her feet slip into the cool water. She wiggled her toes. The pool had been a plus. She'd never learned to swim really well, but had enjoyed evenings spent just like this after she'd moved in with her father. Sometimes, when he was feeling up to it, he would join her, ensconced on a lounger complete with some amber-colored drink over ice that she knew had been forbidden by his doctors. They'd spent a lot of time talking around each other, being civil, trying to behave normally, circumventing the past and ignoring the future. They were like strangers thrown together by circumstance, trying to make the best of an awkward situation.

Savannah considered now that her father had been remarkably accepting of the fact that he was dying. He never once complained about it, didn't show anger or fear, but he also never wanted to talk about it. He did have a lot of stories to tell her, about his work, as if that would explain to her what he wanted her to know about him.

She wasn't sure how long she sat that way, but when the real estate agent came out to find her, her toes were starting to wrinkle.

"Well, that's it. I finally got the last person to leave." She sat on a cushioned deck chair and crossed her knees, smiling in satisfaction. "That went very well, I would say. There was lots of interest, and there were lots of offers. Of course, I told everyone I'd have to speak with the owner as there were other bidders…"

"I've changed my mind."

"Let them think there's stiff competition. It's good for…what did you say?"

Savannah turned to regard the agent whose stunned expression was almost comical. "I'm sorry. I think I've changed my mind. I'm pulling the house off the market."

"You're joking, right? You haven't even heard what the offers are. They're all higher than your asking price. You're going to make a killing on the sale of this house."

Savannah smiled to herself. *Bad turn of phrase,* she thought. She shook her head. "I'm not interested."

"B-but, why? Do you realize how much work has gone into making today happen? And don't even think about going behind my back to sell this place on your own. I want my commission, regardless."

Savannah lifted her feet from the water and pivoted to face the agent, her arms around her bent knees. She felt very calm, very sure of herself. Even her upset stomach had settled down. "I'm not going to sell the house. It's not anything you did or said. I realized when I saw all those people walking in and out that I can't let it go."

The agent looked frustrated and angry. And then confused.

"You could have cleared a million, give or take a hundred thousand. We could probably get a little more."

Savannah got to her feet and looked around the small peaceful enclosed backyard. The pool surface reflected a wrinkled image of part of the house. The slightly humid air held the sweet fragrance of flowers. They were the same kind that had been used at his service.

She could hear her father's raspy laughter.

"It's not about the money," she said simply.

Chapter 1

"Mac, Jeff Peterson is on the line. He said it's important."

The man behind the sleek, modern desk was already on the phone with another call. At the sound of his assistant's voice he sat back and momentarily stopped his note taking on a pile of official documents.

"Mr. Samuels? Sorry to interrupt. Can I put you on hold for a quick moment? Thanks." He frowned at the young man standing in the half-open doorway. "I'll have to get back to him. Didn't you let him know I'm on an important call?"

The young man nodded. "He was insistent. Said he had some crucial information for you, and if you didn't get it you'd probably kick his ass. Sorry, those were his words. And there's a Miss Daly waiting in reception. She doesn't have an appointment but said you're expecting her?" He ended on a question to explain his own lack of knowledge of the unexpected visitor. "I think she has to do with why Mr. Peterson is calling."

"I wouldn't be surprised," McCoy Sutton muttered, already pushing a button on his phone console as his assistant backed out of the office door, closing it behind him.

"Jeff, this is a bad time. I'm in the middle of..."

"Fifteen seconds, I swear. It's about my sister, Cherise Kim Daly. She's twenty-three, was voted Miss Something-or-other in Washington, D.C., has done a few commercials, and she wants to be an actress. Think Vivica Fox, but younger. I sent her over to see you. Did she get there, yet?"

"And you want me to see her because..." Mac began, his annoyance at the interruption held at bay because Jeff Peterson was one of his best friends.

"Because I know you can hook her up."

"Not with me. Not my type, and she's too young."

"Of course not with you. This ain't about booty, Mac. She's trying to break into the business here, and I thought you could help her out a little."

"Jeff," McCoy began with more patience than he was feeling, "I'm not in the business. I don't have anything to do with the movie industry, the studios, the directors, or young women who want to be actresses. *And,* I'm in the middle of a deal."

"You know a lot of people. Just introduce her to one or two and then you can cut her loose."

Mac looked at his watch. "Your fifteen seconds are up. You owe me, Jeff. Bye." He hung up the phone, shaking his head, but nevertheless amused by his friend's affrontery. He called his assistant. "Colin, tell Ms. Daly I'll be with her shortly. Offer her something to drink."

Shortly turned out to be close to an hour.

When McCoy was finally able to go out to the reception area, it was to find that Jeff Peterson's description of his sister had been on target, and Colin had fallen under the spell of the brown-skinned beauty, as was evident by the flush in his cheeks.

"Sorry to keep you waiting so long," Mac said, extending his hand to the very slender, tall and poised young woman who stood up to meet him.

Within the first few seconds McCoy had taken a complete assessment of Cherise Daly and determined that she had at least several key attributes necessary for success in Hollywood. She was tall and Hollywood thin, but with curves in all the places deemed to be important. She had a slightly exotic look, with hazel eyes and long wavy hair. Her features were less African-American than they were kind of multiethnic other. Her skin color was the same as Halle Berry's—brown enough not to be confused for white, but light enough to afford Ms. Daly more opportunities. Mac doubted if all of Ms. Daly's assets were hers, but no one particularly cared anymore about authenticity in Hollywood.

She was totally aware of herself, and with a certain feminine coyness that Mac personally found too studied to be appealing.

"I'm sorry Jeff didn't give you more warning about me." Her smile was warm…and sexy.

Mac tore his gaze from her and looked at Colin who, clearly mesmerized by Cherise, was trying not to appear too dumbstruck.

"What's on my calendar for the rest of today?"

"A three o'clock appointment with Altair Construction over that renovation in Santa Monica, and there's that fundraiser tonight downtown. The dinner starts at eight."

Mac felt a soft light touch on his arm and turned to find Cherise regarding him with limpid eyes. "I know you're very busy. Jeff told me you're an attorney."

"But I'm not an entertainment lawyer," McCoy was quick to clarify. "I'm a commercial real estate attorney."

"But you know a lot of people. He said you did."

"Jeff was exaggerating," he said dryly.

"I don't want to get in the way or anything. Maybe I should come by another day," Cherise offered.

Mac pursed his wide mouth, listening to her practiced apology and offer of sacrifice. He rose to the occasion. "You're here now. Why don't I take you to lunch? You can tell me a little about your professional experience, and what you hope to accomplish in L.A."

Cherise Kim Daly's eyes lit up and, on cue, she tilted her head at McCoy and smiled.

"I'm *going* to be a star, of course."

Of course.

Savannah didn't even flinch when the young man with the stand-up wooly hair leaned over in front of her and planted his hands on her desk to get her attention. She also didn't bother looking up from the treatment she was reading for a coming-of-age story.

"How come you never told nobody you're Will Shelton's daughter?"

"What difference would it make?" Savannah asked, turning a page of the proposal.

"I would have sucked up to you," Tyrone James Sparks said bluntly. "I would have worshipped at your feet and asked for his autograph. I'd have asked to meet the man himself. Damn! Will Shelton's little girl breathing the same air as me."

"Taj, give it a rest," Savannah said, amused. "You know that stuff doesn't work on me."

Taj chuckled at his own failed acting and sat on the edge of Savannah's desk, not concerned that he was interrupting her work. "I didn't even know he'd passed until I saw this little tiny notice in the *back* of *Variety.* In the *back!* I thought we'd gotten over that."

Savannah finally glanced at Taj, who sat shaking his head at the parallel he'd drawn between the civil rights movement and her father's death.

"I'm sorry I didn't say anything," Savannah said with false regret.

"So what was wrong with him?"

For a moment, an entirely different list of shortcomings popped into her mind that had nothing to do with what he'd died of. She shook the thoughts off. "Prostate cancer."

"Ooohh," Taj winced, as if he was suddenly equally afflicted. "When was the service?"

"What service?"

Taj stared at Savannah in disbelief. "You mean to tell me there wasn't a service for Will Shelton? Baby *Girl,* the man was a legend. You can't just put someone like that in the ground and then forget about him."

Savannah sighed and clipped together the pages she'd already reviewed. "I can see I'm not going to get to finish this today."

"It's after six anyway. You're off the clock," Taj reminded her.

"Yeah, but I wanted to get this done before leaving tonight. You've interrupted my schedule."

"You got plans? Maybe you and me can go for a drink or something."

"We've worked together for more than a year, and this is the first time you've suggested anything social, Tyrone. I'm flattered. Or do you just want to pick my brains about my father?"

"That's right," Taj said boldly. "I heard Will Shelton talk to one of my classes at USC. I didn't know anything about him at the time, but after that I tracked down every film he was ever in."

Savannah stared at Taj, at the memory that lit up his eyes with excitement. "I take it he impressed you."

"Look, it's hard out here for black folk. I'm impressed with *anyone* who had a foot in the door, know what I'm saying? Now, I know I'm going to make it. My music is the next wave. I'm working on a demo right now. I'm gonna pitch it to Def Jam when it's done. I know someone inside. Oh. Sorry to hear about your father passing."

"Thanks," Savannah murmured, putting her papers away.

"That why you came out here? You following in his footsteps?"

"I don't have the acting gene, and I was never interested if that's what you mean. I came to California because my father was dying. I took care of him."

"Oh, *man*," Taj shook his head. "I didn't even know."

"Nobody knew. That's the way he wanted it."

Her cell phone began to chime and Savannah dug it out of her purse. "Hello? Yes, this is she. I'm sorry but the house is not for sale. It's been taken off the market.... It doesn't matter what the offer is, I'm really not interested.... I don't think I'll change my mind, but thanks for calling." Savannah hung up and quickly forgot the call. She frowned at her coworker who studied her thoughtfully through his glasses. "Was there something else you wanted to say?"

"How come you never said anything even after he died?"

Savannah stood up, thinking about the past few months since her father's death. She'd felt like she was living between two worlds. Her life, and his. She was still living in his house because she could think of no other place to go. But she still wasn't sure she'd made the right decision.

"I didn't tell anyone because that's the way *I* wanted it."

"You know I can't let you get away with that."

Savannah couldn't help laughing at Taj's audacity. For someone who wasn't that tall, and certainly not distinguished looking, he had a certain fearlessness that always caught her off guard. In an odd way, she also couldn't help admiring him for it.

"Taj, are you threatening me? What are you going to do about it?"

"Baby Girl, I'm going to hound you until you tell me about the man. Sorry, but you can't keep him to yourself. He's like a national treasure or something."

"Will Shelton died months ago, Taj. No one's going to care."

"You buy me a drink and I'll tell you why you're wrong."

Savannah laughed again, as she rose from her desk and gathered her belongings. "A few minutes ago it was, '*We'll* go for a drink.' What happened to the *we* part?"

He shrugged with a grin. "All my money's invested in my music. I'm a poor struggling musician."

"Another time. I do have plans for tonight."

"Don't forget there's a meeting tomorrow morning. The Big T wants to know if we've read anything worth taking seriously."

Savannah was used to Taj's shorthand for their boss, Theodore Russo, all three hundred pounds of the head of development. "I know. That's why I wanted to finish that treatment I was reading."

"Any good?"

She wrinkled her nose. "I've read better. I've read worse. See you in the morning."

"Where you headed? Maybe I'll tag along."

Savannah turned out the light on her desk and headed toward the door of her office. "I have an invitation to see a juried craft show downtown."

Taj split off from her at the door. "See you tomorrow."

Savannah had already pulled out of the lower-level parking garage and was headed toward the expressway when her cell rang again. She answered as she merged into traffic for the twenty-minute drive to the site of the crafts show.

"Hi, Donna. I'm on my way now."

"Don't rush on my account. I can't make it," the girlish voice on the other end announced.

"You're not coming?"

"I just found out the club is hosting a private reception tonight, and I've been asked to stay on."

"Why do they always recruit you at the last minute? Don't you deserve your own social life?"

"Well, I could have said no, Vann, but maybe I'll meet some interesting folks. Forget the crafts show. Why don't you come on over? I'll sneak you in."

"I don't think so. You know those Hollywood-type things make me uncomfortable."

"It's not a Hollywood-type thing. I told you it's a private event. Most of the people are in banking and finance. Maybe I'll meet someone and get them interested in investing in my yoga studio."

"You know that's a long shot," Savannah advised her friend.

"It's an opportunity. Why don't you come? It'll be more fun than that crafts show."

"I'm already in traffic. I'm closer to the show then I am to you. Is Kay going to stand me up, too?"

Donna chortled. "At least I called. She said she had to have drinks tonight with someone from NBC. Kay's angling to do PR in the black community for one of their fall shows. I'm sorry this happened at the last minute, but you know how it is."

"Yeah, I do," Savannah said without rancor.

She had a sudden memory of her father calling when she was about eight to say he couldn't come to see her and Harris because he was about to leave for location on a film. It was a small scene, he'd told her, but he had lines, and that could lead to something else.

"Look, my exit is coming up. Call me tomorrow."

Savannah hung up and moved to the right-hand lane to exit the expressway. For a moment she did consider forgetting about the crafts show as well, and just heading back to her father's house. But it was early, not quite seven, and she envisioned the long evening stretching before her in the quiet house. She could have dinner alone, then sit by the pool and read. Or she could go through the short stack of forms, notices and documents that had been arriving since her father's death, to tie up the loose ends of his business here on earth.

She was tired of dealing with death.

Savannah jumped at the chance to spend an evening doing something just for herself, and signaled as she approached the exit ramp.

When she entered the exhibition hall she felt relief at the sense of the familiar. One of the things Savannah most missed about living in New York was the variety of activities there, the diversity throughout the city that made life interesting, lively and unique. Not at all like Hollywood with its fixation on youth, beauty and make-believe.

Savannah still had trouble understanding a culture based on such superficiality. But even more bewildering to her was how her father could have chosen such a way of life over his family, his children? Why weren't she and Harris and their mother enough to make him happy? Did he find happiness here in La-La Land?

"Everything is reduced thirty percent."

Savannah slowed her steps in front of a vendor who was selling beautifully carved wooden boxes of all sizes. Because he'd gotten her attention she stopped to examine some of his pieces.

"They're great for loose change, jewelry, secret love letters."

Savannah turned one box over to look at the price. Expensive. "This is lovely," she told the man, glancing at him briefly. He had a kind of Malibu look of tanned skin, slender athletic body, and the ubiquitous blond hair that was a bit long and shaggy. But it was also clear that the artisan was not a young man.

"There's only three more days of the show. I need to sell something," he said.

Savannah smiled at him. "Help out a starving artist?"

"Help out a starving actor," he corrected dryly.

She thought he might be in his late thirties, early forties. To her way of thinking, he was a little long in the tooth to still be pursuing an acting career.

"Why don't you just concentrate on your wood carving? You could probably build a cottage industry out of your talent and work."

"Thanks. But this just pays the rent. I had a steady gig about five years ago on TV. You probably heard of the show?"

He not so modestly mentioned a popular sitcom that Savannah not only recognized but had watched herself. But she didn't recognize his face or name. Still, she listened politely and spoke with encouragement.

"I'm sure you'll get something else. You already have experience from a former hit show."

He shrugged. "Yeah, but it's always 'What have you done lately?' I'm a very good actor, but I'm up against a bunch of kids who are barely twenty, know what I mean?"

Savannah nodded, sympathetic to his situation. "Maybe something will turn up soon."

"I hope so. Look, if you really like that box I'll give it to you for fifty percent off. Now, that's a good deal."

It was. Savannah took her time looking through the other styles and designs. She finally chose one that appealed to her, and of a size that could really be useful although she wasn't sure yet how she would use the box. He wrapped the box in newspaper, a section of the Sunday comics, and put it inside a plastic bag from a local supermarket.

"Hey, you enjoy that box."

"Good luck to you," she said, before moving on.

The show had a wide variety of artists displaying and selling their wares, from glass works and handmade gold and silver jewelry, to pottery and even furniture. For her the show was not about buying things, so much as it was a chance to see creative work from talented people. She'd always appreciated anything made by hand.

Since it was a juried show, she passed booths where the artists proudly displayed their winning ribbons. There was a buzz and flurry of activity at a booth one aisle away, and Savannah realized that someone of note was being followed and photographed as she moved along the displays, occasionally stopping to handle work or chat with the artist.

"Do you know what's going on?" she asked a middle-aged woman in oversized eyeglasses selling leather-bound albums and journals.

"Probably an actress," she shrugged with disinterest. "This is the third time since the show opened that one of them has come by. It's a photo op, you know. They move around among the people, doing regular stuff so they seem real and down to earth."

"I'm sure many are," Savannah said.

"Oh, yeah, right. But if I can find out who the actress is," she gestured toward the aisle where the gathering was happening. "I can tell you what they're promoting, what scandal they're trying to gloss over, or what love affair they're recovering from."

"And what if they're just here to enjoy the show, buy some handmade work?"

"Sweetheart, *nothing* that appears natural in Hollywood is. Everything is planned, scripted and coordinated. Now, I'll tell you something else. Tomorrow there will be a big photograph and a short blurb about how so-and-so was 'spotted,'" she made quote marks with her fingers, "at the L.A. crafts show. It's all about publicity and timing."

"Are you an actress, too?" Savannah asked the amusing but cynical woman.

"Not me. It's a crazy business, and a heartbreaker. But my brother works for Disney in the animation department."

Savannah soon said goodbye and wandered away, sure that the woman had missed the irony.

She'd pretty much seen the entire exhibit, stopping at those booths that interested her, when she realized it was after eight o'clock. Despite that odd sensation she always experienced when returning to her father's house, it was time to leave. There was still one aisle remaining, but she decided to skip it. That is, until she spotted, from a distance, a shawl being worn by a young woman at a booth where other woven accessories were displayed. Drawn by vibrant colors that suggested a sunset from a distance, Savannah detoured in the direction of the booth.

The young woman managing the booth was carefully folding another shawl and adding it to a neat stack on a table behind her. On the front table, pinned to a square pillow made of some of the fabric, was a second-place ribbon from the show judges.

"Congratulations," Savannah said.

"Hi. Thanks," the young woman smiled warmly as Savannah began looking at the displayed items. "Everything is woven from original designs. I have shawls, tablecloths, napkins..."

"They're really gorgeous," Savannah said, running her fingers over the folded fabrics. "Are you the artist?"

"Yes, I am. I work on a hand loom with wools and threads I pick up when traveling."

"I love the shawl you're wearing."

The young woman pulled it from her shoulders and held it up so that Savannah could see the full design. "Thank you. It's a good size. I was wearing it as a shawl, but it can also serve as a tablecloth or as a tapestry hung on a wall. I design so that everything has multiple uses. Here. Would you like to try it?"

Savannah accepted the cloth and was immediately surprised by its light weight and warm, soft texture. She stood in front of a rectangular mirror that the artist held for her, and wrapped herself in the shawl. The colors suited her own toffee complexion, and lent an air of the exotic to her features, her slightly slanted dark eyes and wide, well-shaped mouth.

"How much is this one?"

Almost apologetically the young woman named a price. It was higher than Savannah was expecting, but she knew it was very fair. The shawl was one of a kind. She removed it and handed it back to the young woman. Seeing the tiny easel with business cards, she took one from the stand. The card read Domino Designs…for you and your home."

"Are you Domino?" Savannah asked.

The woman nodded with a small shrug, and made a knowing gesture with her hand. "My grandmother gave me that name. You know how some of the folks are. Always digging into the past for these meaningful names.

Savannah looked at her more closely, trying to meld the women's appearance with her surprising mannerisms and the way she talked. She was a little above average height, with the kind of looks that naturally drew stares and compliments. Savannah had noticed at once that she was very thin and fair, with a flawlessly smooth peach complexion. She had an incredible mane of corkscrew blond curls that fairly sprouted from her head down to her shoulders, framing a face that was way-above-average beautiful. Her eyes were a smoky gray color.

"It's an usual name," Savannah observed.

"My real name is Dominique Hamilton. I use Domino Hagan professionally."

"I like it." Savannah narrowed her eyes with a slight frown. "Don't tell me. You're also an actress." To her surprise, Domino laughed in a self-deprecating manner that immediately warmed Savannah to her.

"When I can get the parts, I am. This week I'm an artist. It's hard getting by the gatekeepers—secretaries, assistants and others who have power. I get a lot of, 'You're great, you're got what it takes,' and then I don't get a callback or I'm told I'm not quite right for the role. I get a *lot* of that. This is my fallback plan," she said, referring to the woven items on sale. "I learned from my grandmother."

"I'm so impressed. Your work is fabulous. I love that one." Savannah pointed to the shawl she'd tried on.

"Thanks," Domino said with a pleased grin. "I could give you a small discount..."

"It's worth what you're asking," Savannah said, "But it's more than I can afford right now." She looked speculatively at Domino. "Will you do a layaway?"

"Bet!" Domino nodded decisively, again surprising Savannah.

Savannah wrote out a check for a deposit on the shawl. After once again congratulating Domino on her work and wishing her luck with her acting, she finally headed for the exit.

There was still a lot of traffic on the expressway, but it was moving briskly. Savannah figured that at this hour it would take her thirty minutes to get home. Her mind settled into not only a review of the show she'd just left, but a reminder to herself to call Donna and Kay, the two women friends she'd made since coming to L.A., to encourage them to catch the crafts show before it closed. Donna in particular, a former dancer and now part-time yoga instructor, would appreciate many of the original pieces. Kay, who could ill afford to, loved to spend money.

On autopilot, Savannah switched lanes, preparing for a crossover to another route that took her back to the upscale black community and her father's house. As always, she also considered what was to be done to the house she now lived in but could still not call her own. Why had she continued to stay on, given her ambivalent feelings for a man who'd chosen his career over his family? Even more bewildering to her was why she'd answered his call, and why he'd chosen to ask her to come and be with him in L.A. He'd said he had something important to say to her and wanted to do it in person. Why had she decided to come? And why, once she'd arrived and they'd played at being father and daughter for almost a week, had he decided to tell her he was dying. And the final surprise...would she stay with him until the end?

Savannah blinked away the memory that still had the power to confuse her, to make her feel both anger and regret. Why had he waited so long?

She heard a car horn ahead, and the screech of brakes. The taillights of the car ahead of her came on and its speed abruptly reduced, forcing Savannah to brake sharply. A second later her car was suddenly bumped forward and rocked, and she was forced against the restraints of her seat belt. She'd been hit from behind. She glanced in her rearview mirror to see a man dressed in a black tux getting out of the car. Savannah put her car in Park, put on her hazard blinkers, and did the same.

Chapter 2

Already there was a small pileup of vehicles behind her; the drivers hadn't had time to see what was happening in time to change lanes. The driver of the dark BMW immediately behind Savannah walked toward her. He did two things that annoyed her. He first looked at his watch, and he then examined the front end of his car for damages.

"You just hit my car," Savannah said, her voice indignant and angry. She checked out her vehicle before turning her frowning glare on him. "Why were you tailgating?"

"You stopped short."

"Are you blaming me?"

"I don't see any damage."

"You don't know that. It's too dark to tell for sure," she persisted, standing with a hand on her hip.

Cars around them were blowing their horns, trying to get around the blocked lane, and some drivers were rubbernecking.

"I'm not going to argue with you," the other driver said, talking over the noise of traffic. He looked at the time again, and removed his wallet from an inside pocket of his jacket.

"Am I keeping you from something?" Savannah asked sarcastically.

"As a matter of fact, yes. I'm late for an important event," he said, his voice cool and formal. "Are you hurt?"

"Nice of you to finally ask." Savannah shook her head. "No. I'm okay."

"Good. I'm not hurt, either. So, there's nothing to discuss."

He suddenly looked back to his own car. It was then that Savannah realized there was a passenger in his car. Female. She was young and very pretty, dressed for the night in something gauzy, skimpy but formal. She glanced back to the man and realized he was wearing a tuxedo, with his bow tie made of yellow Kinte cloth.

He didn't exactly apologize for plowing into her, but he also did not engage in an argument with her. Savannah took a moment to look more closely at him. He was maybe six feet tall. He was brown-skinned and clean-shaven. It was hard to tell how old he was, but he certainly wasn't a twentysomething or middle-aged. He had a mature demeanor about him, calm and controlled. He had a clean, precise appearance. *Definitely a Hollywood type,* Savannah thought scathingly. Self-centered and always in a rush.

He handed her a business card, but she couldn't read any of the text in the dark. She walked back to the front seat of her car, reached for her handbag, and found a card of her own to give him in return.

"I don't see any need to call the police and report this. Do you?" he said, putting his wallet away. He was already returning to his driver's-side door.

"What if there are damages to my car?" Savannah asked, feeling as if he was marginalizing what happened.

"Then call me," he said, pointing to the card in her hand.

"How rude! We just got into an accident. You can't just leave."

He was halfway back inside his car, but paused to face her over the top of his open door. "I can tell you're not from L.A. Don't make a big deal of a little fender bender. It happens all the time. Save your indignation for something really important."

Savannah stood speechless as he slammed the door and instantly had his car in gear as he peeled off around her, back into traffic. She stared after his disappearing taillights until she finally lost track of him.

It had all happened in less than five minutes.

Savannah heard another car horn so close behind her

that she jumped. She was standing in a dangerous place and about to cause another accident. She hurried back to her car and got in, continuing on her way. But her hands were shaking, and adrenaline rushed through her body.

Savannah's annoyance, coming on the heels of her reflection about her father's life in Hollywood, was heightened. Thank goodness it hadn't been a serious collision, but the attitude of the driver involved had gotten to her.

"Fool," she murmured scathingly, although it brought little satisfaction.

She suddenly realized she was still holding his slightly bent card in her hand. She squinted at the lettering, making out a name. McCoy Sutton. She tossed it carelessly aside and it landed just inside the top opening of her purse.

He was not so easy to dismiss. Something he'd said echoed in her head, infuriating Savannah with its implication. *I can tell you're not from L.A.*

What the hell did that mean?

By the time she pulled into the driveway of her father's house, she was tense and impatient. The incident on the way back seemed to have settled in her and she couldn't shake it off. They had been lucky that it wasn't more serious. Why couldn't she just let it go? But her reflective mood was not about having been rear-ended by another car. It was what the driver had said to her, because he'd been right.

Savannah let herself into the quiet house and, as

had become a habit, she walked slowly through it, from room to room. The walk still evoked the life and times of Will Shelton. Growing up, she'd come to hate L.A. because she believed that her father loved it more than he did her or her brother Harris. Los Angeles had stolen him right out of her life, and it wasn't enough that he'd called out to her in the last year of his own. How was she ever going to recapture the lost years between?

There were still piles of old industry magazines on the bottom shelves of her father's bookcase. There were mementos and souvenirs from different films or TV programs he'd done. After she'd changed her mind about selling his house, she'd replaced on the walls the photographs of her father taken with industry people, some well-known. He looked handsome and happy.

She'd moved nothing in his bedroom. She hadn't made a shrine of the space, but it was still *his* space. It pretty much remained the same as the day he'd died, although by then her father had been moved to a private hospice where he'd been attached to oxygen and sedated to keep the pain at bay.

The room she occupied was used as a combination guest room and home office. In there were housed the numerous photo albums, scrapbooks, shooting scripts, reviews and notices of his work. She'd more or less taken the room over, sleeping in the comfortable full-sized bed where, almost nightly, she had dreams about her father.

In one he was taking her to the zoo, and then leaving her to wait in the bird house while he went off for an audition or reading, promising to return for her soon. But never doing so.

I can tell you're not from L.A.

How could he tell, exactly? Was it the way she dressed, Savannah wondered? Mostly in New York black, in clothes that were more conservative than her west-coast counterparts. They revealed, she concealed. Was it her get-in-your-face attitude about the accident, rather than just shrugging and saying, as he had, "no harm done." Or was it her inability to get in the mind-set of L.A. culture—live and let live. Don't sweat the small stuff when it was *all* small stuff.

Or had the stranger been able to see into the heart of the matter and recognize what she had not been able to see herself? Cutting some slack, and letting bygones be bygones.

Will Shelton had been a minor actor in Hollywood, low on the food chain with other black actors. He'd survived and built a life and career in a city that manufactured dreams. But had it all been worth the sacrifice?

Savannah started from her introspection when she thought she heard something outside, in the back. She silently made her way to a window and looked out. There was no one there. But she did catch a glimpse of a moving shadow. She went into the kitchen and to the door leading to the yard. She stepped outside. There was another sound. Someone was there, near the door that opened out to the side of the property.

She went to investigate. But by the time Savannah reached the door and unlocked and opened it, the walkway was empty and all was again quiet. About to close it to return to the house she, instead, walked down the flagstone pathway to the curb. She looked to the right, toward the main thoroughfare and traffic two blocks away. To her left, and some distance down the block, she caught sight of a retreating figure. It appeared to be a woman, small in stature with a graceful carriage, wearing slacks, a sweater, with her hair either very short, or pulled back and held with a tie or clip. She was walking purposefully as if trying to get away. Savannah watched her for a while, wondering if she'd been wrong about someone hanging around the house. She finally went back inside.

The phone began to ring and she hurried to answer.

"Hello?"

"How was the crafts show?"

"Hey, Donna. It was fun. Sorry you missed it."

"Did you buy anything?"

"I got talked into buying a carved wooden box. I felt sorry for the artist."

"Unemployed actor, right?"

Savannah laughed in response. "How was the reception?"

"Crowded with a bunch of very skinny beautiful people. People get silly when they drink too much, especially when they're not paying for the drinks. Ooohh, you'll never guess who came in."

"Who?"

"You know that actor who's on the *Law and Order* franchise?"

"I don't know who you're talking about, Donna. I don't watch a lot of television. I would guess that he's very good-looking, with great abs."

"Yep. And full of himself."

"Isn't that true of most of Hollywood?" Savannah asked dryly.

"Not really. A lot of folks in this town are really nice and work hard. Everybody's just trying to make it, and a lot of them aren't going to. You can't blame people for dreaming big. What else did you buy?"

Savannah proceeded to tell Donna about the show, and enthusiastically described the shawl she'd left a down payment for with the artist, Domino.

"And you won't believe what happened to me on the way back to my father's house."

"You met someone?"

Savannah laughed. "Yeah, I did, but you won't believe how. I had an accident."

"Get out! You okay?"

"Yeah, fine. Just ticked off by the driver's attitude."

"What do you mean?"

Savannah went over the details, including the comment of the driver as he was leaving the scene.

"Can you believe his nerve? Acting like the problem

was me 'cause I'm not from here. Then he just left me on the highway while he hurried off to some event. Probably a movie premier."

"Vann, you *are* very down on L.A. You're always making fun of actors and actresses because they're willing to do anything to get noticed."

"It's not like becoming an actor is this great contribution to society."

"Maybe it's not. But it is about having talent and dreams and wanting them to come true. I admire people who risk everything to follow their own hearts. I wanted to perform with the Dance Theater of Harlem, but never made it out of the repertory company and the chorus line of a few Broadway shows. Kay always wanted to be a designer, but she admits she was only really interested in dressing herself, not other women. At least she gave it a shot."

Savannah knew there was no intended criticism of her in Donna's observations, but the barb had struck home, sharply and deeply.

"You said you'd always wanted to be a writer, and that's exactly what you became, right? For a women's magazine back in New York? So, how is what you wanted to do any different?"

"I just feel like he was making fun of me."

"Oh, you mean like—Why don't you lighten up?"

"I think so."

"Look, I know this past year has been rough, taking care of your father and knowing he was going to die and then having him die, and staying in his house. But maybe you do take things too seriously. You need to take up surfing, or riding in cars with boys, or start going to acting class."

Savannah began to laugh.

"Maybe you need to get a tattoo, or get more hair like Diana Ross, or become really eccentric and start walking around with a pet in your purse. It works for Paris Hilton and Beyoncé."

When she'd finished laughing, Savannah felt relief flow through her at the dissipation of her tension and thoughts. "Maybe I'm not the L.A. type. Maybe I really do belong in New York."

"You can belong anywhere you choose to. It's not like you get to pick only one from column A or one from column B. Take them both."

Savannah grew pensive, listening to Donna's pearls of wisdom. It *had* been a hard year.

In that moment, with the accident and the image of a well-dressed, slightly arrogant man fresh on her mind, she made a decision. But it was about much more than wanting to prove to a perfect stranger that he'd gotten it wrong. She could still see her father sitting in his living room slowly looking through his albums with a slight smile and a glow in his eyes for his memories. Earlier that very evening she'd met many artisans at the crafts fair who believed in themselves enough not to give up, who could even make light of their struggles.

When she finished the call from Donna, Savannah

took another look around the living room. Then she went down to the basement in search of boxes or any empty containers. She found enough to get started. She was going to pack her father's albums and books and scripts and history, and store them in the garage for now. She was going to take some of her own belongings, which had been in storage for a year, and set them about the house. She lived here now. This was her home.

Savannah made the decision that she *did* belong in L.A.

No one was going to tell her otherwise.

As Savannah trailed behind Taj, his babbling knowledge of the history of the popular TV series *ER* was lost on her as she indulged in her own thoughts. In the year that she'd been working as a reader for the small independent studio, she'd never been particularly interested in doing a studio back-lot tour. Of course, it could be fairly said that she'd had a lot on her mind during that time.

If she'd been asked beforehand, Savannah knew she would have quipped that everything was done with smoke and mirrors. She would probably have believed that the sets were simple facades, cardboard with surface dressing. She was speechless at how profoundly wrong she was. From the moment she and Taj had passed security, through the good graces of his labyrinthine network of contacts and inside friends, Savannah found herself swept up in the make-believe hospital. Everything possible had been done to make the complex set look like a real emergency room. It was even painted two shades of institutional green. Walking the set and seeing the attention given to the smallest detail, there was no reason for her to believe it wasn't real, but for the minor fact that it *wasn't.*

"Look at this," Taj said, walking over to a gurney in one of the many authentic-looking triage rooms. "They even have used bloody gauze pads on the floor," he pointed out excitedly.

"Awesome," Savannah murmured, queasy at the idea that the dried stains might be the real deal.

"This is one of the best TV sets I've ever seen, and I've seen a lot. You know what's another good one? The set for *The West Wing.* I love when the characters are rushing through the halls and turning corners, and passing through rooms. Man, it's like…where do they put all the cameras?"

Eventually they came to the end of the set and, suddenly, just like that, it ended. It was as if a chain saw had been used to disconnect it and remove it from the rest of the hospital.

"Wow. I'm impressed," Savannah said. And she meant it.

"See, I told you you'd be blown away," Taj boasted.

He finished his guided tour and commentary, and they walked through a large hangar-type space.

"Now, I want to show you another set, but this one is different. It's for a movie with Martin Lawrence."

The next building they entered was more open, and

designed to look like someone's contemporary living room with sliding doors leading out to a backyard patio.

"What do you think?" Taj asked.

Savannah stood in one spot and slowly turned around. She shook her head. "This set doesn't look all that real to me."

"Exactly. That's 'cause it's not the set that's important, but just a place where not much happens between the actors."

After briefly touring that set, and one other for another movie in the making, they left the building and headed off the lot.

"Change your mind?" Taj asked Savannah.

She smiled at her enthusiastic coworker and nodded. "Yeah, I have. I'll probably never look at a TV program or movie the same way again," she said as they got into Taj's car for the short ride back to their office. "Just how did you become so interested in all of this?"

Taj shrugged, driving with the reckless abandon of many twentysomething males. "I didn't much like the real world I was growing up in. I lived in a really bad part of Newark, New Jersey. I loved going to the movies 'cause it helped me forget about sharing a bedroom with my two brothers. We used to listen to gunshots from outside our apartment window at night. The mother of one of my friends was killed walking home from the supermarket. How messed up is that?

"I had no space of my own, man. I always wished I could be someplace else but home. My mom really tried hard and everything, but I wanted *out.* I knew when I was little I wanted to live and work in Hollywood."

"But why Hollywood? Why not New York, or Philadelphia?"

"Different city, same problems. I felt like I could breathe in California." He glanced briefly at Savannah. "People come here because of the weather or to get into the movies. I came to get as far away from Newark as I could. I came to save my life."

Savannah didn't have much to say after that. She couldn't relate to the environment Taj had been raised in, and she had never really felt the need to escape, as he had. But she suddenly found herself applying some of his motivation for coming to L.A., of all places, to her father. She suddenly wondered if that's what it had been like for him? Maybe he wasn't escaping *from* a circumstance, so much as running *to* one that he wanted for himself. But still, there was that nagging question: how could he just up and leave his family to risk everything on a career in Hollywood?

"Thanks for the field trip," Savannah said to Taj, once they'd returned to their own studio.

"Anytime, Baby Girl. Next time, we'll go people watching. I know where all the celebrities hang."

Savannah gave Taj a slightly exasperated look. They were walking down narrow mazelike corridors to their cubicles. "Why do you insist on calling me that?"

"What? Baby Girl? Hey, that's a compliment. You

don't even *know* some of the names I got for folks around here. It's laid-back and all that in L.A., but not everybody is nice. Sorry to say it, but there are lots of brothers and sistahs who get an attitude, know what I'm saying? Jealousy and backstabbing and liars, but you're not like that. You have this sweet innocence...."

Savannah rolled her eyes in amusement. "Oh, please..."

"Like you don't really know what's going on. You're like Alice in Wonderland. Only brown skinned."

His observation made Savannah laugh as she reached her office and turned to thank Taj once again. "I had a really good time. Now I really do owe you a drink sometime."

"Don't worry about it. But it looks like I got big-time competition," he said, walking away.

She frowned. "What are you talking about?"

Taj didn't stop walking and he didn't turn around. "In your office. On your desk."

Savannah did as she was told. On her desk was a bouquet of mixed exotic flowers. The arrangement was so large that it seemed to fill her small space. The rounded glass vase was wrapped in pale mauve cellophane, with streams of pink, blue and purple ribbon tying it in place. She stared in disbelief at the magnificent grouping, certain that a mistake had been made in delivery.

She tried searching for a card enclosure but found none. Sitting down she called the receptionist.

"Kim, there's a giant arrangement of flowers on my

desk. I think it was meant for someone else. Could you check and find out where it was supposed to be delivered? Probably the director's office."

"There's no mistake. I have the delivery notice right here. It has your name on it, and I signed for it."

"But I don't know anyone who would send me something like this," Savannah frowned. "Is there a name on the notice?" With one hand Savannah turned the vase so she could see all the different flowers that had been selected. Some of her favorites were included, and not an ordinary rose in the bunch.

"Just the name of the florist. Want me to call them?"

"Oh, wait a minute. I think I see a card inside the wrapping. Thanks, Kim."

She hung up and wiggled her fingers inside the folds of the cellophane, not wanting to disturb the arrangement too much for when the flowers were passed along to the true recipient. But what Savannah found was a white pack of plant food, and instructions on how to use it to keep the flowers fresh for a week.

Savannah called Kim back.

"When was this delivered?"

"Actually, this morning, but you know how security is. They probably had it sitting in their booth all morning. It wasn't brought here until just after you'd left for lunch."

"Oh. Thanks." Savannah said, disappointed when nothing new was revealed.

And try as hard as she might, she could think of no one who would have made such an elaborate or expensive gesture. She finally moved the flowers to the window ledge. They blocked out a lot of daylight, but her office was filled with delicious fragrances that made her feel it had been converted into a garden. She inhaled with pleasure.

Savannah was typing up her comments and recommendations on a proposal when her phone rang an hour later.

"Hi, this is Savannah," she said absently, cradling the phone between ear and shoulder as she continued to work on her computer.

"Hello. I'm calling to see if you got the flowers."

She came to attention and focused on the rich tenor voice on the other end. "Who is this?"

"Didn't you read the card?" the voice asked.

"There was no card. And I don't know anyone who would send me something so extravagant."

"That's too bad," the voice drawled.

"Who are you? What do you want?" Savannah asked again, not so much annoyed as nervous.

"We met last night on the 405. Does that ring a bell?"

The car accident with a tall handsomely dressed stranger in a hurry. Imperial. Impervious. Impatient. Impossible!

"Oh, it's you. Well, don't think that I forgive you. I could have been injured. Or killed."

"When I asked, you said you were fine," McCoy Sutton responded in a voice of reason.

"That doesn't mean I was. I mean…it was a terrible

experience. You drove away leaving me standing in the middle of the highway, and never once considered that I might get hit."

"That's why I sent the flowers," he said.

"Too late," Savannah said grandly. She hung up.

Her satisfaction instantly evaporated. Her hands were trembling. Blood felt as though it was pounding in her temples. She was overly warm, still angry and still aware that things could have gone a whole lot worse. And now, having worked herself up into royal indignation, she was embarrassed.

The line went dead, and McCoy stared at his cell phone in disbelief. "I'll be damned," he muttered.

A car horn blew behind him, bringing him back to the moment. The previous night's highway incident flashed through his mind. His car was blocking the exit of the parking lot of an upscale restaurant just off Santa Monica Boulevard. He shifted gears and pulled out into traffic, headed back to his office.

His cell phone rang. For a brief second McCoy wondered if it could be Savannah Shelton, calling back to apologize…or to give him a piece of her mind. Steeling himself for a confrontation he answered on speakerphone, so he could drive safely.

"McCoy," he announced firmly.

"Hi, it's Cherise," came the silky, very feminine voice.

The corners of his mouth lifted in a tight little smile. "Cherise. How's it going?"

"Really good. I just wanted to thank you for calling Bob Sinclair and mentioning my work to him. I have an appointment to see him tomorrow," she said, excitement evident in her voice.

"That's great," McCoy responded automatically, but he checked the time to see how close it was to his own next appointment. "I hope it leads to something."

"Oh, I'm sure it will. I told Mr. Sinclair that I've known you for years. He thinks you're my attorney."

A small frown began to gather between McCoy's brows while he considered his response. "Bob Sinclair knows I'm not in the business, Cherise. Be careful what you tell people. This is a very small town and word gets around. You don't have to lie."

"Well, it was a little white lie," she giggled. "I just wanted him to understand that I have someone looking out for me."

A muscle worked in McCoy's jaw. "I think it's a good idea that he knows that. I have a couple of names of entertainment lawyers I can recommend to you. You'll need one sooner or later," he said, to soften his intent.

"But, you'll still help me if I need it, right?"

"I'll do the best I can, but I'm not the right kind of lawyer for what you'll need," McCoy said carefully. "I think you should also be prepared for some, er, setbacks now and then. This is a tough town. We eat our young."

There was silence for a brief moment.

"What?"

McCoy tried again. "I know you'll probably succeed, but keep in mind that not everyone is going to think you're wonderful and gorgeous."

"You think I'm wonderful and gorgeous? That's so sweet," Cherise responded.

As if she didn't know. McCoy silently shook his head. "But a director or producer might not see you as anyone out of the ordinary here in L.A."

"Then I guess it's up to me to convince them how unique I am."

McCoy's brows rose. He heard the ironclad confidence in the coy tone. Also, there was a ring of steel determination. Many a young black starlet came to L.A. with dreams of fame and wealth clouding her judgment. Most of them never got to first base. His guess, however, was that Cherise had quickly figured out how the game was played. He'd be a fool not to bet on her. But she'd be a fool to try and play him for her own ends.

Once again McCoy heard an impatient driver behind, reminding him that the light had changed. He glanced in his rearview mirror at a prototypical California blonde behind huge dark glasses, riding with a buff black man in equally dark shades at the wheel of a Mercedes coupe.

Welcome to the land of make-believe, he thought.

Well, why not? Los Angeles was a town of outsized egos, and even bigger dreams. He knew that a lot of people, black and white, came here because almost anything was possible. L.A. was a place where it was definitely okay to be yourself. Or, someone else. It could be a forgiving place. Short-term memory of past transgressions failed if there was an opportunity to make money.

Off the top of his head McCoy could remember the names and faces of a lot of talented black folks who'd tried to make it here and had failed. He knew from experience that L.A. could break a person's heart.

As he pulled into the garage of the high-rise building where his office was located, McCoy unexpectedly wondered what in the world had brought someone like Savannah Shelton to L.A.?

He didn't believe for a moment that it was to follow a dream.

Chapter 3

Savannah dropped two rolls of paper towel in her shopping cart and slowly continued down the narrow aisle looking for sponges and Formula 409. She found the items, adding them to the growing pile. Then she stood with her arms braced on the handle of the cart, while she perused her list.

But instead of the remaining five or six things she still needed to purchase, Savannah's focus shifted to the memory of the box she'd found in her father's closet. It was a cardboard suit box that she'd thought would contain shirts or sweaters or other clothing he no longer wore. Instead, when untied and opened, the box protected two piles of papers, each carefully wrapped in aging and yellowed tissue.

She'd resigned herself to the necessity of reading the contents to make sure that no important documents would be thrown out. But the papers had turned out to be an astonishing number of letters, articles and several journals, written in a shaky but feminine hand by one Rae Marie Hilton.

At first Savannah had assumed that a former lover had written the saved letters to her father. It was a possibility that was understandable, if demoralizing. There had been no time to read more than a few of them. The tone of the letters was desperate and fearful. They were also very personal, but had nothing to do with a love affair between Rae Marie Hilton and Will Shelton. It was all about Rae Marie's career as an actress, and the terrible secret she guarded that would have destroyed her.

Savannah blinked and stood straight. She was anxious to get back home and resume reading. There was a mystery in its contents that she wanted to get to the bottom of.

Right now, there were food items written on the bottom of her shopping list. Savannah expertly navigated the aisles until she was in the food and produce section of the market.

She was once again slowly scanning the shelves when someone turned the corner ahead. A man ambled along, carrying a handbasket already nearly filled. A quick glance revealed several varieties of cheese, boxes of crackers and cocktail bread, containers of olives and three bottles of wine. The basket looked heavy, and Savannah's curiosity was drawn to the man toting it so effortlessly.

He was wearing black jeans, a pale-yellow polo shirt and Docksides. His sunglasses were folded and hooked into the neckline of his shirt. His only jewelry was a heavy sports watch on his right wrist. His dark hair was thick with a slight wave in the texture, but cut short.

Something about him seemed vaguely familiar. Unable to place him, Savannah shifted her cart to wheel past, as he continued examining the shelves.

He glanced at her briefly, nodded and stepped back to allow her room.

Savannah suddenly became very aware of the fact that she was not dressed as fashionably as the man, even though he was in jeans. She was conscious of her exposed bare legs in a pair of khaki shorts, her olive-green cami visible through the front opening of a white camp shirt. The shirt had been added just before she'd walked out the door because she would have been too self-conscious if her nipples could be discerned through the tank's fabric. As it was, she felt decidedly underdressed in the stranger's presence.

"Excuse me."

Savannah stopped at the voice behind her and looked over her shoulder. His voice sounded familiar, too.

His lips were slightly pursed as he frowned at the stocked shelves.

"Would you happen to know where I'd find the mustard? I like the spicy kind."

"I think it's two aisles that way," Savannah responded, pointing. "French's Brown Spicy..."

He was shaking his head. "Grey Poupon."

"That, too." She turned to continue on her way.

"Excuse me."

Savannah stopped and turned again. He was staring at her.

"Have we met before?"

"That line is so lame," she said easily.

He laughed, sheepishly. "You're right, but..."

There was something in the bend of his head as he briefly glanced down. Something in the shape of his mouth. Now she remembered.

"Yes, we have met before," Savannah spoke up. She recited the day, approximate time and the circumstances. He'd rear-ended her on the expressway almost a week earlier.

"Right, right," he nodded, still staring at her.

This time, Savannah stood still while his gaze made a quick but thorough assessment of her. She tried to read into his silence, as he appeared to be remembering the incident in full. She was prepared to go on the defensive for what happened that night, and for the way she was dressed now. Then she changed her mind. Why should *she* care what he thought?

Another man turned down the aisle, his wagon holding not only food but also two very young children who were happily babbling to each other while their father shopped. He rolled by, his sudden appearance breaking the silent moment.

The man took several steps toward Savannah and suddenly thrust out his arm and hand in a firm take-charge manner.

"McCoy Sutton."

Savannah wasn't sure why, but she felt relief. She did the same, grasping the offered hand.

"Savannah Shelton."

"Well," McCoy said simply.

"Fancying meeting you here," she added dryly.

McCoy hesitated before suddenly breaking out into laughter. Savannah relaxed at his unexpected response, and didn't bother hiding her smile.

His gaze traveled up her, then down, and then up again. He lifted a brow as he looked into her eyes. "You don't look any the worse for that night."

"I'm okay. There's a small dent in my rear fender, but I wasn't going to hunt you down because of it. And you?"

He spread his arms open. "Not a scratch. Same with my car. If you send me an estimate for the repairs to your fender, I'll take care of it."

Savannah, who'd had several conversations with herself about what she'd say to McCoy Sutton if she ever ran into him again, was thrown off guard by the sudden offer.

"That's nice of you," she said stiffly, "but I'm not going to bother. It's a leased car. The dent comes under the heading of normal wear and tear."

"Your call," he conceded. He pointed to her cart. "Doesn't look appetizing. I hope you're not finished."

"No, I..." Savannah hesitated. An explanation would have been too long, and unnecessary. "No."

McCoy partially lifted his basket. "Friends for dinner. This is for the munchies-and-drinks part."

"Oh," she said. She found his explanation amusing. "Why not cater? Isn't that what people do in L.A.?"

"Some do. I like to cook. It's therapeutic."

She was surprised by his confession. The man she'd encountered the night of the accident had hardly seemed the cooking kind. Behind McCoy, Savannah suddenly saw an absolutely beautiful young black woman approaching. She couldn't believe that anyone would actually go shopping dressed as she was.

Her straight and expertly shaped long hair lifted and moved as she walked. She was wearing an above-the-knee fashionable take on the shirtwaist dress in tan, cinched at her small waist with a wide black patent leather belt. It was unbuttoned at the throat to show cleavage. Her sandals were at least three inches high, with thin straps that wrapped around the ankles several times and tied in front. Her finger- and toenails were lacquered to match her lip gloss. She was dressed to be seen...and appreciated.

"I was waiting at the raw bar. What's taking so long?" she opened, tilting her head around McCoy's frame, and smiling into his face.

Belatedly realizing that McCoy had actually been in conversation with someone, the stunning beauty looked at Savannah.

Savannah felt she might just as well have been invisible for all the interest she didn't see in the young woman's eyes. McCoy introduced them.

"This is Cherise Daly," he said. But before he could announce Savannah's name, Cherise spoke.

"Are you in the business, too?"

"The business?" Savannah frowned. "Oh, you mean the film industry. No, I'm not."

"I didn't think so. I've been auditioning like crazy lately. I'm about to sign a contract to do a pilot for a TV show. McCoy's been so great about helping me," she cooed, leaning into his arm.

Savannah forced herself to smile. "Congratulations. I hope you get the part."

Cherise turned her attention to McCoy. "I'm ready to go. What else are you looking for?"

"A few more things and then we're done. Why don't you wait for me at the checkout?"

"Okay. Bye," Cherise threw over her shoulder at Savannah as she swished away.

"She's very beautiful," Savannah said honestly.

"She's very young," was McCoy's response.

"Actress, right?"

"Is there any other kind in this town?" he asked. Then he looked speculatively at Savannah. "But you're not, as you said, in the business."

"By choice, thank you. You'd better go. I think she's getting impatient."

"Before you go I'd like to ask you something, if you don't mind."

Savannah, curious, nodded. "Go ahead."

"Any chance you're related to Will Shelton, the actor?"

It was the last thing Savannah had expected to be asked. But oddly enough the very question gave her a certain satisfaction. And it cemented the resolve she'd recently made not to sell her father's house. The question also confirmed what she was starting to find out about her father. She may have grown up resenting his choices and his career, but clearly there were people who knew and remembered Will Shelton with admiration and respect.

"I'm his daughter," Savannah said.

A slow smile curved McCoy's mouth. "I thought so. It occurred to me a few minutes ago that you looked familiar to me for a reason other than the accident last week. You have your father's eyes and smile. Did you know that?"

She didn't. No one had ever pointed that out before. She felt a sudden wave of emotion that went deep into her genes and family history.

"How could you see something like that? Did you know my father?"

"Only from his movies and TV roles," McCoy said, shaking his head.

"I always thought I looked like my mother," she said.

"Then you come from good-looking parents and got the best of both. You certainly hold your own."

Savannah wondered if McCoy was coyly making fun of her, but saw only light and interest in his gaze.

"I heard that Shelton was ill. How's he doing?"

"He passed away some months ago," Savannah said. Again, she felt on the edge of emotion. She delicately cleared her throat to keep the sudden feelings at bay.

"I didn't know. I don't remember reading anything about his death in the trades."

"There was a small item in his union paper. Other than that he didn't want any announcements. There was only family and a handful of personal friends at the funeral. His agent was the only industry person in attendance."

McCoy frowned. "Why? Sooner or later word will get around. He deserves more attention and recognition."

"I don't know," Savannah said. "He just didn't seem to want to make a big deal about the fact that he was dying."

"I'm sorry for your loss. I'm sure you know your father was a very fine actor. One of the unsung good guys in Hollywood."

"Thanks for saying so."

McCoy merely nodded, not pursuing the questions that Savannah could see he really wanted to ask. She was not about to admit her ignorance of her father's life and career in L.A. Who he knew, and who knew him.

That box of curious letters came to mind. Who was Rae Marie Hilton?

"You're keeping Denise waiting."

"Cherise," McCoy corrected.

Whatever.

"Nice meeting you."

Savannah didn't wait for him to say anything else. This was the part where he might say, *Let's keep in touch* or *I'll be in touch* or *May I have your phone number* or even *It was nice meeting you; good luck, and farewell.*

"I'm sure we'll see each other again. This is really a small town," McCoy said smoothly. "Take care."

They were headed in opposite directions. Savannah suddenly stopped her cart.

"Mr. Sutton," she called out.

McCoy turned. They began walking back toward each other. Savannah had this eerie feeling that the only thing missing from the scene was them jogging in slow motion, with classical music to herald their coming together.

"McCoy. Call me Mac, please."

"Thank you for the flowers."

"Are you sure?"

She shifted uncomfortably.

"I'm just teasing. Frankly, I had visions of you tossing the whole thing in the garbage."

"That would have been criminal. They're beautiful."

"And you hung up on me."

"Don't push your luck," Savannah said.

McCoy shrugged. "Sending flowers was the least I could do after, as you say, deserting you in the middle of the highway. I was in a hurry."

"Yeah, I got that part."

"Look, I was late for a fundraising dinner to benefit a black theater program out in Englewood. I was the MC for the silent auction. But that wasn't your problem, was it?"

"Did you make it?"

A brief look of annoyance clouded his eyes. "Just barely. It was all because of…never mind. I missed the dinner but the auction did well for the program."

Savannah had the feeling that Cherise had been a factor. She remembered that there had been a female passenger in the car with McCoy that night. Was she a trophy? Accessory?

"But that's still no excuse for driving recklessly," he said.

"Okay," Savannah sighed in resignation. "I accept some of the blame. I suppose I should have been paying more attention to the car ahead of me."

"I rest my case," he said unequivocally. But he suddenly winked at her before doing an about-face and finally going off about his business.

Savannah stared after his retreating back. She knew that she'd behaved very badly about the flowers and the phone call. In New York, anyone else might have said I'll-have-my-insurance-agent-call-your-insurance-agent. She remembered from McCoy Sutton's business card that he was an attorney. In New York he might have sued her, and won.

She thought about McCoy Sutton through the rest of

her shopping, and all the way home. Although she was certainly curious about the relationship between him and the gorgeous woman with him, she did not see them again. But his comments about her father reminded Savannah of similar remarks from Taj, and just about anyone else she met who'd heard of him. It gave her an odd feeling to know that her father was also in the public domain.

There was a bulky envelope in the mailbox when she returned to the house, from Simon Raskin, her father's former agent. Curious as to what he would be sending her at this late date, Savannah sat at the kitchen counter to read the contents, even before unpacking her groceries.

Much of the information had to do with her father's pension fund, SAG membership and such. She was about to stuff everything back into the envelope when a small card with a handwritten message fell into her lap. It was a note of regret that her father had not gotten a particular part, but also encouragement and admiration for his talent. It was signed, Sidney.

The possibility of it being from *the* Sidney made Savannah smile. Then she realized that she just might be reacting like a starstruck fan of her own father. His peers had respected him. How cool was that?

All in all, she was very glad she'd kept the flowers sent her by McCoy Sutton. And that she'd stayed in California.

* * *

"How come movies never say The End anymore when it's over? They just start rolling right into the credits," Donna asked, as people around them began shuffling about and leaving the theater.

"You don't need it," Kay responded, as she pushed her seat back into an upright position. "If you're paying attention the action and dialogue tells you that."

"Or the sudden dramatic swelling of music," Savannah added, standing. "I like it better without being told."

"Yeah. That kind of kills the mood, you know?" Kay said.

They began filing out of their row, Kay in the lead and Savannah picking up the rear, along with the three hundred other viewers.

"Thanks for getting us into the screening," Savannah said to Kay, once they'd made it to the lobby.

"No problem. It's one of the perks of my job. I can't remember the last time I had to pay to see a film," Kay said.

"I'm so glad you're my friend," Donna yawned.

The Special Screening Tonight sign was still on the marquee. Savannah watched as Kay said hello to a number of people she recognized from the audience, all of them involved in the movie business in one way or another; from extras to gophers, to grips and camera crew people, they had come out to see the fruits of their labors.

Savannah looked around. She was sure she'd seen

Taj enter and take a seat with a friend before the lights had gone down. But she didn't see him anywhere. She did, however, spot a very pretty young woman with blond corkscrew hair whom she remembered from the crafts show, and just as quickly lost her in the crowd.

"Where should we go to eat?" Donna asked, as the three of them stood outside the theater.

"I don't care," Kay said. "But I don't feel like going all the way to Santa Monica. It's so hard to find parking down there…"

Savannah listened as Kay and Donna debated, deferring to their superior knowledge of L.A. and places to eat. She would have been content with a small quiet café, off the beaten track and away from the chance that celebrities, even those of minor fame, frequented it. But she knew that both Kay and Donna loved that aspect of dining out, just so they could boast who they'd had dinner with.

Donna and Kay had now moved on to what kind of food they wanted. Savannah waited patiently, taking the opportunity to look more closely at the people around her. Only recently had she been curious to know what kind of people lived in L.A. Where had they all come from? Since she'd yet to meet anyone who had actually been born here. And why were so many of them hell-bent on making it? On the other hand, the lyrics to a Frank Sinatra song, "New York, New York," popped into her head with the famous line about "if I can make it there, I'll make it anywhere…" Savannah smiled to herself. That could hold true for the City of Angels.

"Hi."

Savannah turned around at the greeting. She found herself face-to-face with Domino, the fabric artist.

"Oh, hi," Savannah replied. "I thought I saw you before. It's nice to see you."

"Thanks. Did you just leave the screening?"

"Yes. I came with two girlfriends. One of them is in PR and got us into the film. How'd you like it?"

"It's a great story. I'm a little disappointed in my performance."

Savannah frowned. "You were in the film? Where? How did I miss you?"

Domino chuckled. "It wasn't hard. I was wearing a brunette wig. I was the girlfriend of the main protagonist at the very beginning. He left me for a singer."

Savannah's eyes widened. "Oh, you're kidding. Was that you? I couldn't tell."

"Yeah, I know, but you probably weren't looking to see me, either," Domino said. "It was a small part, but I want people to know it was me."

"I feel badly that I didn't recognize you, but you did a good job in the part. I felt so sorry when your boyfriend took off with the other woman. I liked that you got mad at him and not her." Savannah said.

"Thanks for saying so. Actually, that part led to an audition for something else the director is doing, so I'm pleased."

"We decided on a little place over in West Hollywood near the UCLA campus," Donna said, as she and Kay joined Savannah. She noticed the other woman and stared at her for a moment. "You look familiar."

Savannah beckoned Domino closer. "This is Dominique..."

"Hamilton," Dominique supplied.

"You're an actress. Now, where have I seen you before?" Kay said more to herself, narrowing her gaze on the young actress.

"How about in the last hundred and ten minutes," Donna suggested. "Did you play the part of the girlfriend at the beginning?"

Domino smiled calmly. "That's me."

"Well, I give you credit for being so nice to the jerk. Man, I would have kicked his ass if he'd done that to me," Donna said with female indignation.

"I suggested something like that to the director, but he said her character wouldn't do that. He was right. She had to remain likeable."

"Listen, we're going for some dinner. Would you like to join us?" Kay asked Domino.

"I was just going to suggest that," Savannah said.

Domino hesitated. "You're having a girlfriends' night out. I don't want to mess up your plans."

"We'd love to have you," Donna added. "Besides, I want to know some of the inside dirt on getting work. I'm a dancer...."

Savannah let Kay and Donna bombard Dominique

with questions about the trade. But there was a lot of laughing, and a lot of harmless gossip. She mostly listened, liking Dominique more and more for her open friendliness and for the balanced life she'd managed to achieve while she waited to be discovered. Savannah was impressed when Dominique stated she had no burning desire to become a big-name movie star. She just wanted to act, to work as long as she could. Savannah could see at least one problem the actress might be encountering. There didn't seem to be anything superficial or calculating about her. The lovely young thing with McCoy Sutton came to mind. Savannah had the feeling that Cherise was more like the industry standard. She was a little disappointed that McCoy seemed to go for that type.

It also made her wonder about Rae Marie Hilton. Who was she and what was her connection to her father? Especially since Rae Marie was white.

They were waiting for after-dinner coffee and cappuccino to be served when Donna suddenly planted her elbows on the table and leaned across to regard Dominique closely.

"I bet you never get asked to play the black female roles."

Kay looked dumbfounded at Donna's comment. But for Savannah, suddenly a lot of things she'd witnessed about Dominique's gestures and body language, her use of certain phrases, made sense. She looked at Dominique more closely. There was nothing to make the average person believe she was anything but white. But there were the slightly full lips. Were they real or was it collagen? Her hair texture appeared curly, but might also have been slightly relaxed to make it more manageable. There was nothing in Dominique's expression that would have said otherwise.

"No, I don't. Even when I prove I can talk the talk."

"What are you trying to say?" Kay asked.

"It's not really about how you sound. It's about how you look," Donna said knowledgeably.

Savannah nodded. "I wondered myself. Are you biracial?"

"I'm African-American." Dominique said, not hesitating for a second. "Most people don't notice, or don't ask. I don't volunteer that I'm black, but I don't deny it."

Savannah wondered what Dominique thought as she, Kay and Donna stared openly at her, fascinated by this little phenomenon of nature, genes and history.

"I'm sorry. I know it's rude to stare, but I just can't get over it. I've never seen anyone like you, but I *knew* you had to be black," Donna said.

"How?" Kay asked. "I can't tell."

Donna shrugged. "I don't know. It's just one of those things I felt. I kind of connected to the way you talked, and maybe how comfortable you seemed with us right from the start."

"Yeah, that's what I felt," Kay nodded. "You just seem to fit right in."

"I wasn't trying to put something over on you..."

"No, no. That's not it," Savannah spoke up. "But we all grew up hearing or reading about black men and women who are light enough to pass."

"But I'm not trying to pass for white," Dominique clarified. "I'm always myself, and I don't *pretend* to be anything else but black. But people never ask. It's all about the color of my skin, hair and eyes. Most people don't see anything else."

"Look, forget the cappuccino," Kay said, signaling for the waiter. "I'm ordering another bottle of wine."

They all burst out laughing.

"I'm sorry if I put you on the spot," Donna said earnestly.

"You didn't, I promise. If I can't handle what people think or believe about me, what they come to find out about me, then I'm in trouble and in the wrong business. Being an actress is all about becoming other people."

"But how do you get work?" Savannah asked.

"It's hard. I can play and pass for a lot of different ethnic types with makeup and wigs. But getting someone to believe I can play an African-American doesn't fly. The audience wants to see someone who looks a lot like them. I don't.

"One of my friends in high school used to tell me I'm a fake..."

There was an audible gasp around the table.

"She used to say I didn't have a clue what it was like being black, 'cause I wasn't. "

"Yeah, and I bet she got on your case because all the boys flocked around you like bees to honey."

"I bet not," Savannah conjectured. "I bet they were afraid of you."

"Right," Dominique nodded firmly. "If they were seen with me they might be accused by their homeboys of preferring white girls. I don't think I should have to explain or defend who I am."

"I hear that," Donna nodded.

"So, how are you doing? Are you from L.A.?" Kay wanted to know.

"I graduated Yale, but I was born in Texas. I'm okay. I work."

"Domino is also a wonderful fabric artist," Savannah interjected, wanting to get away from the subject that seemed to be an interrogation of Dominique, even a friendly one.

"Really?" Donna asked, surprise. "Like what?"

"Like this shawl I brought with me," Domino said, and pulled from her large tote bag one of her own creations.

Savannah sat smiling, as Donna and Kay exclaimed over the fine woven cloth. Then she told them she had a shawl on layaway, and took out her checkbook to write a second payment to Domino.

"You have my card. You can come by my studio anytime to make the final payment and pick it up," Domino said to Savannah, then turned to Donna and Kay. "Sorry to be taking care of business during your dinner out."

"Well, I want to know how I can get one, too," Kay said, examining the work on Domino's shawl. "This is really nice."

"Me, too," Donna joined in.

The conversation turned to the recent crafts show. Kay was doubly sorry she'd missed the exhibit now that she and Donna had had a chance to see Domino's work.

"Thank you for inviting me to join you tonight. This was really great," Domino said, as they finally walked out to the parking lot.

"I'm sorry for getting in your business the way I did," Donna said.

"I didn't take it that way."

"Now that we've met, I have to rent all the movies you've been in. Give me some titles," Kay demanded.

Dominique laughed as she recited several.

Savannah was the last to say goodbye to Domino, while Donna and Kay got in Donna's car and waited for her.

"And you thought you were just going for dinner," she smiled ruefully at Dominique.

"It was all good. I have black friends here in the business, but it's very competitive. I don't expect anyone to have sympathy for what I have to go through. I'm going up to Vancouver day after tomorrow to shoot a small part."

"I'm glad," Savannah said warmly.

"But I'm not giving up my day job yet." They

laughed. "Good night," Dominique waved, walking away to her car.

"Good night," Savannah called after her, before climbing into the backseat of Donna's car.

"Well! Surprise, surprise," Kay said.

"I like her," said Donna, who had a very good bull-shit detector.

"Me, too," Savannah said. Then added reflectively. "This is the first time I've gotten a true sense of how hard it is to get your foot in the door without getting it slammed on. She reminds me of someone else who came out here to act."

"That twinkie-dink guy you work with? What's his name? Taj?"

Savannah chuckled. "No, not Taj. Anyway, I have no doubts he's going to make it. I don't know how talented he is, but he's so determined. I'm thinking of someone else."

My father.

Chapter 4

Savannah untied the red string around the first bundle in the box found in her father's closet. Little bits of dried and brittle paper flaked off from the edges of newspaper articles, layered in between letters, tear sheets and one composition notebook that looked as if it might be a journal. The dust spoke of the age of the materials and the need to be careful not to damage them further. She gently blew the dust away. Now, where to begin?

Savannah decided against any attempt to put the papers in some sort of order. For all she knew, they were already in order, just one that wasn't readily apparent. Right away a line in the top sheet caught her attention.

It seemed to be a continuation of a review from some publication, the start of the piece either missing, or out of place in the two piles.

> ...Miss Hilton, a young starlet of astonishing beauty, with her abundant Raphaelite hair and mesmerizing green eyes, is miscast in the role of the flirtatious neighbor's daughter. Her demeanor is too nervous, too self-conscious. But I wouldn't count her out as a rising star. She is talented, and sometimes affecting. I see great things in her future, given the right project and the right director who can coax genuine emotion from the young actress....

Savannah settled back more comfortably in the poolside lounger, preparing to spend the next hour reading about a white actress who had obviously come in contact with her father and developed a relationship. The partial review was older than she was. Did that mean her father knew Rae Marie Hilton before he'd left the east coast for Hollywood, or had met her afterward?

It was necessary for Savannah to shift her chair several times as the sun crossed the sky and the day slipped away. She ignored the telephone when it rang twice as she was reading. She distantly heard the front doorbell but made no attempt to find out who the caller was. She gave no thought to the chores she'd lined up for the day, and it never once occurred to her to put the documents aside, even for an hour or two. She was riveted by the unveiling portrait of a young Hollywood hopeful who was desperate for recognition from film power brokers, but who lived under some sort of cloud of uncertainty and fear.

When her cell phone rang around four o'clock, Savannah reached for the unit, conveniently placed on the flagstone patio next to her chair. She quickly tried to finish a sentence in which it was reported that Rae Marie was suspected of having an affair with one of Warner Brothers' hot young male properties, a blond former athlete with action-film aspirations.

"Hello?" Savannah answered absently.

"Where are you? I thought you were going to call me this morning."

Savannah's concentration was abruptly broken. "Harris. I'm so sorry. I forgot all about calling."

"Thanks a lot," her brother said dryly. "I hope you had a good reason."

"I don't know about that. I was going through some of Daddy's papers. I didn't want to just throw them out."

"Sure, I understand. Find anything important?"

Savannah gnawed the inside of her jaw. "So far, the usual stuff. Plus, there are a lot of things from his career. Maybe not so much important as interesting. How are you?"

"Great. On my way to Germany."

"Really? What's in Germany?"

"I'm going over to work with the foreign service contingent to train them in new government procedures."

"Well, that sounds like fun," she said.

"It's not, but it is Germany. It'll be my first time there. Just wanted to check in with you to see how it was going before I go."

"Is Janet going with you?"

"Not this time. I'm only going to be away two weeks, and the boys are close to the end of the school year. She wants to be around for last-minute tests and projects.

"I thought I might fly out and see you when I get back. Maybe for a long weekend. Is that okay with you?"

"That would be great."

"We can take care of whatever else needs to be done about Dad's affairs and spend some time together. Must be a little hard living in the house now that he's gone," Harris observed.

Savannah sighed and tilted her head back against the cushioned lounger. "Not as bad as I thought it would be. I love the house, Harris, but right now it still feels like I'm just a visitor. I've decided it's time to put Daddy's things away. Since I'm going to stay in L.A., I don't want this house to look like a shrine. Have any thoughts about what I should do with everything?"

"I'd like to have some of the photographs, especially those of him with Poitier, Sammy Davis, Jr., and I think there was one with Lena Horne. Oh, and can I have any scripts you find?"

"Sure. What else?"

"That's all I can think of for the moment. But keep anything else that looks interesting until I come out."

"I will. Harris, I have to ask you something. Do you know if Daddy was involved with anyone else? I mean, romanticwise, after he and Mommy separated?"

Harris laughed. "Are you kidding? The man was a good-looking dude. I'm sure there were lots of women who wouldn't necessarily kick him out of bed."

"Yeah, but, do you think there was anyone in particular?"

"Probably more than one over the years, but he never talked about anyone special to me. Why all these questions about Dad's love life?"

"I'm just curious. I realize now how little I knew about his life out here."

Harris sighed. "To be honest, Vann, you never seemed all that interested. I don't think you ever forgave him for going to L.A. to become an actor, and leaving us behind."

"I know. I lost a lot of time, didn't I?" Savannah said quietly. "I wish I did know more. I wish now I hadn't stayed angry for so long."

"It was hard for him, too. But he understood why you blamed him. He just didn't know what to do about it."

"How do you know all that?"

"We talked about it. Whenever I came out to spend time with him it was about me and him, not him and his acting career. It really hurt him that for so many years you wouldn't give him a chance to show how much he loved you. He felt guilty about not being there while we were growing up, but I never blamed him for that."

Savannah felt her throat starting to close. The feeling had come over her several times since her father had died. As if she was having a delayed reaction to the loss.

"I get the feeling there was a lot more to the story I didn't know about."

"Maybe Dad didn't want us to. But when he knew he was dying he asked you to come out to L.A. and be with him. Not anyone else. And you went. That says something, don't you think?"

She swallowed hard, and took a deep breath. "I'm glad I came. I hope it's not too late."

"Too late for what?"

"I…don't know exactly. That's just how I feel."

"Let me know if I can do anything to help."

"I do have another question. Did you ever hear Daddy talk about someone named Rae Marie Hilton? I think she was an actress he knew."

"Doesn't ring a bell. Why?"

"Daddy has a lot of letters and papers from her. The thing is, she was white. Nothing romantic, as far as I can tell, but I'm curious."

"No. Can't say that the name means anything."

After Harris said goodbye, Savannah decided to take a break and run some errands. She'd decided, after going through all of her father's papers and records, that she would organize them. For a while she'd been thinking about giving some to her brother, and keeping some for herself. But she considered that his Hollywood history, particularly as a black actor, might be useful somewhere. Savannah considered that New York's Schomburg Center for the study of African-American history might be a good place.

A few hours later, when she returned to the house, she noticed that there was a small shopping bag that someone had left at the top of the driveway, just outside the wrought-iron gate to the property. Annoyed that someone would be so thoughtless as to leave garbage behind, Savannah parked her car, and then walked back to remove the bag. She was going to dump it in the trash bin when the weight of the bag made her curious. Glancing cautiously inside, she was surprised to find that it contained a potted plant. Reaching into the bag, Savannah carefully removed the contents, an African violet with rich purple blossoms and lush green leaves. It was beautifully planted in what seemed to be a blue and white ceramic sugar bowl.

Savannah glanced up and down the street, helplessly trying to figure out if the plant had been left by a neighbor or someone else. And why? The residential street was quiet and deserted. She looked inside the bag to see if there was a note or card, but it was empty. Puzzled, Savannah took the plant inside with her, trying to decide what to do about it. The phone was ringing as she entered the house through the garage.

"Hello," she answered.

"Hi. It's McCoy."

Savannah experienced an unexpected and instant reaction to McCoy identifying himself. It was a combination of surprise, wariness, and pleasure.

"Am I interrupting anything?" he asked, when she didn't immediately respond.

"No, not really. I just got back from taking care of a few things."

"Good. I thought I'd check and see how things are going."

She frowned. "How things are going? Like, what?"

"Well, I know your father died recently, so I'm assuming you're still dealing with that, his business and estate. You know. Are you managing okay?"

"Oh. Why do you want to know?"

After a second's pause, McCoy began to chuckle. "You know, I'm the one who's usually giving people the third degree. You missed your calling."

"I don't mean to sound rude, but I…I don't understand, frankly, why you're calling me."

"You don't. Of course not," he seemed to say more to himself than to her.

"I do have a question for you, since you called. I know this is going to sound strange, but did you leave a plant at my house sometime today?"

"Nice idea. But I don't know where you live," McCoy responded. "And I remember what happened the last time I sent you flowers."

Savannah felt like she was blushing, and was glad he couldn't see her expression. "That was different."

"If you say so."

She could hear the amusement in his voice.

"So, you found a plant. Maybe it's from a secret admirer."

"Are you making fun of me?" she asked, keeping her tone light.

"Why don't you think that's possible?"

"I don't know that many people in L.A. I've only been here a little over a year."

"Then I can't help you. But I wish I could."

Again Savannah felt the urge to blush, the banter between them taking on a curious personal exchange.

"So…you're calling because…"

"I have something for you. No, it's not a plant, but I think you'd like to have what it is. I was going through some old programs and invitations, and I found several from events involving your father. He was either performing or sitting on a panel, or hosting. Are you interested?"

"Yes. Of course. I'm going through boxes right now of things he'd kept about his career."

"Maybe we can get together and I can give you what I have. Are you doing anything this evening?"

"No, I'm not."

"What's a good time?"

Although she was glad for the opportunity to receive anything of her father's, Savannah hesitated to accept McCoy's offer. She'd never had visitors to the house, certainly not while her father was ill. So much of the past year or more had been spent seeing to his needs that Savannah realized she was a bit out of practice when it came to entertaining. Donna and Kay notwithstanding, she hadn't been much in the mood.

"Well..."

"Look, we can meet somewhere, if you like. This shouldn't take that long."

Of course he'd have other plans for the evening, Savannah considered. L.A., like New York, was a very social city. She didn't doubt for a minute that McCoy never lacked for things to do or places to be, or companionship. And while she'd not been all that impressed with some of the men she'd met here, Savannah had to be fair and admit that McCoy did not come across as being self-absorbed.

She agreed to meet him, and gave McCoy the name and location of one of the many cafés that lined the boulevard several blocks from the house. They set a time and said goodbye to each other.

After completing his call with Savannah, McCoy sat staring thoughtfully at his cordless telephone before replacing it in its cradle. A rueful smile lifted one corner of his mouth. Man, she'd really made him work for the privilege of getting together with her. And as annoying as that might be on the one hand, on the other it was a novelty and refreshing. Savannah Shelton was intriguing, her independence and attractiveness a sharp contrast to the Hollywood fetish of most women he tended to meet, with their it's-all-about-me focus.

He got up from the kitchen island, where he'd made the call. He picked up the chilled glass of his own version of Long Island Iced Tea, and wandered out to the spacious balcony of his duplex condo, overlooking the Pacific. Sipping his drink, McCoy looked out at the stunning beauty of the ocean. From his apartment, he could pretend that L.A. lived up to its name as the City of Angels, and was as serene as the ocean view suggested. He could forget about the congestion on the freeways, and the L.A. energy that could try your patience when dealing with folks who were only watching out for themselves and what you could do for them. And the women…but it wasn't like he didn't already know the deal. As his grandmother would say, if you can't stand the heat, get out of the kitchen; may she rest in peace.

McCoy finished his drink and returned the glass to the kitchen. He had a weekly housekeeper, but his upbringing automatically led him to rinse out the used glass and place it in the dishwasher. He went in search of his car keys, his wallet, and the manila envelope containing the materials he had to give Savannah Shelton.

As he left his apartment, donning his sunglasses against the sun lowering in the western sky, McCoy was reluctant to admit that not only was he looking forward to an opportunity to see Savannah Shelton again, he knew he had to be careful. She was not the kind of woman to try to get one over on.

He was the first to arrive at the restaurant, and he'd planned it that way. He wanted to acclimate himself to his surroundings. McCoy had a sense that Savannah lived nearby. He liked what he saw of the neighborhood. It was definitely upscale, but not pretentious. He could tell from the passersby that it was mostly African-Americans who inhabited the local homes and, while they might not be rich by Beverly Hills standards, they were clearly doing very well. It was attractive, quiet, clean and comfortable.

McCoy spotted Savannah before she saw him. She was approaching the corner, and looking both ways for a chance to cross the street. Relaxing in the iron bistro chair, he took his time to update the first impression, and the second, he'd had of Savannah. He had to admit, it was getting better and better.

She wasn't tall or leggy, or a size 2. She was average height, slender but with curves. Actually, he considered as she began to cross the street, Savannah was very nicely proportioned and put together. If he put his arms around her he knew he wouldn't feel like he had to be careful about crushing delicate bones. McCoy also did not berate himself for enjoying the physical aspect of seeing her, reminding himself, righteously, that it was her self-possession and clear personal boundaries that had ultimately gotten his attention. Seeing her now as an appealing woman was a bonus.

Savannah was wearing a pair of capri pants, a cheerful print on a black background. He knew the pants to be popular, but had *never* seen any women in the industry dare to dress down in them. Her light summer top had a wide boatneck opening, exposing a long neck around which was a simple heart-shaped gold pendant with a pearl in its center. Her earrings were large, thin gold hoops. No diamonds. No precious gemstones. She was wearing ballet flats in orange, one of the colors on her pants.

Her hair was also distinctive from most of the women he knew. Savannah wore hers natural, fuller on the top and front, and shorter in the back. The texture appeared to be light and soft, the cut giving her an interesting and tasteful punklike look. McCoy would guess that Savannah wasn't aware, nor would she necessarily care, that her personal style made her stand out from the usual L.A. fare.

She saw him. He stood up as she approached, her eyes hidden behind her dark glasses. But so were his.

"Am I late? Thank you," she said, as he held out a chair for her to sit. She looked all around, as if expecting to also see someone else with him.

He chose to ignore her silent inquiry. "No, not at all. I wasn't sure how long it was going to take me to drive over, so I was a few minutes early."

Immediately a waiter appeared. They both ordered wine.

McCoy glanced around again. "Nice community. Do you live here?" He watched as she considered his question and her answer.

"I'm not that far away," she murmured. "And you?"

"Santa Monica."

"Nice. Expensive," she said.

"I was lucky. I moved in when it was still affordable."

"Moved in from where?"

"I'm not from L.A.," McCoy confessed easily. "I grew up in Long Beach, attended Princeton..."

"Really?"

"...But came back to California following an opportunity."

"She must have been some opportunity," Savannah said quietly with a slight smile.

McCoy pursed his lips in appreciation. "At the time she was. She became my wife, but that was then."

"And now?"

He shrugged, waiting until their wine was served before responding. He picked up his glass but didn't immediately take a drink.

"We were young. We divorced, she went on to fame and fortune, and I went into real estate law. Here's to the past, present and future."

Savannah raised her glass and they clinked the rims together.

"What a strange toast," she said.

"It pretty much covers everything. From how we met, which you have to admit was usual, to this moment, to whatever comes next."

She nodded silently and took a sip of her wine.

With the flurry of greeting and small talk out of the

way, McCoy felt an unexpected awkwardness settle over them. He quickly spoke to bridge the silence.

"Where did you grow up?"

"East Coast. Mostly my mother raised my brother and me. My parents divorced when I was about seven. I've only been in Los Angeles a little under two years. I came out to be with my father after I learned he was terminal."

"And you decided to stay?"

McCoy watched as she glanced around, took a deep breath and another sip of wine, and nodded. "I think so. Life is much easier out here. The weather is better. I didn't give up much in New York."

"What do you do out here?"

"I work for a studio. Surprised?"

"A little. I got the impression you don't think much of L.A."

"It's not L.A. as a place. It's the movie industry that I don't care much for."

"What do you know about the industry?" McCoy quickly asked. She looked embarrassed.

"Well, not a lot, I admit. My father was an actor."

"But he left the family to become one out here. I'm sure that didn't sit well."

"It didn't, but I think I'm beginning to understand what it meant to him to follow his dreams. He might have regretted it his whole life if he'd never tried."

"It's good that you realize that. But you had no desire to follow in his footsteps?"

"I'm a writer. In New York I was a contributing editor

to a magazine. Out here I read proposals and treatments and write critiques and coverages and make recommendations. I actually like what I do."

He held up his glass again. "I hope you like it well enough to stay."

Savannah grinned. "You know, you're the first person who's said that. Thank you."

"Now, let me show you what I have for you..."

McCoy took the envelope, which had been leaning against the leg of his chair, and placed it on the table. He opened it and slid out nearly a dozen pieces of printed material. Both he and Savannah removed their sunglasses as they looked over the contents. There were invitations to programs and events held at theaters or college campuses. There was an announcement for a book signing at the famed black bookstore, Eso Won, with author Donald Bogle, known for his bestselling books about blacks in Hollywood. Will Shelton had moderated that event.

He explained what each event had been about, and Will Shelton's contributions. As he spoke, offering details and impressions, McCoy was aware of Savannah's intense interest in each piece of material she looked at. She was especially fascinated with the photos and brief bios of her father that had been printed in each case. She looked long and hard and lovingly, he thought, at one image of her father as he was photographed surrounded by a dozen or so students, both black and white.

"That's at UCLA," McCoy explained, pointing to the

brochure Savannah was examining. "Your father was a guest lecturer one semester. He basically used himself as an example to show students how difficult it is to break into the industry by talking anecdotally about his own career. I attended two of the sessions."

"I didn't know he was in a play," Savannah murmured, looking at the program for a limited run of *A Soldier's Story.*

"Listen, like a lot of black actors and actresses, your father probably took any decent work he could find. The run of that play got good reviews and was extended an extra two weeks. I'm sorry you missed his performance."

"Me, too," Savannah said. "I was away at school during the play's run. I can't thank you enough for showing these to me."

"They're yours. Put them in your scrapbook."

She smiled but shook her head. "I never kept a scrapbook about my father. But I'd like to add these to what I've already found in his house."

"Of course you can have them. Now I'm glad I never threw them away."

"Why didn't you?"

"I guess I thought that it would all be important information one day. I was hoping to eventually give it to some black organization. I never got around to it."

"I'm like to do something like that myself. It seems to me that my father had a long and productive career, don't you think? He made a contribution."

"Absolutely," McCoy nodded. "If you like, I can help you research some organizations that might be interested in his archives."

"I appreciate that," Savannah said, putting everything back into the envelope. "I don't know how to thank you. I never realized before how active my father was out here. He did a lot."

"Yes, he did. And he gave back as much as he got. Do you know there's a small neighborhood theater in Englewood that's named after him?"

Savannah silently stared at him, maybe embarrassed and horrified that there was so much she didn't know about her father's life in L.A. But McCoy could understand that all she might have cared about was the Will Shelton who was her father, not necessarily Will Shelton the actor, whom she had to share with a cast of thousands. He leaned forward.

"Whenever you have some time, I'd be glad to take you out to see it. It's a nice little theater."

Savannah rubbed her temple. "A lot of people knew him, didn't they?"

"Of course. Or knew about him. But I don't think many people realize that he's dead."

She was thoughtful, staring blindly into her now-empty wineglass. McCoy gently touched the back of her hand.

"Hey," he said quietly.

He knew that Savannah did not realize the poignant picture she made, reflecting on her father's public life. But he wondered what else she was thinking.

Savannah blinked at him. "Don't worry. I'm going to make sure he gets the recognition he deserves."

Savannah stretched and yawned. A glance at her clock radio showed 2:17 a.m. She knew she should have turned out her lights and gone to sleep hours ago. But the secret box with its two neatly tied bundles of paper had become too fascinating and revealing to put down.

What she had thought would be a quick exchange of materials with McCoy Sutton had turned into a few hours. He'd talked her into having dinner with him, right where they were. It was an unexpected invitation, but one that she welcomed.

It surprised Savannah how easy it was to be in McCoy's company. She could relax after her initial suspicion of his motives because it wasn't all about him. And he seemed remarkably easygoing given her first impression of him. To go right back home, she realized, surrounded by everything that was her father, might have been too much. In the end Savannah was grateful for the distraction.

And McCoy had done something else that she would always be grateful for. He had not spent the evening talking about Hollywood or the famous people he knew. No mention was made of the beautiful young woman she'd seen him with on two occasions. Instead, he told some pretty funny stories about getting started as a lawyer, and the mistakes he'd made believing he knew more than he did. He talked about his family: a mother who was deceased, a father who was a retired eye doctor living in Oakland, and a younger brother. He glossed quickly over the fact that he'd been married himself and divorced, only saying, 'I was young, in love and stupid.'

McCoy's willingness to talk about himself laid the groundwork for Savannah to tell him something of her life in New York, and why she wasn't necessarily sad about leaving it all behind for L.A. And, as she honestly said to McCoy, L.A. was growing on her. He'd laughingly accused her of being an East-Coast snob. Savannah smiled now as she recalled laughing as well, taking his comment in the manner in which he intended.

She yawned again. She knew the smart thing would be to turn out her light and get to sleep. But with only a few more pages to go, Savannah promised herself that she'd just finish the last of the letters from the first bundle.

Based on what she'd read so far she concluded that Rae Marie Hilton and her father had not been lovers, but professional friends. She did wonder how they'd been able to pull that off without any gossip or publicity. Had it been possible for a black man and white woman to just be friends in Hollywood back then? They'd met while costarring on a short-lived TV show in the 1980s. Savannah was surprised to read that Rae Marie had obviously trusted her father, and had made him her confidant. Her letters said, in so many words, that there was no one else she could talk to in all of Tinseltown.

Savannah also read, with sympathy, the desperation with which Rae Marie seemed to have lived her life. She wanted to be a star and was willing to do anything to achieve that. She wanted the adoration, the fame and the recognition that come with being someone the public loves. She was insecure but determined. She was beautiful and saw her beauty as a tool to achieve what she wanted so badly. She wrote that she'd done things she was ashamed of, compromising, as she stated, her upbringing and family values. There was even one poignant plea that God would forgive her.

But it was a simple quickly stated truth, scrawled in one of the journals, which finally clarified for Savannah Rae Marie's fundamentally unhappy life, and how the power and seductiveness of a dream had led her to use Will Shelton as a sounding board and the keeper of her deepest most horrific secret.

> I went to an audition this morning. The casting director actually walked around me, examining me like I was a horse. Touched my hair, pushed it from my face and stared at it. Then he looked at me and said, 'It's very curly, isn't it?' I laughed and said he should know hair could be made straight or curly. That was the end of it, but the way he looked at me scared me silly. Afterward I ran to the ladies' room and stared in the mirror. What else had he noticed? I'd never had any problems before, but I wondered if he could tell. Is it

something about my nose or my lips? What if he'd asked me about my background?

My friend Will said he could tell when we first met that I wasn't white. He said it was the way I talked and sometimes what I said. I have to be more careful. Will said it wasn't his place to judge what other people did with their lives. I told him I was just using what God had given me. Hell, in one way I've been acting all my life to get by. I think Will sometimes feels sorry for me, but he also tries to watch out for me. He said everybody's got something they're trying to live up to, or live down....

Chapter 5

Savannah stared at her screen, trying to keep track of the various links that had generated from her Google search for the name *Rae Marie Hilton.*

She'd been surprised by the number of possible hits, but the past hour spent checking out some of them had produced only the mention of Rae Marie's name from cast lists, dated reviews and several old profiles. None of the information had been revealing, or even very personal. The one thing Savannah had not been able to find out was whether the actress was dead or alive.

"Hey, Baby Girl. What's up?" Taj asked, stepping into her office space and planting himself in the extra chair.

Taj's sudden appearance made Savannah jump with guilt. She didn't want anyone to know why she was researching an obscure actress who probably hadn't been heard of in two decades. He was wearing one earplug from an iPod while the other swung free in front of his chest. From the tiny amplifier came the screechy distorted sounds of a rap song.

"What are you listening to?" She asked.

"Great new group out of Compton called MoJo. They're starting to get a lot of play and some press. I'm thinkin' of contacting them and offering my services as a producer. What you working on?"

"Oh...er...I just finished writing a critique of a treatment. It was good enough that I wanted to see what I could find on the Internet about the author."

Taj snickered. "Don't waste your time. He could be an ax murderer, but if the studio bosses think they can make a buck off this guy's story that's all that matters."

"You're too young to be so cynical," Savannah said, as she logged back into her e-mail, and stared at the screen. There was a message from McCoy.

"And you're too...*mature* to be so innocent," Taj said carefully.

Savannah chuckled. "I need a favor from you since, by your own proclamation, you know everything and everyone in Hollywood."

"Anything for you, you know that."

"I'm trying to find out about a former actress by the name of Rae Marie Hilton. She would have been in the business about twenty-five years ago. And she's white," Savannah concluded smoothly.

"Never heard of her but I'll see what I can dig up for you. You should also check out the American Film Institute. They've got records on everybody who was anybody in this town, from way back."

"That's a good idea," Savannah said, making a note. But it occurred to her that she might also use that source to see what more she could learn about Will Shelton.

"I got something for you," Taj suddenly said in a sweet, coy voice.

"Really?"

"Sure do. It's on my desk. I'll be right back…"

He was out the door in a shot, and Savannah turned at once to her e-mail, opening with great curiosity the one from McCoy.

Enjoyed our impromptu get-together last weekend. I'm glad the lawyer in me saved some of the programs from your father's performances, believing they could one day be important. I hope they add to your memories of him. Perhaps one day you'd like to see the evidence of his influence as an actor and teacher. I'll be in touch. Mac.

Savannah read the message several times. It was friendly and gracious and such a nice surprise.

Was he asking her out?

"What are you grinning at?"

Savannah shrugged but said nothing to enlighten Taj as he returned to her office and again took up residence in her one chair. He held out a DVD jewel box.

"What is this?" she asked, taking it.

"You probably never heard of the movie, but Will Shelton is in it. See. His name is right there on the label."

Savannah scrutinized the information and sure enough, there was the name of Will Shelton along with all the other cast. "You're right, I'm not familiar with this film."

"It was never released," Taj informed Savannah. "When they finished shooting it, it was canned. It just got converted to DVD because some of the other people in it are now famous."

"How did you get it?"

"I have my sources," Taj said mysteriously.

"Well, thank you. I'll return it as soon as I…"

"Don't worry about it. That copy is yours to keep. Good movie."

"Thank you, Taj. This is really nice of you."

"You didn't find a copy of the original video in your father's stuff?"

"I haven't finished going through his things, yet. It's funny. Every time I meet someone it turns out they're familiar with my father. I didn't think he was all that famous."

"Well, maybe he wasn't *famous,* like getting nominated for the Golden Globes and Oscars or pictured in your *TV Guide*, but, yeah, his name rings a lot of bells in this town. I'm so glad he never did any of those corny sitcoms. That would have been embarrassing."

"Why? A lot of them were popular shows,"

Taj slumped down in his seat. "Yeah, but it's, like, a lot of former actors are so desperate to still be seen that they became part of a game show, or have these cameo appearances. Man!"

She gently pursed her lips. "Sounds like you know a lot about it."

"Don't get me wrong. I used to watch some of those shows, but if I'd been respected as a serious actor I wouldn't do it."

"Maybe some actors feel differently about it. Maybe being seen as often as possible is really important."

"I know, I know. I'm just glad Will Shelton never did it. The man had class and pride. His reputation stands solidly on the body of his work. All *you* gotta do is keep both of 'em alive."

Savannah considered Taj's comment as she held the DVD he'd just given her. *His reputation stands solidly on the body of his work.*

Savannah frowned over one of the source books she'd borrowed from the library. The essential information was the same in all of them, that a script consists pretty much of 120 pages, the story told in three acts, with beats in the script indicating transactions in the story. A shorter script length was possible, and suggested more action taking place and less dialogue. Her head was spinning with all the new information.

She'd also gone onto the Internet from home, researching script format. In the end it was easier to borrow several old shooting scripts from her own office and study them. Ever since she'd come across the revealing truth about Rae Marie Hilton's life, Savannah knew it was a story begging to be told. And now, she couldn't stop thinking about it and how it could be done. Savannah was astonished by the realization of what a terrible strain it must have been for the beautiful actress, living the life of a woman she'd completely made up.

It rained the next day, adding to her pensive mood on so many levels. Savannah tried to imagine the loneliness of Rae Marie's life, always watching over her shoulder for the something or someone who could out her, bringing an end to her dreams. Did she ever marry and have children? Where was she from? What happened to her?

A development meeting was called as soon as she arrived at work, and all the while that Savannah was presenting some of the story ideas she'd recently read and analyzed from other writers, for the first time she began to get a sense of the excitement each writer felt for their project. Back in her office there was evidence that Taj had stopped by. He'd left a folder behind on her desk with *R M Hilton* written on it in black marker.

Savannah breathlessly snatched up the folder. It seemed far too thin to contain anything, but inside there was a single sheet of paper, a photocopied document that was the original application for membership into the Screen Actors Guild in the name of Rae Marie Hilton. She'd been twenty-two at the time. A black-and-white headshot was printed on the reverse side. Savannah was struck by how beautiful she was. And how very easy it would have been, based on the exquisite features in the photograph, to assume she was white.

It was a disappointing amount of information, but at least, Savannah realized, she had actual proof that, in the realm of filmmaking, Rae Marie had existed. The document, along with all she'd learned about the young actress from her letters and journals, confirmed for Savannah her growing desire to know more about Rae Marie—not only as an actress, but as a young woman, a black woman with a big dream that might have cost her her soul.

"What do you think of that property?"

"It's not bad," McCoy responded as he and two associates approached a corner. They were on their way back to the office after lunch. "The location is convenient, and that old factory building has possibilities. I can see a condo with commercial businesses on the street level."

"The area is slated for gentrification," said the third man as they were finally able to cross the street, "So this is a good time to get in."

"It's worth considering, but I need to see some figures and architectural plans, and I'd want to know about the other investors. So, what next? Who do we talk to?" McCoy asked.

When he didn't get a response, McCoy looked to check out what had caused the other two men to fall silent. He wasn't surprised to find it was a lovely young female, standing near the security desk of their office building. In fact, it was Cherise Daly.

"Isn't she your new client?" the first man asked, but with telling amusement in his tone.

"She's not a client. She's the sister of one of my best friends," McCoy clarified calmly although he was annoyed that his associates insisted on putting their own spin on the situation.

"I don't have a best friend or even someone I hate that has relatives who look like her," the first man said with a sly drawl.

McCoy put up with the teasing without comment as they entered the lobby, conscious of the admiring glances that Cherise drew so effortlessly. He knew that she loved the attention, playing up the part of the beautiful ingénue to the max, coming across in an appealing mixture of innocence and ambition. Cherise stepped forward.

"I wasn't expecting you," McCoy opened.

"I need to talk to you," she said quietly to him.

He could hear the anxiety in her voice.

"John, Ben. You remember Cherise Daly," McCoy said.

Cherise smiled pleasantly and absently murmured a greeting to the two men.

"Come on up," McCoy said to Cherise as the group entered an elevator. He looked at his watch. "I have a client to see in twenty minutes."

Attempts at light conversation fell flat, and the rest of the elevator ride was conducted in awkward silence. Ben and John got off first, McCoy promising to call them later. After reaching his own floor McCoy escorted Cherise into his office. He didn't wait for her to speak first.

"Cherise, I'm at work. You can't continue to interrupt—"

"Mac, you have to do something. They want to give my part to another girl. It was already promised to me. I even had fittings in wardrobe. I'm so upset. It's not fair. Can you call the director for me? Please?"

McCoy took a deep breath as he listened. Cherise was clearly upset, as evidenced by her shimmering green eyes hovering on tears, the quivering voice managing to keep control over a wellspring of emotions, the slender graceful hands clasped nervously. He frowned at her thoughtfully.

She was good. She was *very,* very good.

"Okay, calm down. Why don't you tell me what happened?" he suggested solicitously, but did no more to comfort her.

She pulled a tissue from her purse and dabbed gently at an eye, careful not to ruin her makeup.

"I'm sorry. I should have called first, but this is an emergency."

McCoy sat observing Cherise as she continued to complain about the conniving little bitch who was going to get the part that she'd auditioned for and been told she had. Her rant was not obnoxious, and she still managed to come across as totally sympathetic. But he couldn't help but suddenly compare Cherise's manipulations to the straightforward I-will-not-back-down approach of Savannah Shelton. The highway encounter was indelibly imprinted in his mind, as was the graceful and thoughtful way in which she'd accepted the envelopes of programs he'd given her about her father. Cherise's ability to command attention was undeniable and entertaining. But what he'd liked about Savannah was that she didn't care if she got his attention or not. That was not only intriguing, it presented a challenge.

When Cherise finished outlining her complaint she sat waiting with a silent plea for his help.

"Welcome to Hollywood," he began simply. "You don't just waltz into town with great looks and talent, and it's a given that everything will go your way. I told you that from the beginning."

"I know, but I already had the part."

"And your point?" McCoy asked dryly. He sat forward, bracing his forearms on his desk as he faced her earnestly. "Look, this business is not about being fair. Directors and producers in this town have notoriously short memories. They're like kids in a candy store. There is *always* another pretty face to grab their attention and twist their libido."

As he talked McCoy could see the change come over Cherise. It was fascinating to watch as she switched from drama queen to cool and calculating, taking in the cold hard facts. He was not unsympathetic to her complaint, but he wasn't going to gloss over the reality.

"I don't know if there's much I can do to run interference for you, Cherise. I'm not in the business by choice, and for a good reason. I don't like playing games, and I don't like kissing ass. Sorry to be so crass, but you have to understand what you're getting into. The only question now is, how badly do you want this role, and what are you willing to do to get it?"

"I deserve this role," Cherise said bluntly. "And I'm the best actress for it."

"Fine. How are you going to convince the studio?"

She pursed her beautiful mouth, deep in thought, and finally arched a brow at him.

"I'm going to demand that they honor their commitment."

"And?"

She blinked, thinking again. "I'm going to remind them that I have a signed contract."

"Better. What else?"

"I'm going to ask the producer if the other actress was being considered because she's white."

"That's a daring move, but be careful about pulling the race card. It could backfire badly, and you can never use it again. Blackmail has its limits, even here."

Cherise pulled herself straight, looking more like

the determined young starlet who'd walked into his office for the first time more than a month earlier.

"Maybe I won't have to go that far this time. I'm going to show them my audition tape and point out why I'm the best actress for the part. Then I'm going to suggest they give the other actress another part…or write one for her."

"Now you sound like a pro. Have your agent or manager review the contract. If all else fails you got them there," McCoy advised.

"Oooh. This is the life."

Savannah smiled at Donna's contented sigh. Through her dark glasses she watched as Donna came up on her elbows from her prone position in a poolside lounge chair. She shook her head; the woman had the *nerve* to be wearing not just a two-piece swimsuit, but an actual bikini. Fortunately, she observed, Donna also still had the lithe toned body of the dancer she used to be. Her short wild hair was tied back from her face with a bright scarf, and she wore oversized dangly earrings.

"It *is* a beautiful day," Savannah said, stretching out her own slender legs and resting the notepad she'd been writing in on her thighs.

"No, it's not just a beautiful day. It's a *fabulous* California day," Donna corrected, gracefully righting her body to a sitting position, and adjusting the top of her suit that covered her boyishly flat chest. "There's a huge difference. I can't believe I was reluctant to leave New York."

"It's a major dance center. That's where your career was," Savannah reminded her.

"Yeah, but New York had weather," Donna said dryly. "The first thing I wanted to do when I moved out here was sell my boots and umbrellas." Savannah laughed. "And the first time I flew back east to visit family I thought I would die from the cold. And it was only September. Maybe I'm a California girl at heart."

"Maybe. If you were blonde, from the valley or 90210."

Savannah and Donna turned their attention to Kay, who'd been napping, stretched out on her stomach on another lounger under the partial shade of a jacaranda tree. Kay rolled her curvy bod and adjusted her chair to a more upright position. A straw hat and sunglasses protected her toffee-colored features.

Donna made a dismissive gesture. "Most people in L.A. are from somewhere else. Just like in New York."

"I'm from Atlanta, but I belong here." Kay nodded.

"Makes no difference where you're from. People go to New York because of publishing or theater or fashion or art or dance," Donna said.

"But you're here," Savannah reminded her. "Why did you come here? Why does anyone come to L.A.? I mean, yeah, there's the film business but most people don't make it, do they?"

Donna and Kay exchanged silent considering glances. Donna shrugged.

"I don't know. Maybe because they think they're going to make it. It's all about having a dream. In California anything is possible. I came because I was in the chorus of the film version of a Broadway musical. I thought I'd just go on getting work, so I never left."

"In L.A. it's okay to fail," Kay added. "I mean, not that failing is such a great thing, but there's always something else you can do. People give you a second chance. They don't much care what you've been or done before."

"Is this all about your father?" Donna asked, squinting at Savannah as she reached for her plastic tumbler of lemonade.

Savannah rested her head back against her chair. "Maybe a little. You know he left his family behind to come out here and act."

"Yeah, and all things considered, Vann, he did good. He had a career," Donna said.

"He did keep in touch, didn't he? You did see him and spend time with him over the years, right?" Kay asked, but didn't wait for an answer. "You're so lucky, Vann. Some folks get the bug and forget all about where they came from. You know the kind I'm talking about."

Savannah didn't answer. She had the feeling that Kay was not talking about the likes of a Rae Marie Hilton. After all, how many people could there have been like her who managed to slip in under the radar and not get found out eventually? Savannah knew that there were movie people who made a lot of money, and rubbed elbows with the Hollywood elite, who acted like they'd gotten where they were on talent alone. But she also knew that was almost never the case.

"What are you writing? You've been scribbling all afternoon. Working on a biography of your father?" Donna asked. She got up and walked to the edge of the pool, where she sat and dangled her legs in the cool water.

Savannah glanced down at the legal pad she'd been writing on. She lifted the pad and hugged it close to her chest, as if guarding her work. "Just notes. I'm still sorting through his papers and there are a couple of things I want to remember to follow up on."

A cell phone suddenly rang. Realizing it was hers, Savannah answered with an absent hello.

"I hope you're doing something fun."

It was a second before she recognized McCoy's voice. "Oh, hi." Did she sound pleased to hear from him again?

"I'm not interrupting anything, am I?"

It crossed her mind that he might be fishing, but couldn't understand why he would feel the need to. "Not at all. I'm just hanging out at the pool in my backyard with some girlfriends," Savannah said, watching as Kay joined Donna at the pool edge to begin their own animated conversation. "And you?"

"I'm at my office."

"Don't you know it's Saturday?"

"I had some work to take care of. This call is the one break I've allowed myself."

Savannah hesitated, finally smiling. "I guess I should be flattered."

"I hope you don't mind if I get a vicarious thrill from your afternoon with friends."

Savannah laughed lightly. "I'm sure you can do better than this. And there isn't anything I can do about, er, giving you a thrill."

"Sure there is. Invite me over."

She was silent for a brief moment. It seemed a very provocative suggestion. Was he serious? "You mean you don't have one of your own? I'm talking about a pool. I thought it was a law that anyone living in L.A. had to have a pool." Now it was McCoy's turn to laugh.

"Actually, I do. There's one on the roof of my condo in Santa Monica. I think the last time I was actually in it was five or six months ago."

"Poor baby. Woogie woogie?" Savannah cooed, as if she was comforting a contrite child.

McCoy cracked up.

His hearty laugh made her smile. She'd surprised even herself by goading and teasing him.

"You're right. I shouldn't complain."

Then she realized that Donna and Kay were listening to her one-sided conversation with baffled expressions. Savannah lowered her voice and grew serious.

"McCoy, thanks again for all that stuff you gave me. I really appreciate it."

"Mac, please. I thought it would mean more to you than to me. I'm a fan of your father's work, but you're family and will want to keep as much as you can for posterity, right?"

"I'm thinking of organizing all the programs and announcements and newspaper articles into some sort of usable system. Maybe by years, or maybe by individual projects."

"That's a great idea. Are you also planning on giving some or all of it to a library or college? That way people will be able to research his career."

Savannah drew up her knees and leaned forward, her legal pad now sandwiched between her chest and thighs. "Do you think people will really be interested in the collected works of Will Shelton?"

"Absolutely. For a black actor especially, who's been around for more than twenty years, there's not only his contribution, but his major influence on other blacks in the industry. Your father made it. He survived. He will be remembered."

"Thank you," Savannah said quietly.

"For what?"

"Reminding me that Will Shelton was more than just my father. I can't keep him all to myself, can I? I have to share who and what he was."

"No need to thank me. I think you already knew that. Otherwise you wouldn't be taking your time to sort through what would otherwise be a bunch of old papers and notices. Find anything interesting?"

Savannah thought immediately of the box found in her father's closet. She glanced covertly at Kay and Donna again, but both had now slipped into the pool to gently swirl about as they talked and laughed together.

"I'm not sure. I'm reading through so much right now, I'm just trying to get my head around all the information."

"I understand. Well, let me cut you loose to enjoy the rest of the day. I have at least another hour here before I can leave."

"Would you like to come over and join us?" she blurted out suddenly.

"I appreciate the invitation, but I do have plans for later. Thanks anyway."

"Sure."

"Can I get a rain check?" McCoy asked quietly.

"A rain check?"

"Can I hold that invitation for a later date, to be announced?"

Savannah shrugged, not believing for a minute that McCoy was being anything but polite. "I guess."

"Good. You take care."

"Thanks. You, too."

Savannah barely had time to put her cell phone down before Donna and Kay were wading to the side of the pool nearest her chair. Standing side by side, both women rested their forearms and hands on the tiles and regarded her steadily, just their heads visible, their oversized sunglasses making them look like aliens.

"What?" she asked, trying to give her attention back to her writing, but only hearing McCoy's laughter as she did an instant replay of their conversation.

"Don't give me that wide-eyed 'what,'" Donna said. "Who was that and why haven't we heard about him before now?"

"Yeah. And what's up with that baby talk?" Kay added.

Savannah felt flustered but maintained her calm demeanor. She shook her head. "No one important."

Donna and Kay hummed a droll "uh-huh" in unison, indicating their skepticism.

Savannah gave in, exasperated. "That was the other driver from that accident I had. I told you about it. He just wanted to make sure I was okay. I thought that was pretty decent of him."

Donna climbed out of the pool, dripping water as she walked to her lounger to retrieve a towel. "Correct me if I'm wrong, but didn't you declare the man a major jerk at the time of the accident?"

Kay followed behind Donna, her hips and breasts swaying with a soft sensuality capable of effortlessly drawing men to her. "That accident was over a month ago. How long does it take to apologize?"

"He can't be that much of a jerk if you stayed on the phone with him for almost twenty minutes, laughing at what he had to say," Donna said coyly, settling gracefully again on her lounger.

"I'm still waiting to hear about the baby talk," Kay said.

Savannah merely smiled at the good-natured ribbing of her girlfriends. She realized that she liked having a harmless secret that kept them guessing. Of course, she had to wonder herself. McCoy was a good-looking man, more than gainfully employed, and he was straight. He was already a Master of the Universe, on the black side. Not bad. Not bad at all.

Given the incomparable Cherise, and all the other '10' women that came by the hundreds every day to L.A., why had McCoy called her?

"I invited him to join us," Savannah said nonchalantly. Donna and Kay came immediately to attention.

"You did?" Kay asked.

"He's coming here? What did you say his name was again?" Donna asked.

"Down, girls," Savannah chuckled. "He can't make it."

"Oh," Donna said, disappointed.

"You know I wasn't about to throw over my girlfriends just for some man," Savannah added.

Donna chortled, adjusting her glasses as she settled down in her chair. "I would."

Savannah finished typing in the last line from the last page of her notes. She read it back and sighed with satisfaction. She was done.

She sat back in her chair. As she moved, the gentle ache in her lower back warned her she'd been sitting for too long in the same position. She slowly rose from her chair and stretched, and began pacing back and forth in the confines of the kitchen, where she'd set up a work space for herself on the counter. Her laptop, articles and photographs and the journals from the box she'd found were scattered all over the counter surface. Some had fallen to the floor where Savannah had left them, unwilling to break her train of thought as she'd worked.

It had taken almost a month, but Savannah felt a giddy

sense of accomplishment as she gazed down at the short stack of pages that was her first attempt ever to write a film script. She flipped through the first draft, with its red editorial markings and notes. The changes would have to wait for another night. It was almost four in the morning. She was dead tired, but too excited to go to bed and fall asleep. An anticlimactic energy made her feel she should be doing something more.

Savannah sat down again and read through the last known journal she had for Rae Marie Hilton. As it turned out, it was the very last of anything written by Rae Marie that she'd found among her father's possessions. In Rae Marie's own words she was preparing to perform in a new project. She'd written about having to make a trip, but also of being tired and wondering what was going to happen to her when she returned. She'd written about the fact that suddenly, black actors and actresses were becoming the vogue in Hollywood. They'd finally arrived, and projects geared to the black viewing audience were proliferating.

What was she going to do?

Savannah yawned. She picked up a banana from a basket as she wandered aimlessly into the living room. The silence of the middle of the night was so complete that it was like being in a vacuum. For now, she was hermetically sealed off from the rest of the world. She felt oddly at peace.

On the bookcase she saw the African violet, which had been mysteriously left outside the house weeks earlier. It had grown and thrived. On the bottom shelf of the bookcase that lined either side of the window, Savannah spotted three albums. She'd known they were there, but she'd never before removed them from the shelf to look through them, always assuming that they were just more of her father's memorabilia. But what if they weren't?

Putting aside her snack, Savannah had to get down on her knees in order to reach the albums. She sat on an ottoman with the first one on her lap and opened it. Almost at once Savannah realized that the photographs were not of colleagues, co-stars, crew, fans or anything else having to do with Hollywood. Stunned, she knew she was looking at a photographic record of her own life, and that of her brother Harris, saved and preserved by her father.

Savannah recognized nearly all of the pictures, but she had no idea how they'd come to be in her father's possession. There were annual class photos from second through fourth grade, a picture of her in costume from a school play. Lots of images from Christmases and birthdays and other family gatherings that Will Shelton had not been present at. But one picture showed her with her father as he knelt beside her. She was scowling disagreeably into the camera. Savannah remembered that one. It was taken at the airport as she was about to be put on a plane back home after a visit with him. Harris, four years older, was standing and smiling behind her. Everyone but she seemed to be enjoying the moment. Had she not wanted to leave?

Savannah frowned as she examined the photo. She no longer remembered what she had been feeling. The disappointment of a little girl had somehow morphed into the understanding of a woman. In the last two years she'd slowly come to see that her father's life made complete sense and could not have been any other way. Another thought also occurred to her. Surely her mother had played a part in the family's breakup.

Why hadn't she come to L.A. with her husband so the family could stay together?

By the time she'd leafed through the second album, Savannah had a sense of closure as well. Her father had made his own memories, and he'd never willfully forgotten his children and what had been left behind. She smiled at her own pun and yawned again. Dawn was starting to lighten the sky outside the window.

She closed the album. The last one would have to wait. Savannah knew that unless she got at least a few hours sleep, she was going to be catatonic by midday.

Exhaustion finally began to catch up to her as she slipped into bed and sighed contentedly. She suddenly felt a real closeness to her father, and a sense of pride. For the first time she understood exactly what a sacrifice he'd made, and what it might have cost him. For the first time Savannah felt compassion for people who were compelled to follow a dream against all odds, their lives succeeding or failing mostly by chance.

People like the tortured Rae Marie Hilton, caught impossibly between two worlds and never really belonging to either one.

Chapter 6

Savannah cruised slowly past the low-rise garden apartments, the kind of residential building complex that had proliferated throughout L.A. in the fifties and sixties, and that housed aspiring young actors and actresses. After parking her car, she approached and walked through the wrought-iron-gate entrance. Inside, the pathway was lined with lush palms and other plants. It led past the management office to three wings of apartment suites each three stories high. They were designed so that all the units opened out onto a common terrace on each level that overlooked the small square swimming pool in the center of the complex. Half a dozen young adults in a hot tub were having a lively conversation.

The one thing that Savannah had not been able to get used to in L.A. was the number of adults who apparently had blocks of free time in the middle of the day to lounge around the pool. It was almost six, but she had the sense that the young adults hanging out did not hold traditional jobs.

Their laughter followed her as she walked up to the second level and found Domino's apartment. The doorbell was answered almost immediately.

"Hi. Thanks for stopping by," Domino said, somewhat breathlessly.

"Hi," Savannah said, hesitating when Domino beckoned her in. "Are you in the middle of something? I can come back another time..."

"No, this is fine. I just got in myself. I had a callback and it went longer than I expected. Come on in. Sorry about the mess."

Savannah stepped into the apartment, glancing around. She had no idea what "mess" Domino was referring to. The entrance gallery, which led to a sizeable open living room and dining room combination, was comfortable and charming. The only mess was a stack of what appeared to be scripts, a large weaving frame and several baskets filled to overflowing with different kinds of yarns and threads.

"What's a callback?" Savannah asked, as she sat on a canvas-covered love seat.

"It's after you first audition for a part and the producers like your reading well enough to ask you to come back and read again, sometimes with actors that have already been chosen, sometimes against someone else they're also considering. It's nerve-racking. Here's your shawl," Domino said, as she unwrapped the one that Savannah had selected at the craft show two months earlier.

Savannah pulled a check from her tote bag and they made the exchange. "Thank you," she said, admiring the shawl as if it was the first time she was seeing it. "I don't know when my girlfriends Donna and Kay are going to get around to seeing what you have, but I know they're still interested."

"They can come over anytime. There's a chance I might go on location for a few weeks, but I don't have the shooting schedule yet."

"What happened at the callback this afternoon?" Savannah asked, as she rewrapped her shawl and put it into her tote.

Domino shrugged. "I won't hear anything for a few days, but I probably didn't get the part."

"Why?"

"I wasn't the right type. I wasn't brown enough."

"Excuse me?"

Domino grimaced good-naturedly. If she was disappointed it certainly didn't show. "Someone did the Ms. Thang part better than I could. Well, maybe not better, just more convincingly."

"What do you mean?" Savannah asked.

Domino sat on the edge of the chair opposite her

and looked directly at Savannah. "Close your eyes and listen."

Savannah did as she was told. After a moment's pause, Domino launched into the dialect and intonation of the street, complete with inflections, vocal attitude and current slang. Savannah grinned.

"You sound very good to me."

"Okay, now watch me."

With Savannah watching, Domino repeated the dialogue. The effect was jarring. Savannah heard the words in exactly the same way, but coming out of Domino's mouth, with her blond curls and white skin, it all seemed a put-on, a fake.

Savannah winced, and Domino reacted to her inadvertent response.

"See what I mean?"

"I'm sorry."

"I'm used to it," Domino said smoothly. "It is what it is. I am what I am."

"Who do you think will get the part?"

"A newcomer. She's gorgeous, of course, but she also has props and authentic ethnic creeds, if you know what I mean. Even her name works. Cherise Kim Daly."

"Oh. I know..." Savannah began, but quickly swallowed what she was about to say. "It seems unfair, doesn't it?"

"Not really. This is not a fair business," Domino said dryly.

Savannah couldn't help, in that moment, but to draw

a parallel between Domino and Rae Marie Hilton. Domino seemed to have a levelheaded understanding of what she was up against, and didn't rage over what she couldn't control. Rae Marie, on the other hand, had lived uneasily in her own skin, trying to invent herself and fool the eye. It still wasn't clear to Savannah whether the actress had ever succeeded at either.

"If you don't get the part?"

"I move on to something else. That's the nature of the business. I'm doing a TV commercial next month and a few print ads. They pay the rent."

"Well, I certainly admire your focus."

"Sometimes I think I'm just kidding myself," Domino said honestly. "Sometimes, I do think about giving up and going back home. I can always open my own shop with my weaving,"

Savannah stared at Domino with understanding. "But that's not what you want to do. You'd never forgive yourself if you didn't stick it out 'til the bitter end."

"Exactly. What if I give up one day or one month too soon? And to be honest, sometimes it's not about how talented you are, but about whether you have the right look. Cherise has what the producer is looking for, for this project. He could change his mind next week."

Savannah sighed at the uncertainty of it all, and stood up. "Well, I'm not going to stay. What do you do when you're told you're not the one?"

"I don't take it personally," Domino said, walking Savannah to the door. "It's not about me, it's about the work. Anyway, I *am* getting work, and I *will* be filming out of town soon. Gotta keep moving," she chuckled.

"Do you think this other actress has what it takes to become a star?"

Domino was thoughtful as she opened the door. "Maybe. She could make it on her looks, that's for sure. You know, there are lots of folks who get all the great notices and the spot in *People* magazine and the great parts, and then suddenly you never hear from them again. There is always another pretty face, or a buff pair of biceps and great abs. There is always, as the saying goes, 'someone waiting in the wings.'"

"My father was an actor," Savannah confessed, somewhat sheepishly.

"I know. Your last name sounded familiar and I checked it out," Domino said. "He was great."

"To be honest, when my brother and I were kids I hated that my father was an actor. But now I realize how brave he was to risk so much."

"Sounds to me like you're not interested in following in his footsteps."

Savannah shook her head. "I don't think so."

Domino laughed. "It's kind of refreshing to meet someone who doesn't have stardust in their eyes. I'm sure your father warned you about the craziness of the business."

"No, he didn't do that," Savannah said. "But he did say that one of these days I would know what it's like to hold fast to a dream and not let it go."

"Hasn't happened yet?" Domino asked.

"Actually, I think I"m working on it," Savannah said spontaneously. "You're the first to know, but I've just written a film script."

"Really? What's it about?"

Savannah hesitated, but Domino's interest sounded real. "Well, in shorthand, it's about how a woman's life is ruined when she lies her way into a career, and how she saves herself." Domino frowned. "I guess that wasn't a good pitch, and I'm not telling it well, but I think it's a timely sotry."

"I think I understand your theme. Would you mind letting me read it?" Domino asked.

Savannah felt a jolt of excitement that seemed to light her from the inside; like a premonition.

"If you really want to. I'd love to get your feedback."

"I'd be glad to," Domino said.

Savannah held the envelope tightly in her hands and stared at it. The contents represented weeks of writing in a format that was foreign and confusing and much more structured than she was used to. It also represented someone's life and a cautionary tale of being careful what you wish for. Most of all, as far as Savannah was concerned, the one hundred and seventeen pages also represented a concession to the lure of L.A. and the single-minded dedication it takes to make it. The script she'd written was about coming to Hollywood obsessed with succeeding, blinded by imminent failure. It's about what happens when the two meet head-on and the end result is not only painful, but self-destructive.

What happens to the dream then?

Savannah realized that her stomach felt queasy. She quickly stuffed the envelope back into her tote, and shoved it under her desk. That's where it stayed until just after lunch, when she'd finished reading her third treatment of the day for the development director. The script ideas had been universally terrible, and she'd written as much in her critiques. And yet, the one thing that consistently surprised her was the incredible amount of belief all the writers had in themselves and in their stories. Enough to write them, submit them and take a big chance on rejection, ridicule and the criticism of total strangers.

Her own father had done it. Domino Hagan did it every day. Even Taj had an outsized belief in himself that had yet to be tested and proven. But it didn't stop him from having big plans. Cherise Daly apparently had enough gall for several people, and because she did, Savannah was now convinced that the young woman would succeed.

Coward, Savannah admonished herself. What was the worse thing that could happen to her for having tried to write a film script?

Savannah waited until the end of the day to decide she had absolutely nothing to lose. And in any case, "nothing ventured, nothing gained," became a mantra that she used to build courage as she walked down a corridor that suddenly seemed endless. The office door almost near the end was open and Taj sat at his desk playing with the on-line digital mixing of music that only he could hear through his big Bose headphones.

"Whuzzup, Baby Girl?" he asked, his glasses sitting low on the bridge of his nose as his shoulders moved and rolled to the music he was listening to.

"You're busy. I can come back," Savannah said, a sudden feeling of insecurity sweeping over her.

"Naw, you're already here." Taj pressed a button and the noises leaking from his headphones stopped. He pulled them off and left them looped around his neck. "Talk to me."

Savannah looked at him earnestly. "I need you to do me a favor."

"You know, I do a whole lot of favors for you. When you gonna treat me to that drink you owe me?"

"Think of it as having a running tab with me. I'll add this favor to the list."

"I'm down with that. What do you need?"

Savannah slowly held out the envelope to Taj. "I want you to read something for me." Taj reached for the envelope but she quickly drew it back. "I want you to be straight with me, Taj. If it sucks, don't be afraid to say so."

He peered at her over the top rim of his glasses. "You wrote it?"

"Yes. But I don't want that to influence you."

"It won't," he promised, reaching for the envelope.

Savannah pulled it back again. "I'm serious."

"I hear you," he said patiently. Arm extended, he wiggled his fingers at her, waiting.

"Another thing…"

"Baby Girl, I'm getting *old* sitting here. If this is something you wrote I promise I will protect it with my *life*. How's that?"

"You don't have to go that far," Savannah said, although her voice suggested otherwise. "I just want you to keep in mind I've never done this before and I'm completely open to advice."

Taj snatched the envelope. "You will not be open to advice. I haven't met a writer out here yet who doesn't think they've written a masterpiece. That said, I will read it and I'll be honest, so be prepared."

"Thanks," Savannah said.

"Hey, I'm taking a chance too, you know. This could be the end of a beautiful relationship."

Savannah grimaced at him. "You watch too many movies."

But now that the script was out of her hands, she was overcome with fear. Who did she think she was? Hollywood was littered with the walking wounded who claimed to be writers and who believed they had a great project. How many of those projects actually got sold? How many made it into films? How many writers turned their talents to other ways of making a living while they waited for a break? How many gave up, only to slink away in defeat, their dreams and spirits crushed?

Savannah sighed. "Thanks, Taj. What are you working on?" she asked, as a distraction from her own small concerns.

"I'm mixing something I wrote with the lyrics from a friend of mine. It ain't half-bad."

"Can I listen to it?"

He hesitated. "I'll make you a deal," he said. "I'll read your work first, and then, after you hear what I have to say, if you still want a shot at getting even, I'll play it for you."

"I guess that's fair," Savannah said. "Well, take your time. There's no rush or anything."

"Yeah. But hurry up," he added.

Savannah chuckled. She turned from Taj and headed out of his office as he laid the envelope aside and went back to his music.

"Hey," he called out behind her.

She stopped at the door and glanced back at him silently.

"What's it called?"

"*Fade to Black,*" Savannah said, spontaneously coming up with a title to her work.

Taj nodded sagely. "Good title."

Is this what people go through? Savannah wondered as she finally walked away. Anxiety and self-consciousness, combined with a false confidence and a starry-eyed fantasy that what they'd created was the greatest thing since chocolate milk?

She felt sick to her stomach. But she also recognized why.

Savannah remembered something her father had said that had never resonated with her until this moment. They'd just returned from a doctor's appointment that had been difficult for him. He was exhausted by the time they'd returned to the house, but he'd insisted on reclining on a lounger by the pool, dozing off and on during the day as it slipped into a magnificent sunset. She'd brought him out a glass of iced tea, ignoring his requests for something stiffer that would have anesthetized some of his pain. He'd stared at her with a sad smile.

"Thank you, Vann, I'm really glad you're here."

"You don't owe me any thanks."

"I think I do. I cheated you out of a father. I have a lot to make up for and no time left to do it. Honey, I don't think I had a choice. I had to do what I did. I don't know if you can ever understand that."

"Daddy? Do you ever have any regrets about how everything worked out?"

"Umph. That's the first time you've called me Daddy since you've been here. Does that mean you've forgiven me?"

Savannah squirmed under his wistful question.

"Vann, regret is expensive," he'd murmured heavily. "I don't regret coming out here to L.A. and giving it a shot. I did okay. But I missed you and Harris. More than you'll ever know. There's a moral to my story, baby. I want you to hear it from me before I'm gone."

"What?"

"Hollywood is called an alternative universe for a reason. It's not grounded in the real world. It's all about make-believe. Smoke and mirrors. Pipe dreams. Do or die, maybe not in body, but in your soul. Being out here taught me something. Without dreams to chase after, you're missing out on half of what life's all about. It's not about arriving. It's about the bumpy road to getting there." He chuckled quietly. "It's been a helluva ride."

Savannah was just pulling out of the parking lot of her studio when her cell phone rang.

She adjusted her earpiece and flipped open the unit as she drove. "Hello?"

"Did I catch you at a bad time?"

Savannah pursed her mouth at the sound of McCoy's deep voice. "Hi. I'm just leaving work."

"So you're on the road."

"Yes. Does it matter?"

"I wouldn't want you to have an accident because you're distracted."

"You don't want to go there," Savannah said, but recognized that McCoy was teasing her.

"You're right. And I don't want to give you a reason to hang up on me. Tell you why I'm calling. Any chance you're free sometime this week?"

"Depends on why you want to know," Savannah said, frowning at the slow traffic ahead. She made a spur-of-the-moment decision to get off the expressway and take local streets.

"I thought we'd do a field trip out to Inglewood so I can show you the theater named after your father."

"Oh."

"And I thought that as long as we were out of L.A., we'd drive down to Long Beach. There's a junior college there where Will Shelton was an adjunct. That's where I'm from. I know the area."

"I knew about the college. I didn't think there was any reason to see it."

"You might be surprised. Interested?"

"Yes, of course. But are you sure you really want to spend your time chauffeuring me around the county?"

"Is that a quaint way of saying you'd rather not go, or you'd rather not go with me?"

Savannah navigated an unexpected end to the street she was on, and quickly made a series of turns. She sighed when she recognized Santa Monica Boulevard.

"Why would you say that?"

"We didn't exactly meet under the best of circumstances."

"I thought we'd gotten past that. Don't forget, I invited you to my house to use the pool."

"And I'm going to hold you to it," McCoy said. "How's this Saturday for the field trip?"

"Well..." Savannah hesitated, then suddenly hit her brakes and her horn as another car attempted to cut her off short.

"I heard that," McCoy said. "Are you okay?"

"Yes. I got off the expressway but the side streets are just as bad right now."

"Where are you?"

"Somewhere near Century City."

"Wave as you drive by. I'm still at the office."

She shook her head but smiled at his foolish suggestion. "Where were we?"

"Saturday. Inglewood and Long Beach."

"It's very nice of you to make the offer. Are you sure you want to do this?"

"Are you fishing for a hidden motive?"

"Yes."

He laughed. "You don't pull any punches, do you?"

"I don't want to sound ungrateful, but you're talking about giving up a day of your weekend. That's pretty valuable time. And I'm sure you have better things to do. And I wouldn't want to interfere with any plans you already had."

"You know, this wasn't supposed to be that difficult," McCoy said with dry humor.

"I'm sorry."

"Don't be. Maybe you just don't want to be in my company."

"That's not it at all."

"Good. Then all you have to do is say yes, Savannah."

"Yes, Savannah," she grinned broadly,

McCoy chuckled in her ear. "See you Saturday. I'll pick you up around ten."

It began to rain late Friday night, and was still drizzling on Saturday morning. Savannah fully expected McCoy to call and cancel. But by nine-thirty she had not gotten a call from him. Having failed at second-guessing him she hurried to get ready, donning a pair of stretch black pants, a lime-green cami worn under a white blouse that belted at the waist. Her ballet flats were faux leopard skin.

Savannah sat in the kitchen nursing an almost-cold cup of coffee, trying to pretend this little outing was no big deal. However, she was acutely aware of the fact that McCoy had been the one to reach out and touch her and extend the invitation. And she couldn't deny that she was trying to figure out why.

While it was true that McCoy hardly acted like the Hollywood type with an ego and a short attention span, she couldn't quite figure him out. He certainly had turned out to be more relaxed and laid-back than any of the men she'd met recently, here or on the east coast. And he had a sense of humor. And he was good-looking.

What was she missing?

The doorbell rang and Savannah nearly dropped the mug as she got up from the kitchen counter. She hastily placed it in the sink and went to answer the door. Passing a small mirror mounted on the wall near the entrance, she checked herself out. She used her fingers to tease up her short hair, and rubbed her lips together to redistribute what remained of her gloss.

Savannah opened the door.

McCoy was standing under the entrance, holding a closed wet umbrella. He was partially turned away, looking about the surrounding street with interest. He turned to face her, and for just a moment they silently appraised each other. His expression was easy and thoughtful, his eyes showing instant appreciation for her appearance.

Take that, Cherise Too-Gorgeous-To-Be-Real.

Savannah realized that this was only the third time she was actually seeing McCoy face-to-face, but she no longer felt as though he were a stranger. As a matter of fact, she was overcome with a sense of the familiar, and the uncertainty she'd experienced while waiting in the kitchen now gave way to shyness based entirely on something else.

"This is a really nice street," McCoy opened.

Savannah felt relief at how smoothly he'd gotten them over that tiny awkward moment.

"Yes, it is. I like it here."

He studied her thoughtfully. "Will Shelton was obviously not into big and pretentious."

"Thank goodness. His house is not on the map of where the stars live, either," she said. "Would you like to come in?"

"Another time. I thought we'd get started."

"Are you sure you still want to go?"

"Are you trying to back out?" he arched a brow.

"No, I…"

"Then let's go." He deftly popped open the umbrella and held it up.

Savannah reached behind her for her handbag and a lightweight cardigan, on the chair near the door. She closed the door and locked it. McCoy kept the umbrella aloft to protect them both as they headed down the walkway to his car, idling on the curb.

"Sorry I couldn't provide you with a sunny day, but it could clear up later," McCoy said.

Savannah cut him a questioning glance. "If you had that kind of power I'd address you differently."

His cell phone rang. He reached for it with one hand, and with the other held the passenger door open for her.

"Yes," he answered shortly.

Savannah paid no attention to his conversation. She'd just caught a glimpse of a petite woman getting into an older car some ways down the block. The woman looked familiar.

"Is there a problem?" McCoy spoke into his cell phone. There was a pause. "Then I'll speak with you later." He snapped it close.

Down the block Savannah watched as the car door closed and the female driver turned over the engine. She quickly sat herself in McCoy's car and waited until he joined her. She half turned in her seat to him.

"I know this is going to sound crazy, but...could you follow that car?"

He looked at her blankly. "You want me to what?"

Savannah glanced out the rear window. The car was already pulling away from the curb. "That silver car behind us. Quick! She's leaving."

McCoy put his car in gear and made a U-turn to head in the other direction behind the departing vehicle.

"Yes, ma'am. Follow that car. What movie is that line from?"

"I have to find out who that woman is. I'm sure I've seen her several times near the house."

"Really. Is she stalking you?"

"Not me. I'm pretty sure her coming around has to do with my father."

McCoy kept a safe distance, even allowing a car or two to get between his and the silver-gray Infiniti. The driver eventually entered another community of quiet, small but stately looking homes. It was a more modest version of where she lived, Savannah conjectured. The driver of the car now directly ahead of them eventually slowed down and signaled to turn into a driveway. The garage was detached from a split-level Cape Cod frame house, charming and neat, on about a quarter of an acre of land. The front of the house had been painstakingly landscaped with a variety of semitropical plants that thrived in southern California temperatures.

Savannah quickly made note of the street and the house number.

"Got it," she sighed, settling back in her seat as they continued to roll slowly along the street.

"That's it? You don't want to confront her and find out who she is?"

Savannah felt conflicted. "I don't want to scare her.

She's not a threat, and now's not the time. I think it'll be best if I introduce myself later."

McCoy looked at her, concern etched in his eyes, and nodded his understanding.

"Thanks, Mac," Savannah said with a wry smile. "I promise I'll let you know what happens."

"Whenever you're ready. Now you've got me curious."

Anxious to get past the unexpected detour and the mysterious lady, Savannah asked McCoy where they were headed first.

"Fortunately, this little side trip has put us pretty much where we want to be. Inglewood is the next town south of here," he informed her.

While he drove, McCoy talked a little about the predominantly black community they were passing through. Much of the area looked not only dated, but in some cases blighted. There was a stark contrast between here and where her father had chosen to live, Savannah realized, or the neighborhood where the lady of mystery apparently lived.

"This is an economically challenged area," McCoy said, driving slowly. "It just needs incentives, some interest, ideas and cold cash to be revitalized. The folks around here are wary of that word. It generally means buying up property and homes and fixing up the neighborhood so someone else can move in."

"I know. It was a big problem in New York once Harlem was targeted for gentrification. I have a friend who lives near Abyssinian Baptist Church who said she'd never seen so many white people in her life up there until they started coming north to buy the brownstones."

"That's the nature of progress," McCoy said to her. "It's not a racial thing, it's economic. What used to be commercial gets reinvented and rezoned for residential. What used to be a ghetto suddenly becomes chic and upscale."

"Try telling that to a displaced family," Savannah sighed.

"I have," McCoy said quietly, as she shot him a curious glance. He didn't elaborate.

McCoy finally pulled up in front of a storefront. It was clearly named, the Shelton Repertory Theater Company.

"Here we are," he said, parking near the corner just beyond the building entrance.

The rain had stopped, although it was still overcast and the air was humid and muggy. They got out of the car and walked back to the theater. As McCoy reached for the door, it suddenly swung open and two young adults exited together, so deep in conversation they never saw Savannah and McCoy before them. McCoy held the door to let Savannah precede him into the tiny foyer.

To her left was an open half door to what appeared to be a storage space doubling as a coat check. To her right was another door with a glass window that functioned as the ticket counter.

Savannah's attention was immediately drawn to the framed posters hung on the walls. She stepped closer to one that showed her father seated on a stool, surrounded by actors and actresses in costume from a play set in the twenties or thirties. Another photo showed him cutting the ribbon in a ceremony signifying the opening of the theater. She felt an unexpected lift of pride at her father's prominence in both pictures.

"Wait here," McCoy said, lightly touching her shoulder. "I'm going to see who's around."

He disappeared through a double door. Savannah vaguely heard voices in the distance just before the door closed shut behind him.

A small plaque on the wall over the ticket window read, *Founded 1987 by the Inglewood Troupers. Named in 1991 after Will Shelton, noted actor and teacher, for his guidance, support and unwavering commitment to the community.*

Savannah read the sign several times. She had mixed emotions about the dedication her father clearly had for this theater, and for his efforts not only to bring entertainment but also to encourage the craft of acting right here. It was a side of him that she'd missed out on. The door to the interior of the theater opened again. McCoy called out to her.

"They're rehearsing, but the director would like to meet you. Come on in," he coaxed her.

Somewhat dazed, Savannah allowed herself to be led. The theater itself was old, the seats wooden, the carpeting worn and torn in places. The house lights were on, and the space had a tired look, but she doubted if any of that mattered to the half-dozen people on the small stage who stood waiting for her.

Savannah glanced, nervous and apprehensive, at McCoy. He winked and placed his hand on her back, urging her forward.

"They're doing *Two Trains Running,* one of August Wilson's plays," he whispered in an aside as they approached the front of the stage.

A middle-aged man stepped forward, hand extended, a broad smile on his tobacco-brown face. "Ms. Shelton, this is a real honor."

And then, everyone on stage broke out into applause.

Chapter 7

Savannah walked silently beside McCoy, watching their shadows in the sand. The sun had come out after all, but it was still humid. The gentle hissing of the ocean, not even a hundred feet away, was calming. She'd expected the sand to be squishy and hot, but at this end of the beach, as it began to narrow inland, it was packed hard and was cool on the soles of her feet.

She tilted her face upward toward the sky, enjoying the melting warmth of the sun on her face. She felt a wonderful sense of well-being, peace and giddiness. Savannah couldn't help smiling to herself as she replayed in her head the way the small group of repertory actors had greeted her. She knew it wasn't really about her but about her father. Nonetheless, Savannah had experienced great satisfaction from hearing the clapping and had suddenly sensed what it must be like for actors to get that response from an audience. She'd done nothing to deserve the recognition, but part of her welcomed it.

She stole a glance at McCoy, who seemed just as pensive, yet comfortable with the silence between them. He had her shoes, each one stuffed into a pocket of his slacks. He held his own Docksides in one hand, gently swinging them with his gait. The lower legs of his pants were haphazardly rolled up to midcalf as he sloshed through the bubbling surf that rolled in from the Pacific Ocean.

"Long Beach was a great place to grow up," he reminisced. "It has beaches, restaurants, a boardwalk, and it's just far enough away from L.A. to make going there easy when I wanted to go in for some fun."

"But you're glad you didn't grow up in L.A.?"

"That's right."

"I'm surprised to hear you say so. You live there now."

"Now it's by choice. I have a practice that's thriving in L.A. I live in a part of town that's really a different side of L.A. It's quiet and almost completely residential. There is the Third St. Promenade and the mall, there's still access to the beach, although that's become a major tourist attraction, but it's not intrusive."

"I like it here. I can see and feel the difference," Savannah commented. "Do you still have family here?"

"My younger brother lives in San Francisco. He's an architect. My mom is dead and my father, who's retired, lives in Oakland. My brother and I still own the house we grew up in. I don't stay there much anymore, but Cody uses it as a weekend getaway."

They'd just finished lunch, although it was almost three-thirty, and McCoy had suggested they walk for a while. Suggesting the beach had been a nice surprise in Savannah's eyes. She'd only gotten to go to the beach once since coming to L.A., and only then because Donna had dragged her along shortly after they'd met at a yoga class Savannah had attended.

"This is my first time back here in probably six months," McCoy said in a surprised tone.

"Are you saying this trip was just for my sake?"

"Mine, too. I was glad for a reason to come. And I did want to show you the college where your father taught."

"I thought he just gave a lecture or two. I didn't realize he taught on a fairly regular basis," she murmured.

"You sound a little resentful," McCoy observed gently.

She shrugged. "I don't mean to. I'm really proud that my father apparently gave back so much. I'm glad that he was so admired and loved."

McCoy glanced at her. "I hear a *but* coming."

She shook her head. "No *but.* I guess I'm still getting used to the fact that I really know so little about his life in L.A."

"I'm sorry. I never considered that doing this would be painful for you."

Savannah smiled up at him. "Not painful. Embarrassing. I should have taken time to learn. I should have cared more."

"I suppose you might say he could have done the same about you."

"There's enough blame to go around, but what's the point?"

"How do you feel about his being a actor? Coming to L.A. and perhaps making a difference?"

Savannah swallowed before answering. "Awed," she got out, letting it go at that. So much of what she was feeling simply could not be put into words, yet.

"The college here is where I first heard him speak. I wasn't into acting or anything. I just wanted to hear what the man had to say. The funny thing is, he didn't really talk about being an actor. He talked about making decisions and taking responsibility for those decisions. And something about having a backup plan when the first one explodes in your face," McCoy chuckled.

"Heads up!"

Savannah and McCoy both turned sharply at the sound of the warning in time to see a volleyball arching through the air in their direction. Savannah dropped her shoulder bag and positioned herself below the falling ball.

"I got it," she shouted, deftly catching it.

About to toss it back to a waiting player, Savannah suddenly changed her mind. She turned her body, held the ball in her open left palm, and with a calculated toss into the air, she sent it back toward the players with an underhanded punch of her clasped fists.

It put the ball right back into play, and the two sides gave her a cheer.

"Good move," McCoy complimented her.

She turned to him, smiling and self-satisfied. "I'm not much of an actress, but I grew up pretty good at sports. I had to, to keep up with my brother and father when I was little. That was before my parents separated, of course, and he came out here."

"A jockette," McCoy mused, twisting away from her attempt to punch him in the arm.

Savannah retrieved her purse and fell back into step next to him. His cell phone rang again. The shrill sound intruded on the moment, and Savannah accepted that McCoy was popular and busy with lots of friends and contacts…and others.

"Go ahead and answer," she said when he continued to ignore the ringing phone.

He did.

"Yes? I'm not in town right now…. I'm sorry, it will have to wait…. Not for another few hours…"

Savannah tried to pretend she wasn't listening, but it was hard not to construe the other half of the conversation. She slowed her steps, putting a small distance between herself and McCoy and his caller. If it wasn't who she thought it was on the other end, it was someone similar. She felt annoyed about the intrusion, even though she knew she had no right to.

"Look, I'll call you later.... I don't think that's a good idea. It'll be too late.... Fine...when I get back."

When the call was finished McCoy did not apologize as she thought he might. She hazarded a sideways glance at him, wondering if he'd forgotten her presence. Taking a deep breath Savannah decided that the interruption was not worth spoiling what had, so far, been an interesting and fun outing.

She picked up right where they'd left off before McCoy's cell call, determined not to spoil the day.

"You said you're glad you grew up in Long Beach. What have you got against L.A.? Are you telling me you don't buy into its reputation?"

"Do you?"

"No, but I have an excuse. I'm from the east coast and a newbie. Maybe I just don't get it."

McCoy lifted a corner of his mouth into a half-hearted smile. He was silent for a long time, staring down at the sand then out to the Pacific Ocean, before responding.

"Life in L.A. isn't as easy and carefree as it seems. It can take up a lot of energy. You spend a lot of time trying to figure out if a person is for real, or if they have some angle they're working, an agenda. Everybody wants something from somebody else."

"I'm surprised to hear you say that."

"Why?"

"You're a lawyer. Don't you ever stop to think how people see your motives? You happen to live in L.A., but you could be anywhere and people might feel the same about you. Lawyers are self-serving. In it for the money."

"Touché," McCoy murmured.

"That's not how I meant it, Mac. I spent a lot of years hating L.A. because it took my father away from me. But that's not what happened. L.A. is just a town that promises to make your dreams come true. People buy into that. Sometimes it happens and sometimes not. I bet there are as many heartbreaking disappointments as success stories, but who wants to hear about those?"

He stopped walking to look at her. "Does that mean you forgive your father?"

"Yes. I think I have, finally. I understand what drove him better than I used to. I still wish he'd stayed with us back east, but that's the little girl in me talking. Now I know why it wasn't possible for him."

"Then you don't mind me showing you some of the places where he left his mark?"

"Of course not. I needed a different perspective. It was all good." She smiled up at him. "Really good."

He stopped to face her.

"We probably should start heading back."

She nodded silently, remembering the recent call. Of course he had plans for tonight.

"I know this is short notice, but would you see a film with me tonight?"

She was instantly surprised and alert. "A movie?"

THE EDITOR'S "THANK YOU" FREE GIFTS INCLUDE:

- Two NEW Kimani Romance™ Novels
- Two exciting surprise gifts

YES! I have placed my Editor's "Thank You" Free Gifts seal in the space provided at right. Please send me 2 FREE books, and my 2 FREE Mystery Gifts. I understand that I am under no obligation to purchase anything further, as explained on the back of this card.

PLACE FREE GIFTS SEAL HERE

168 XDL ELWZ

368 XDL ELXZ

FIRST NAME

LAST NAME

ADDRESS

APT.#

CITY

STATE/PROV.

ZIP/POSTAL CODE

Thank You!

Offer limited to one per household and not valid to current subscribers of Kimani Romance.
Your Privacy – Kimani Press is committed to protecting your privacy. Our Privacy Policy is available online at www.eHarlequin.com or upon request from the Reader Service. From time to time we make our lists of customers available to reputable firms who may have a product or service of interest to you. If you would prefer for us not to share your name and address, please check here. ☐

▼ DETACH AND MAIL CARD TODAY! ▼

He smiled. "You make it sound like you haven't seen one in so long you've forgotten the experience. Or the film."

"I do go to screenings sometimes, thanks to my friend Kay."

"What else have you been doing for fun?"

"You don't want to know. Nothing very exciting." But the craft show did come to mind. She'd met Domino Hagan that night. And McCoy.

"Then you're overdue. How about it? If you're free."

"Thanks. I'd like that."

They turned around and retraced their steps down the beach until they reached the point where they'd entered. By the time they got back to McCoy's car, Savannah was feeling genuinely pleased about having been asked to the movies. The curious phone call notwithstanding, she felt as if she'd just been asked out on a date, a first since arriving in L.A.

How sad is that? she thought wryly.

The drive back to L.A. was chatty and casual, the conversation covering a wide range of topics, everything from how she'd met Donna and Kay to McCoy's out-loud thinking about whether or not to get a cat. Savannah was surprised and showed it. She hadn't thought of McCoy the lawyer as a pet person, but the idea once again changed her perception of him. Up several more notches for the better.

She paid no attention to the traffic or where they were headed since she wasn't the one driving. Savannah was eventually aware of the fact that McCoy was a more careful and defensive driver than she would have given him credit for. To be honest, Savannah also recognized that she was enjoying being a passenger in his car. She enjoyed being with him.

"Oh, I know where we are. The Third Street Promenade is a few blocks from here," she announced, once they'd gotten off the Santa Monica Freeway.

"Correct."

"Are we going to the Cineplex there? What movie did you have in mind?"

"We're not going to the Cineplex. And I want the film to be a surprise," McCoy said.

Savannah's curiosity was heightened even more when they continued driving right through the commercial area of Santa Monica, and into the community itself. She frowned.

"McCoy, where are you…?"

As he turned off the street into the driveway of a four-storied building, and the iron gate began to retract electronically, Savannah realized this was where he lived.

She was still trying to digest this and the implications, when he parked his car in a designated space and turned off the engine. He turned to look sharply at her.

"I hope you don't mind. I should have been more clear…."

"Yes, you should have."

"But to be honest, I also wanted to surprise you. If

you're still okay with this, you'll find out what I mean when we go inside."

Savannah looked long and hard into his eyes searching for subterfuge, or even a message. But McCoy's gaze met hers openly and steadily. No flinching, no suave posturing, no overblown confidence or expectations. She relaxed and nodded.

"You're being a bit melodramatic, but…this is L.A. Let's go."

The building where McCoy lived was a modern wonder of white and glass. When he told her there were only two apartments per floor, she understood at once that her father's entire house could probably fit in McCoy's square footage. She would have been right.

The rooms were large, open, with the windows facing south and southwest. That meant his apartment got the cooler afternoon sunlight and spectacular sunsets. The furnishings were modern but comfortable. A leather sofa and love seat, faux suede club chairs. And there was a nice kind of hominess to the way his possessions lay about that made the space warm and lived-in. It did not have the look and feel of someone who was into acquiring material objects. But Savannah could see that there were several older pieces, possibly family heirlooms, hand-me-downs or antiques that fit in nicely.

"Sorry," he said easily. "The cleaning person didn't come today."

"That's okay. Doesn't look like there's a lot for her to do."

"In here," he called out, disappearing into another room and turning on a light.

Savannah slowly followed him and found herself in a kind of library and media room. There was a flat-screen HDTV in the cubby space of a wall unit that also housed CD/DVD equipment, books, discs, lots of framed photographs and several awards that indicated that in high school and college McCoy had been a pretty accomplished tennis player.

"What are we going to watch?" she asked, as he looked through a stack of DVDs and removed one of the jewel cases.

"It's called, *Into the Night.* It's a police drama. Will Shelton is one of the players."

"Oh, I've heard of that. One of my coworkers lent it to me, but I haven't had a chance to watch it. Taj…that's the guy I work with…said it was never released. I don't know why."

McCoy shook his head. "It's a shame. Sometimes the decision not to put a movie in theaters is political. Or there might be some scandal involving some of the players. Or someone pissed someone else off. Who knows?"

"How'd you get a copy?" Savannah asked, as he turned on the TV, then the DVD player, and put the disc in.

"I mentioned Will Shelton's name to someone I know and he said he had something he wanted me to see." He looked at her. "I haven't watched it yet, either.

Have a seat." He indicated one of two very roomy and comfortable lounge chairs.

She literally climbed into her chair, kicked off her shoes and curled her feet and legs into the cushions as well.

"Here, read this. It tells a little about the plot and characters. I'll be right back."

Savannah took the page, which was clearly a computer printout from a Web site. The information seemed to be a press release, and was dated nearly fifteen years earlier. The plot was a kind of standard big-city police drama about a cover-up to protect a cop's affair with the beautiful wife of a powerful local politician. Will Shelton played the role of Detective Toni Freeman.

By the time Savannah finished reading the pages, McCoy had returned carrying a tray.

"I didn't know there was a concession stand," Savannah said, delighted.

"Hey, I know how to do it up right," he said. "Gotta have popcorn. This has *real* butter, not that yellow oily stuff from the movie theater."

"I know it's deadly, but I love it."

"Me, too," McCoy admitted, making her laugh.

He placed the tray between the two chairs, on a small occasional table. Besides the big glass bowl brimming with popcorn, there was a bottle of wine and two glasses.

"Is wine okay, or would you like something else?" he asked, already opening the bottle.

"I prefer the wine. It adds a little extra class."

Grabbing some popcorn in one hand, McCoy dimmed the lights, picked up several remotes and settled into his own chair. He hit Play and focused on the screen.

Savannah became absorbed in the story as soon as the opening credits were over. Her surroundings faded as the actors took over and she followed their adventure closely. But it was Will Shelton's presence that really held her attention, his and that of an actress who played a secretary to the politician. The attractive blonde was having an affair with her boss that even those cronies closest to him knew nothing about. The young actress in the role was young and beautiful, effortlessly presenting her character as more than just the other woman.

Something about her was vaguely familiar, but Savannah couldn't say that she really recognized the blond actress. Her character, however, was sympathetic, and Savannah silently cheered for her when she had the strength to end the relationship and walk away.

Yet, it was the strangest sensation to see her father speaking and acting as a different person, while knowing that it wasn't really *him*. The actor, Will Shelton, convinced her that he was a cop, street smart, and didn't take crap from anyone. He was profane, tough, and edgy in the role. That's not what he was like in the real world.

The film ended, and Savannah realized she wanted more of the actors and their on-screen story.

McCoy reached for the remote to stop the play of the DVD.

"I'd like to see the credits, if you don't mind."

"If you want," McCoy said.

While she watched the rolling list of names involved in the production of the movie, McCoy removed the remains of the popcorn and wine. She nodded when the name *Rae Marie Hilton* scrolled by as the actress playing the secretary. Seeing the actress interplay on screen with performers who were both black and white, Savannah had to admit that there had never been a moment when she didn't believe the actress in the part was white. Now that she'd seen Rae Marie in a role on screen, Savannah sat contemplating what her life must have been like, hiding such a big secret about herself.

Savannah wasn't about to judge her. But she didn't envy Rae Marie and the choices she'd had to make, either.

"What did you think of the movie?" McCoy asked, reappearing.

Savannah slipped on her shoes and stretched as she stood to face him. "It was a good drama. But I can't figure out why they wouldn't release it after all the time and work that went into it."

"Yeah, I wondered about that myself. In any case..."

"Yes, in any case it's time for me to get home."

She waited near the front of the apartment while McCoy turned off his DVD player and the lights. In just a few minutes they were back in his car and on their way to her home.

Savannah realized that neither of them seemed inclined to chat much during the drive, which was fine with her. She was still seeing both her father and Rae Marie on screen. She already knew that they'd worked together on a TV show, but didn't know if that had happened before or after the movie. Her father had known from the beginning what Rae Marie's secret was. She'd written so in her journal. How had he found out? At what point had their professional lives developed into a personal friendship? How had her father felt about Rae Marie's secret?

"Tired?"

Savannah sighed. "No, not really. I guess I should be."

"It's been a long day."

"Probably longer than you intended. I'm sorry for taking up all of it."

McCoy shot her a brief glance. "You forget it was my invitation."

"I know, but I really didn't expect it to be so full." Savannah looked at his profile. "Thank you, Mac. Today was…it meant a lot to me," she said almost shyly.

"My pleasure. I learned a few things myself."

Savannah didn't ask what.

His cell phone rang then. It wasn't until that moment that she realized she'd been hoping that there would be no more interruptions. And although McCoy did look at the unit, he apparently decided the call could wait or wasn't important because he didn't bother to answer. Had he done that for her sake or his own?

She suddenly began to feel awkward and uncertain as they pulled up in front of the house. All conversation between them had stopped after that last phone call. McCoy turned onto her street. It was very late and very quiet, even more so once he turned off his engine. She was aware of her own heartbeat as he escorted her to the door.

Savannah had no idea what else to say to him, but the end of the evening felt anticlimactic. Just saying good night somehow seemed trite and formal. She certainly wasn't going to shake his hand, for the same reasons.

She stood between him and the now-unlocked door, his tall frame casting a shadow over her. Savannah took a deep breath and turned to face him. She felt, literally, backed against the wall.

"You know, one of these days you'll have to tell me exactly what it is you do." McCoy made the preemptive first strike, making her smile nervously.

"Nothing very exciting. It's a job. I was an editor back on the east coast."

"No interest in acting at all?'

"None. Zero. I don't think I have the talent or the guts."

"No guts? I don't think I agree with that," he drawled, amused.

He looked at her thoughtfully. Even in the dark, Savannah could tell he was studying her, as if trying to read her expression and words.

"So you've decided you're going to stay here. For how long?"

"As long as the weather stays nice," she joked. "Maybe until I get my father's affairs in order. I have to decide what to do with all the memorabilia. Maybe forever."

"Is it just the weather that could keep you here?"

Savannah was alert to the sensual tone of the question. It made her slightly breathless and McCoy's presence felt a little too close.

"I've made some good friends. Everything seems easier here. I never thought I'd say it, but I think L.A. is starting to grow on me."

"I'm glad to hear that," McCoy said.

When he began to lower his head toward her, one of his hands warm around her upper arm, Savannah had already anticipated that this was the way the day might end. The question was not *would* McCoy kiss her, but *how.* She stood still, her body poised between self-consciousness and curiosity. She felt the gentle pressure of his lips on her cheek, near the corner of her mouth. It was sweet. Nice. Safe. Just as Savannah was deciding she was a little disappointed, surprising herself with a sudden bold yearning, McCoy shifted to settle his lips on hers.

His touch this time was firm, light. She sighed as she

closed her eyes and her mouth became mobile, fitting more naturally to his and experiencing the full shape of his lips. This felt better. And just enough.

McCoy straightened, rubbing her arm lightly before letting her go.

"I'm not an estate attorney but if there's anything I can do to help sort out your father's affairs, let me know."

"Thanks. I will."

He pushed open the door with one hand, urging her to go on inside, making sure she was safe before leaving.

"Whatever your reasons are, I'm glad you're here."

He didn't wait for her response, which was just as well since Savannah had none. She watched as he headed back to his car. What, exactly, did he mean by that last comment?

She closed the door, leaning against it until she heard him drive away, and all fell quiet again.

There was something prophetic about the fact that she woke up to rain again on Sunday. Savannah was sure, however, that there would be no miraculous clearing in the early afternoon, as there had been the day before with McCoy. It was going to be the kind of day that encouraged staying inside, getting things done…reflecting, which she did.

It had been a long night, disturbing and restless, much of it spent thinking about McCoy. Savannah realized that the afternoon and evening in his company had completely changed her opinion of him. Everything she was learning about McCoy showed her someone who did not fit her stereotyped idea of the L.A. man, an opportunistic, self-absorbed and shallow person. But could she trust her own judgment? Savannah thought her track record indicated otherwise. Certain things about her past were another reason why she couldn't sleep.

Savannah, sitting in the living room paying bills, with the TV on as background white noise, also kept thinking of the woman she and McCoy had followed home the day before. Who was she? What was her story? More importantly, what was *her* connection to her father?

Then, just as suddenly, a wave of humiliation rolled over Savannah as she zeroed in on the image of another man, Jordan Nash. She'd known Jordan Nash in New York, and he'd also been accomplished and polished and convincing, like McCoy. She'd been in love with him and had believed Jordan felt the same. Two years is a long time not to have been given a reason to suspect anything else.

She experienced old feelings, old resentments surfacing quickly and, just as quickly, fading. She still smarted under the cold hard truth that Jordan had actually been playing her off against another relationship he'd been conducting at the same time. He'd literally been weighing his options, calculating which of the two women would win his hand.

Eenie, meenie, minie, moe.

Even worse, Savannah recalled that it wasn't as if she could have confronted Jordan on his cruel behavior. There had never been any promise of marriage exactly, but why should she have thought otherwise of someone who got high marks in the arts of courting, caring and affection? Why shouldn't she have believed him when he smoothly whispered, "I love you" at all the right moments?

Savannah put aside her small stack of bills. She stood abruptly and began pacing the room. She wandered to a window and looked out onto the slick wet street. Now the image of that tiny graceful woman getting into her car and hurrying away came to mind.

Had Will Shelton broken *her* heart, too?

Savannah started sharply. How had she gone from the memory of Jordan Nash disappointing her to her father's possible relationship with another woman? Two other women? And what did *any* of it have to do with McCoy Sutton?

Savannah continued her pacing for another moment. She suddenly stopped, staring into space before making a decision and coming back to the moment. Clicking off the TV she got her purse and keys and headed for the door. She could get answers to at least one of her questions right now.

At the last moment she returned to the living room to get one of her father's albums. It was filled with pictures of people she couldn't identify. She was sure some of them were of that lady.

Once on the road, Savannah headed out in the same direction she and McCoy had used to follow behind a silver-gray Infiniti the day before. Keeping the scrap of paper with her notes handy she made her way to the street and the Cape Cod house. A light was on in the front room next to the door. The silver car was in the driveway. Savannah parked right in front of the house.

Huddled under her umbrella, Savannah approached the house. She held the album under her arm to protect it from the weather. She rang the bell and waited. She couldn't hear anything from inside, but belatedly she reasoned that the woman could have gone to a neighbor's house, or walked to a nearby church for Sunday service, or gone to the market.

Just as she was starting to have doubts about the wisdom of turning up on the woman's doorstep, the door was unlocked and opened, and a pretty, petite woman stood peering at her with caution from behind the edge of the door.

Her hair was relatively short but pulled back into a ponytail. The style made her look younger than Savannah knew she had to be. The appearance of gray at her hairline indicated that she colored her hair, but it was the only obvious sign of aging. Her eyes were dark, her medium brown skin smooth.

"I'm sorry to bother you," Savannah began at once, "You don't know who I am, but I've seen you before near my house and, well, I just wanted to introduce myself and find out…"

"What I was doing there," the woman completed.

"…if there was anything I can do for you," Savannah carefully corrected.

The woman regarded her silently and then nodded. "I know who you are. You're Will's daughter. Come in," she said quietly and stood back.

Leaving her umbrella outside the door Savannah did as she was ordered.

Savannah followed the woman through a center foyer, a sitting room and a kitchen to another room at the back of the house. It was a solarium, small and cozy despite the gray skies beyond the wraparound windows. Savannah could see that on a clear, sunny day the space would be flooded with light. The woman sat in a wicker chair with floral cushions, the high curved back making her look even smaller. She silently pointed to a matching wicker chair opposite, on the other side of a small table.

Savannah became aware that there was music playing very softly and she looked around for a CD player or turntable but saw neither. She did see a console table against an adjacent wall where nearly a dozen framed photographs were arranged. Savannah spotted several images of her father posing alone, or of him and the lady together, she gazing up rather lovingly into his smiling face. She sat forward on the edge of her chair and turned to the other woman.

"I'm Savannah."

"The youngest child. I'm Caroline Spencer. Your father called me Carrie."

"Oh, my God. In the last month of my father's life when he was often sedated, he kept saying to me, 'carry, carry.' I thought he wanted me to take something away, or bring something to him. I didn't know he was asking for you."

Carrie closed her eyes briefly, as though the image of Will Shelton asking for her as he lay dying was too much to bear.

Savannah stared at her. Now that she was in the woman's presence she couldn't seem to formulate any intelligent questions. Too late, it occurred to her that questions might be too personal, an invasion not only of Carrie's privacy but perhaps a revelation of yet more secrets. Her father seemed to have been quite good at keeping those.

"I'm glad to know he remembered me."

"Right up until the very end. Why didn't you come to see him?"

"I did, almost every day," Carrie murmured. "He'd call me when you left for work. I'd drive over and stay with him a few hours. I know it was terrible not to let you know. But toward the end, I wanted him to myself for as long as I could."

Savannah was speechless that the clandestine meetings had gone on for so long without her knowledge.

"No wonder he was sometimes so cheerful in the evenings," she mused.

"When you agreed to come out here to be with him, Will was beside himself. He saw it as a sign that you'd forgiven him."

"You sound like you know a lot about me and my family."

"Oh, yes," Carrie admitted. "Will talked about you and your brother all the time. He was very proud of you both. And he gave all the credit to your mother."

"I…I…" Savannah started. The mention of her mother, and of her father obviously speaking openly about her, caught her off guard.

"You want to know why I keep returning to the house. I was hoping I wouldn't be seen, but—" Carrie shrugged as if to say, 'so be it.' "—I couldn't go to the funeral. It was too hard."

"I would have remembered you, I'm sure," Savannah said. "You loved my father very much." Savannah spoke kindly, but was surprised when tears almost instantly shimmered in Carrie's eyes.

"We loved each other," she said quietly. "But I didn't want you and your brother to know anything about me. I felt you would resent me. Will told me about the break-up of the family when he decided to try acting. He never stopped feeling guilty about it. He knew that you, especially, were very angry with him. I didn't want to make things worse."

Savannah frowned. "How long have you and my father been toge— involved?"

Carrie raised her chin slightly, the little ball of it quivering as she held her emotions in check. "More than fifteen years. I was personal assistant to an actress who was well known at the time. Will was in one of her movies. We met on the set."

"Fifteen years?" Savannah repeated, astonished.

"You want to know why we didn't marry," Carrie said, staring into space, her eyes sad but shining with memories. "I was still married at the time. My husband and I weren't getting along well. Our only child had been killed while on a tour of duty with the navy. My husband began drinking. A number of years ago he was in a car accident, but survived. He's been in a special facility ever since.

"Then, it just seemed that it was too late for me and Will. I couldn't leave my husband. We tried to make the best of things. Will did ask me to marry him, all the time. He was a real gentleman. Wanted to do the right thing. But I kept saying no."

"Are you sorry you did?" Savannah asked quietly.

Carrie silently nodded as the tears rolled down her cheeks.

Savannah was far from feeling resentful. She was heartbroken for the couple, stirred by the story of unfulfilled love, poor timing and perhaps a misplaced sense of honor. Remembering the photo album, she retrieved it from the floor next to her feet and silently passed it to Carrie. She accepted it, holding it tightly to her chest.

Savannah knew she would have said thank you if she'd been able to.

It grew dark outside and continued to rain. Savannah helped Carrie make tea and sandwiches and they returned to the solarium to share it together. After the initial shock of learning who she was wore off, she found that she liked Carrie a lot. She could tell that the older woman must have been pretty in her younger day, with the kind of delicacy that would make a man want to protect her. But there was no doubt in Savannah's mind that Carrie was a strong woman, decisive and clear thinking, and still in love with Will Shelton.

Inside the solarium, where Savannah suspected her father and Carrie had spent many quiet comfortable evenings together, she found out even more about her father's life in L.A., the side that had nothing to do with moviemaking. Carrie told her that he'd been careful to keep the professional and private sides of his life separate.

Savannah didn't dare ask if Carrie knew anything about Rae Marie Hilton.

"He should have married you," Savannah voiced at one point.

"I believe that things happen the way they are supposed to," Carrie mused philosophically. "I only regret one thing."

"What?"

Carrie looked at her wistfully. "That I never got pregnant again with Will while I was still young enough. I might have agreed to marriage then."

Savannah didn't hear any self-pity in the announcement. But it did make her feel even more for her father and Carrie. It should have been so easy, and it wasn't.

She finally stood to leave, offering to help clean up, but Carrie insisted it wasn't necessary. Savannah was surprised to find that she didn't want to leave. She liked the older woman, with her quiet strength and graceful demeanor.

At the door Savannah asked, "Will you come for dinner sometime?"

"You don't have to worry about me. I miss Will, but I'm fine, really."

"I'd like to think you and I can be friends."

Carrie smiled at her but already she was closing the door.

"Call me, and we'll see."

Chapter 8

"Donna, that is so great. I'm happy for you."

"Thanks. Rehearsals start this week and there will only be three or four, so I really need to be on point."

Savannah bit into her banana and, on her cell phone, listened to the exuberant details as Donna told of her latest opportunity.

"That's not a problem is it? I mean, you are a professional dancer."

"Well, yeah. But I didn't tell my contact that I haven't done any real pro dancing in three years. Who knows? Performing at the awards show could lead to something else. First, I need to get my butt in gear. I'm up against women who are younger than me, a lot of them just coming off Broadway shows and regional tours. They're in better shape."

Savannah continued to listen to Donna's comments as she finished her lunch and gathered the remains in the brown bag. She adjusted her sunglasses against the bright California sun, marveling that in February she could spend her lunch hour outside on a bench under the shade of a tree. Even as she responded to Donna's excitement, she smiled secretly to herself, enjoying the moment. The news that morning reported a storm on the east coast that had so far dropped nine inches of snow in the metropolitan area of New York.

"How did you find out about the dance number for the awards show?" she asked Donna.

"Well, as luck would have it, one of the choreographers is in my yoga class. He misses more classes then he actually attends, but I'm pretty laid-back about him coming and going. He's always preparing for something so he's in good shape anyway."

"You never told me about him before."

Donna sighed. "Unfortunately he and I play in different leagues, if you get my meaning."

"He's gay."

"And in a relationship."

"With an actor?" Savannah hazarded a guess with the knowledge she'd gained about the culture of Hollywood.

"Personal trainer. But you were close. He's also a

wannabe actor. Isn't everybody? Except you and Kay," Donna chuckled.

Savannah joined in.

And McCoy, she silently added. Otherwise, it was true. The film industry was definitely the biggest employer in the city, and everybody wanted in. She stood up and deposited the used lunch bag into a nearby bin.

"Why don't you come to the taping of the awards? I could probably get you in," Donna said.

Savannah grimaced even though Donna could not see her reaction. "Sounds too red carpety for me. Too crowded. Too 'it's all about me.' I'll watch it on TV."

"I hope you change your mind. It'll be fun to get all dressed up and be seen. A lot of the big names come out for this one."

"You know I'm not impressed by that."

"Kay said we should come over to the restaurant tonight to celebrate. Are you busy?"

Savannah began a leisurely stroll back to the security entrance to the studio, displayed her ID and walked through the gate. "I was going over to the Film Institute to do some research."

"Bo-o-ring."

"I'm working on something, and I can only get to the Institute after work for a fast hour."

"So take tonight off. Come have drinks with us."

"Fine," Savannah gave in. "I'll see you there. Bye."

Savannah was well aware of the importance of the particular awards to African-Americans, and the ceremony that Donna would be performing for. She'd watched it on TV herself, recognizing well-known actors and actresses, singers and musicians, and a host of up-and-coming talent. She had not spent a lot of thought on all the young hopefuls who were in the limelight, up on stage accepting awards or being interviewed and photographed as if they were visiting royalty. She was well aware that, for many, it was their fifteen minutes of fame.

Where were they now?

What happens to dreams deferred, or deflated?

"Savannah, wait up."

Getting off the elevator and hearing her name, Savannah glanced over her shoulder. Jogging down the corridor to meet her was Taj.

"I've been looking for you."

"I'm just getting back from lunch. Why?"

Together, they walked in the direction of Savannah's cubicle.

"I got some information for you."

Once inside her small office, Taj began searching through his jeans pockets until he found a business card, bent and slightly soiled. He held it out to Savannah. She looked at it skeptically.

"What's that for?"

"Read it and you'll find out," Taj suggested.

Savannah gingerly took the card and frowned at the information.

"Who's Punch Wagoner?"

"You're kidding, right?" Taj responded, as if she was out of her mind. "The man is one of the hottest agents in L.A. He handles a lot of black talent. He became famous about ten or twelve years ago when he made the careers of several folks."

Taj rattled off three or four names.

Savannah handed the card back to him. "So?"

"Baby *Girl,*" Taj said dramatically, as if she was breaking his heart. "Don't you get it? The man read your script, *Fade to Black.* He wants to meet with you ASAP."

Savannah stared at Taj and swallowed. "You're serious?"

"As a heart attack," Taj said, using an old phrase to make his point.

"What did he say about it?"

"Nothing to me. I'm just the messenger. You gave me your script to read, I thought it was good enough to show Punch. He thought it was good enough to send you his card. I've been trying to catch you for the last two days. If I were you I'd call him *yesterday.*"

"Oh, my God," Savannah murmured.

She actually had very mixed emotions to Taj's news, one of which was uncertainty. Another was elation. Another, fear. She'd only wanted Taj to read her work because she knew he'd be honest. Was the writing good or bad? Did the story make any sense? It was quite a leap from that to a professional and, at least by Taj's comment, famous agent showing interest. What, exactly, did that mean?

"I thought you'd be excited," Taj said, somewhat bewildered. "That's why you wanted me to read your script, right?"

"I don't know. I just wanted your opinion. I guess I'm just a bit overwhelmed. This is like two or three steps ahead of me," Savannah said quietly, looking at the business card. Then she forced herself to smile at Taj. "You've been great. Thank you for reading it, and for showing it to…to…"

"Punch Wagoner," Taj helped her out. He shook his head at the irony. "Do you know how many people would kill to have a meeting with him?"

"How do you know him?"

"I interned with him when I was in college. It's because of him that I got this job. He read your script because I asked him to."

"Then I'll give him a call." Savannah said, coming to her senses and talking rationally.

"And?" Taj coaxed broadly, waiting.

Savannah looked at him and began to laugh. "I owe you drinks."

"Keep this up, Baby Girl, you'll have to buy me the whole damn bottle."

Disappointed, McCoy snapped shut his cell phone without bothering to leave a message. He didn't want to leaves messages for Savannah. He enjoyed getting her on the line and hearing the surprise in her voice when she recognized it was him.

Not only did that stroke his ego, it made him feel he was right about her. She was not like the thousand and one other people who arrive in L.A. in droves looking to grab the gold ring. *Any* gold ring that signified success, fame and fortune. It pleased him that, as far as he could tell, Savannah Shelton couldn't care less. For someone whose father had been famous in a brutal business, that was no mean feat.

McCoy looked at his watch and knew he'd have to leave. He was out of time to try to reach Savannah and ask her out to dinner. As a matter of fact he'd so anticipated being able to reach her and have her say yes that he'd gone ahead and made reservations. So much for putting the cart before the horse, he thought wryly.

At his desk McCoy pushed a button on his phone console and his assistant answered.

"I'm about to leave. Call Jeff Peterson at the Four Seasons. If he's not there yet, leave a message that I'm on my way. He's to stay put until I get there. We have some issues to discuss."

"Will do."

"Have there been any other calls for me while I was out at the building site? Any messages?"

"Just the client you're representing on the sale of that commercial building on Sepulveda, about the closing next week."

"Right," McCoy said, leaning over his desk and swiveling his desk calendar so that he could read it. "Call Mr. Pierce back and let him know it's Tuesday at eleven. I've got the paperwork. Remind him to bring his checkbook."

The assistant chuckled. "Sure. Oh, and Ms. Daly called again."

McCoy grew alert. "You didn't tell her I was seeing Jeff Peterson tonight, did you?"

"Never said a word. She thinks her brother is arriving tomorrow. I guess he had his reasons."

"Good," McCoy said brusquely, relieved.

"She did say she'd try to reach you at home later."

"Thanks for the warning. Not that I needed it."

"She is persistent and single-minded. You have to give her that," Colin volunteered his opinion.

"Unfortunately, that's exactly what it takes."

Forty minutes later McCoy stepped out of his car, handing the keys over to the valet. He strode with purpose past the liveried doorman, who nodded to him politely as he entered the lobby. It was an elegant, traditional-looking setting that spoke not only of wealth and privilege, but also of good taste. A beautiful older woman followed by three or four assistants passed by, leaving in her wake the scent of expensive perfume. McCoy never gave her a second look, although he recognized her as an Oscar-winning actress and Hollywood icon. He headed right to the front desk to have Jeff Peterson paged. The desk clerk handed him the house phone.

"Hey, man… I'm down at the front desk… Suite 1532? I'm on my way up."

Thanking the clerk, McCoy headed for the elevators.

He was pleased and proud that one of his best friends had done well enough for himself professionally to be able to afford the nosebleed rate of a five-star hotel, as well as all the other toys and distractions that money can buy. But places like this made him uncomfortable. McCoy recognized that with power, fame, status or political pull came world-class benefits. To his way of thinking they also meant giving up privacy and more than a little bit of yourself. He'd never believed that the trade-off was worth it.

The door to the suite opened as McCoy stood poised to knock. An athletic giant filled the frame, a broad grin exposing perfect teeth in a celebrity-handsome face. He was dressed in Armani slacks and polo top. The soft suede loafers on his boat-sized feet had probably been specially ordered and made in Italy.

"My broth-*ah*," the deep voice boomed, ending on a laugh as he opened his arms.

"Jeff. Good to see you," McCoy acknowledged the man, who was easily three or four inches taller than he.

The two men clasped hands and drew together in a chest- and shoulder-press greeting.

"Come on in."

Jeff Peterson had already settled into the absurdly large room, his presence spread everywhere. An expensive leather suitcase was open on a luggage stand, an equally expensive attaché rested on the bar top. The forty-two-inch flat-screen TV was tuned in to a basketball game, and every light in the room was on, as well as those in a connecting room. There was also a room-service cart beautifully laid out with a platter of snacks. In an ice bucket rested a bottle of champagne.

"When did you get in?" McCoy asked in wonder, looking at the extravagant spread.

"About twenty minutes ago. I had someone call ahead."

"Nice to have money," McCoy cracked, sending Jeff into a boisterous laugh.

"You're not exactly a pauper yourself. Remember when we were freshmen we used to talk about living large?"

"Let's just say we have different ways of enjoying the fruits of our labors," McCoy grinned, seating himself in one of the fancy, but not very comfortable, chairs.

"Look, bro. You know I'm always glad to see you and hang out, but I have this thing going on a little later."

"Who is she?"

Jeff hemmed and hawed. "She's in broadcast TV out here. One of those newsmagazine shows."

McCoy shook his head indulgently. "You just got here. When did you have time to meet someone?"

"She recognized me at the airport. You know LAX is always crawling with photographers. Someone was taking pictures and she came over and introduced herself. Wanted to know if I'd consent to an interview later. *Hell, yeah.*"

"What happened to…what was her name again?"

Jeff waved a dismissive hand. "That's over, man. I felt the noose tightening. After three dinners a lot of these woman expect you to propose. Now, you know I don't roll with that. I'm too young," Jeff chortled.

McCoy listened and merely nodded. He decided against reminding his friend that he'd probably married too young the first time, just after signing with a national team and going pro. But it didn't help that Jeff had then stepped out on his young wife with the first groupie who'd played to his ego.

"Have you decided to accept the offer to do the on-air commentary for that sports program?" McCoy asked, switching subjects.

"I'm close. That's why I'm out here. It was bad luck to bust up my knee like that last season. I think I could have played another three years, but this could work out for the best. Not as much money, but hey, I could have a longer career."

"I still think it's a good thing that you got your MBA."

Jeff looked pained. "It was a struggle, Mac."

"It might come in handy down the road, and it looks good on your résumé. You won't always be able to use the basketball background to impress people."

"Yeah, I know. I'm glad you kicked my ass and made me stick with the program. That was good looking-out. But I'm hoping this commentary gig will get me some cameo parts on TV or in the movies. I'm meeting with the network people tomorrow.

"What about Evan?"

"He's cool. I'm taking care of my son, man. I'm trying to make sure he makes better decisions than I did. His mama is still trying to get sole custody. It ain't gonna happen." Jeff's mood suddenly changed and he pressed his fingertips together, staring at McCoy. "What's up with Cherise?"

"Your baby sister is doing great. She's wasted no time since she got here."

"Sounds like Cherise. Grab the moment, and all you can get. Puts her mind to something and goes after it like a bulldog. Told me about some awards show she's trying to get to. Good place to be seen, and all that. Ain't she something else?" Jeff asked with obvious pride and affection.

"She certainly is," McCoy murmured dryly. "I know you've always been very protective of your half sister."

"I never think of her that way. She's my little sister. Period. I'd do anything for her, but since I don't know the lay of the land out here, I'm relying on you to take care of her, Mac."

"I'd say Cherise is pretty good at taking care of herself. But let me fill you in with some important details. She's got a couple of contracts that could lead to bigger things…."

Half an hour and the bottle of champagne later, former basketball pro Jeff Peterson was satisfied with the news that little sis Cherise was being given due respect, and parts, in accordance with his wishes and her ambition. McCoy had always been amused by Jeff's big-brother act when it came to his younger sister. But, in truth, it was also something to be admired. Jeff was fiercely loyal to his family and friends.

Jeff looked at the time.

"I gotta get out of here. Quick. What's up with you? Anything going on?"

"By 'going on' I take it you don't mean work. You know how I feel about a lot of the women in L.A. They're beautiful, I'll give you that. But that's not enough for me."

"Why you gotta be so picky? Ever since you and Paula broke up you've been playing hard to get," Jeff grinned.

McCoy held back from asking Jeff why he always went for the superficial. "I'm not saying I don't get any action. But I'm selective. Nothing wrong with that."

Jeff bent forward from his chair and affectionately tapped his fist on McCoy's knee. "You know I'm just messin' with you. Ever since Paula you've been too careful, man. There ain't a whole lot of women out there can live up to your high standards. What's wrong with someone just being damned gorgeous?"

McCoy wasn't about to go into the difference between his and Jeff's outlook toward women. They'd both set their own standards in the past, and they'd both been wrong, even if it was for different reasons. But Jeff's question was a fair one. He knew that if you used Cherise as an example the answer would have to be, nothing. The girl was all that. But for him personally, the answer would have to be, *everything*. He had yet to discover anything that Cherise held an informed opinion on, cared about, wanted to change or improve that didn't center solely around herself.

McCoy wasn't exactly surprised when an image of Savannah materialized—the way she had looked as they'd walked through his old home turf of Long Beach. The way she'd been so intensely interested in talking to one of her father's former students at the college where he taught. Actually, letting *him* talk while she listened. The way she'd so genuinely thanked the repertory group in Inglewood for their warm greeting, while demurring that she didn't deserve it because it was her father who'd had the real impact on their lives.

And that good-night kiss.

It hadn't been particularly passionate, or even a standard for foreplay. But it had felt real good, and it held promise.

"I don't need a whole lot of women," McCoy said, a vague smile playing around his mouth. "The right one would be enough."

While he waited for his car to be brought around, McCoy used his cell phone to call Savannah. He was glad when he heard her voice, but he also suddenly hesitated, pulling back a little as his natural instinct toward caution came into play. It was like he was waiting for some revelation that would once again prove his comment to Jeff—that he wasn't much impressed by

L.A. women—to be right. Of course, he was glad that Jeff had never asked if Cherise fell into that category. So far, Savannah Shelton was in a class all by herself. McCoy had to admit that he still didn't know what that was, but he was definitely intrigued.

"Hi, this is Savannah."

"I'd love to hear the story behind your name. I know it has to be something interesting," McCoy said by way of greeting.

"What's wrong with Savannah?"

"I never said there was anything wrong with it. But you have to admit it's a far cry from a lot of current names. How are you? Have I caught you at a bad time?"

"On the road again. I'm headed home from the Film Institute."

"That's not good. You behind the wheel of a car and talking at the same time..."

"Easy solution. I'll hang up."

He grinned, enjoying the banter that seemed so natural and easy between them.

"You understand I'm only thinking of your safety."

"Uh-huh," Savannah responded with exaggerated skepticism. "I appreciate your concern, but until the night you ran into me I'd never been in an accident."

"Got me. I surrender."

"Do I get a prize?"

He laughed. "How about drinks?"

"When?"

"Right now. I'm just leaving a meeting. There's a

nice spot on the Promenade in Santa Monica. But if you're anxious to get home…"

"You know, drinks would be nice. I'd love to join you."

"Good. Where are you right now?"

After hearing the information, McCoy gave Savannah simple directions to Santa Monica, and told her where to meet him. When he was back in his car and headed in that direction himself, he became reflective once more, wondering what it was, exactly, that had triggered the invitation. And what was it about Savannah that kept drawing him back to her?

Chapter 9

"Sorry, I have to take this call."

Savannah nodded and made to get up from her chair to leave the office, but the man behind the desk, black agent Punch Wagoner, indicated with his hand that she should stay. She assumed by the big greeting and laughter that it was a friend he was talking with, and her mind began to drift away from the conversation and into her own thoughts. They took her back to three nights ago when she'd met McCoy at a café for drinks and dinner. His cell-phone invitation had been a surprise, but agreeing to it had come as even more of a surprise, Savannah considered now.

"Well, we'll have to see about that. I'll have a chat

with the producer and see what I can hold over him to get you back on board...."

Savannah frowned at the slight tone of threat in Punch's voice, even as he smiled and appeared calm. She wasn't naive about the deals that are cut in Hollywood in order for things to get done. But to actually witness it happening made her feel uneasy. The conversation suddenly steered away from business and Savannah went back to her own reflections, the memory of that evening now making her smile to herself.

When she'd met up with McCoy, Savannah's first thought was of the brief kiss they'd shared the last time they'd been together. But there was absolutely no reference to cause any awkward moment, and they'd relaxed nicely into an evening of conversation and laughter. McCoy managed to get the story out of her about having been named for the city of Savannah where, according to her mother, she'd been conceived during a forced two-day stormy stay over in the middle of a hurricane that had brushed the coast.

Savannah's smile grew as she recalled McCoy's skepticism, convinced that the story was made up. There had followed his own versions that had kept her laughing through most of the evening.

From the outdoor seating of the café they'd people watched, and Savannah had again been entertained by McCoy's on-the-spot reading of passersby—which ones were tourists, which were locals trying to pass for someone of importance and which were newcomers playing at being locals. He wasn't being mean-spirited, but Savannah suspected a pretty accurate accounting of the thousands of people who pass through the city all the time.

She'd been sorry to have to remind him that she, at least, had to report at a certain time for work in the morning. She had her own car, so there was no question of McCoy driving her home. But in the parking lot, as they waited for their respective cars, the moment of truth happened.

"Thanks for dinner," Savannah said.

"Thanks for accepting my last-minute invitation."

"I almost didn't. I had to wash my hair and..."

Her attempt at humor was only mildly successful. McCoy was waiting for more.

"Why did you?" he asked, fixing her with a look of intense inquiry.

She'd thought about how much she wanted to reveal, and finally she said, "I learn lots of things from you about L.A. I enjoy the conversations. And I like your company."

She'd said it. Immediately Savannah wondered if she'd said too much. He was staring at her, almost to the point of making her uncomfortable.

The valet returned with her car first, pulling up next to Savannah and getting out, only to go racing off to find McCoy's. All the time Savannah was thanking the valet and tipping him she was aware of McCoy's scrutiny. Finally, she turned to him again and shrugged.

"I hope that was enough reason."

"It will do just fine," he said. "I promise next time to give you advance warning."

Savannah grinned. *Next time.*

"Don't wait too long," she teased. "My social calendar fills up quickly."

"I'll remember that."

The valet drove up with McCoy's car. After he'd left them, Savannah stood poised to get into hers as she was saying a final good-night. McCoy had other ideas. He lightly grabbed her hand and pulled her away from the safe shield of her driver's-side door into the circle of his own arms. Instinctively Savannah's arms returned the embrace.

As with their first kiss, this hug had more a feel of warmth and affection than it did a blatant play on sexual tension. For a moment she couldn't decide if she was pleased by McCoy's restraint or merely surprised that he was restrained. The embrace allowed Savannah to feel the strength in his arms as well as the gentleness of his hands on her back. She wasn't crushed against his chest, but could still feel its firm planes through his dove-gray business shirt. He'd slid one hand up her spine to cup the back of her neck. The gesture created an unexpected languid yearning as he turned his head to plant a kiss, again briefly, on her mouth.

"Be careful driving home," McCoy had cautioned, releasing her and standing back as she'd gotten into her car.

She'd waved as McCoy had stood watching until she'd driven out of the parking lot....

"Miss Shelton? Miss Shelton?"

Her head jerked up and Savannah gaze at the puzzled expression on Punch Wagoner's face. "I'm sorry. I guess I was daydreaming."

"My fault for keeping you waiting. Sorry for the long interruption. Now, let's get down to business." He picked up a stack of papers held with metal fasteners and thumbed through the pages quickly. "I read your script. Have you ever written one before?"

"No, I haven't."

"How did you know the structure?"

"I wrote mine according to the format of several published scripts I'd read."

He seemed astonished.

"That's it? You've never taken a film-writing class or anything like that? Did you get some pointers from other writers?"

Savannah shook her head. "I don't know any script-writers. I just wrote it."

Punch stared at her. "Unbelievable," he murmured.

She didn't know what that meant. As a matter of fact, Savannah didn't quite know what to make of Punch Wagoner. His name, for one, sounded like something made up, but it really suited the man. He had a lively open personality that was slick but likeable. His brown skin was clean shaven; he was of average height and, although stocky, appeared to be very fit. Based on what Taj had told her about the agent, Savannah guessed that he was in his late forties or even older, but he looked much younger. Taj had also told her that Punch was a force to be reckoned with. He had a successful history in Hollywood.

Punch dropped the script on his desk and used his curled knuckles to knock on the top page for emphasis. "I've read a lot of scripts, but this is the first one by a total novice that was this well done." He shook his head. "Let me correct myself. You're not a total outsider. You probably have a very good idea of how things work in Hollywood because of your father. I knew Will Shelton casually. Sorry to hear of his passing."

"You were right the first time. I am an outsider. My father never discussed his career with me and, frankly, I've never been interested myself in a Hollywood career."

"But you wrote this script. Why not a novel? Essay?"

"I guess it could have been done as either of those. But, the idea came to me in pictures. I could see the action."

"It's one hell of an idea. Where did it come from?"

Savannah hesitated. She had no clue what might have happened to Rae Marie Hilton, but felt the need to be protective of the former actress's name and history.

"I wrote it as a what-if story. I saw it as a cautionary tale about how far people are willing to go to get what they want and the price to be paid. We make deals and compromises all the time in our lives. When you add in the race card and Hollywood, a place that's all about make-believe and encouraging people to pretend to be someone else, then I think my story has really tragic consequences."

As she was talking, Savannah was aware of the way Punch was watching her. She wasn't sure he was really listening to what she had to say. He seemed to be assessing her for his own reasons.

"Fantastic," he said thoughtfully. Then he sat back. "You know, when Tyrone asked me to read the script I blew him off. I can't tell you how many times I'm asked to read someone's script. Of course, that's what I'm supposed to do. That's how I find people who might stand a chance in L.A. Most of what I read, unfortunately, is pretty bad. I like your writing. I like what you have to say in your story," Punch said, again knocking the top of the script to make his point.

"Thank you," Savannah said, pleased.

"Of course, you want to know what to do with it, and what I can do to help. I have some minor changes to suggest."

"Well, actually..." she began and was cut off.

"It's still not easy getting projects by black writers green-lighted in this town, unless you have a popular rapper, rising star or someone the studios are interested in pushing attached." He leaned across his desk, eyeing her. "Who do you see as the female lead?"

Savannah stared blankly at him. "I don't know. I only wanted to..."

"Well, now's a good time to start thinking about that.

It's going to take a particular kind of female. Someone like Alicia Keyes has the look."

Savannah frowned. Alicia Keyes would be all wrong.

"But she might not want this as her first film vehicle. Too serious. We'd lose the fifteen-to-thirty audience."

"You talk as if my script is definitely going to be a movie," Savannah said, with a trace of excitement in her voice.

Punch Wagoner was moving ahead fast, and her head was spinning.

"Isn't that what you want? Yeah, it could happen. It's going to take some work and persuading. This isn't an easy story to tell or sell, and it's bound to get a lot of folks upset."

Punch was looking for something else on his somewhat unorganized desk when his phone rang. He picked up immediately, announcing his name briskly as a greeting. It was the way he'd answered the phone when she'd finally called two days earlier.

"Sorry, I have to take this call," Punch told her for the second time since she'd sat down with him.

He found what he was looking for and passed it across the desk for her to read while she waited. Savannah saw that she'd been given a contract that laid out the terms of his willingness to represent her as a manager for the purpose of working to secure an option on, and subsequent sale of her work, *Fade to Black,* to a studio to be produced as a feature film or made-for-TV movie.

Savannah felt her stomach roil as she read the paper.

It was formal. The language was intimidating and precise. She was being moved out of her comfort zone of Rae Marie's life just being an idea for a script. It now had the potential to become a viable project. When she'd started writing she hadn't forseen the project getting this far. If not, why had she bothered writing the story at all?

"It's a boilerplate contract," Punch Wagoner's voice broke into her thoughts. "If you agree to let me represent you I'll go out and pitch the idea to a short list of directors and producers. I'll let a few of them read your script to generate interest. After that I try to get you a good option payment against the outright purchase price. You don't have to understand all of that right now. After you sign the agreement I can get started. I already have one producer in mind. He has a three-picture deal with…"

His voice faded, and the words on the form began to run together and blur until they had no meaning. Savannah glanced up at Punch. He was waiting for her answer.

"Can I have a few days to read through this and think about it?"

"Don't wait too long," was his response. "I have a lot of things I'm working on with a lot of folks, so you have to act quickly. Can you get back to me this week?"

He made his announcement with a kind of offhanded indifference that made Savannah waver for a moment. She felt pressured and didn't much like the feeling. She stood up to leave.

"Thank you for your time. I know you're very busy."

"Like I said, I think you have a strong script and a good story. I'm sure I can sell it for you. Let me know what you want me to do," Punch said, getting up to walk her to the door. "And tell Tyrone that I'm still waiting for that demo disc he's been promising to play for me."

Savannah was expecting that he'd say more to put her mind at rest instead of talking as if projects and writers like her were a dime a dozen. But she recognized that there was a real opportunity being offered here. What would her father advise her to do?

"I'll call you as soon as I can," Savannah promised.

At his office door Punch Wagoner already appeared distracted. "You do that," he said, closing the door on her.

Confused and annoyed, Savannah left the building knowing that although she'd managed to wrangle some extra time she wasn't really sure what her next move should be.

Back in her car, Savannah just sat, going over the entire exchange with Punch Wagoner. For a minute she came *that close* to signing the contract he'd given her and telling him to do whatever he could. She felt an adrenaline rush, spurred by Punch's obvious enthusiasm. She felt almost light-headed at the prospect of actually having her story taken seriously, and Rae Marie's life vindicated.

Suddenly, Savannah thought of her father, and all he must have gone through over the years. The hard work it had taken not only trying to prove his own talent, but also building the right kind of support around him to make his career possible. It couldn't have been easy, and maybe it wasn't supposed to be. It was ironic that it seemed to be happening so fast for her. Was this what she wanted for her own life? To be caught up in the Hollywood fantasy machine?

Could she be any less brave then Rae Marie, or her own father?

Savannah opened her cell phone and entered McCoy's office number. The assistant answered and informed her that Mr. Sutton was out of the office for most of the day, but he'd be sure to give him her message when he called in.

"Please tell Mr. Sutton that I need his advice on a contract I've been given to sign," Savannah added.

"Will he know what it's about?"

"No," Savannah admitted. "But I have it with me. Can I drop a copy off for him?"

"That's a good idea and will save time. Do you have the address?"

Savannah drove to McCoy's Century City office. The male assistant met her in the reception area where she handed him the contract. He glanced quickly over the first page.

"Is this about a real estate deal?"

"It's about this," Savannah said, pulling a copy of the script from her tote bag.

"Fine," he said. "I'll make a copy of the contract and give the original back to you. It'll just take a minute."

Savannah thanked him for his trouble, and in less than fifteen minutes she was back in her car and on her way to her office. It was only then that she felt somewhat relieved and began to settle down. Only then did she believe as well that everything would work out.

It was almost three-thirty when McCoy called her.

"Sorry I couldn't get back to you sooner," he said.

"I'm sorry I called on such short notice."

"I haven't had a chance to read through those papers yet, but I wanted to make sure you're okay." McCoy said.

"Yes, I'm fine. I just didn't want to sign anything without checking it out first."

"Smart move."

"But it can wait for a day or two," Savannah offered.

"No, let's deal with it now. Can you come by my office later? I'll have the contract read by then and we can talk."

Savannah hesitated. Of course she wanted to know what McCoy thought, and to get his insights, but she felt uncomfortable, nonetheless, asking him.

"I can be there by six."

"Good. See you then."

After hearing from McCoy, Savannah's anxiety returned, and she couldn't say why. There was certainly a sense of anticipation, but also something else that was harder to define. For a while she even wondered if it had been a good idea to call McCoy at all, to involve him, but there was no one else she felt she could trust to be honest with her.

Well, maybe her father's former agent, Simon Raskin, but that also did not sit well with Savannah.

As the rest of the afternoon unfolded it finally occurred to her to call Taj with the latest information about her script.

"The Man himself is willing to take you on? Hey, I'm not surprised. That's why I went to him. Are you going to sign an agreement?" Taj asked Savannah.

"I'm thinking about it, Taj. The contract looked a little complicated and I want to take my time reading it to make sure I understood."

"You can't get no better than Punch Wagoner, Baby Girl, and he's one of us. He'll watch out for you."

"You're probably right, but he was okay with me getting back to him."

"I guess I should congratulate you."

"Taj, I haven't done anything yet. Right now it's still just a script."

"I'll make you a bet that something happens with it."

"What are you willing to bet?" Savannah asked, getting into the spirit of the moment.

"Double or nothing. If you're right, and the deal dies a quick and natural death, then you don't owe me anything. But if I win, then it's the whole nine yards times *two*."

"Even if I'm right, Taj, then I'll have to do something for you. I wouldn't have gotten this far without your help."

"You know, maybe I should become an agent like

Punch. Hell, you could've been my first client," Taj bemoaned the loss, making Savannah laugh.

But when she arrived later that afternoon at McCoy's office the humor of that moment had vanished. She was still no less anxious to hear what he had to say about the management agreement Punch Wagoner wanted her to sign.

The assistant was waiting and led her right into McCoy's office. Savannah tried not to read anything into the fact that Mac hadn't met her himself. As a matter of fact, when she entered his office, he was not seated at his desk or standing in front of it to greet her. Instead, Savannah found him staring out the window, his back to her.

"Ms. Shelton is here," the assistant announced.

"Thanks," Savannah said to him as he left, closing the door behind him.

It was only a matter of seconds before McCoy finally turned from the window but to her it seemed interminable. Something felt off, and she felt the need to apologize.

"If this isn't a good time, I..."

"This is as good a time as any," McCoy said, sitting down at his desk, and indicating one of the two chairs in front of it where she was to take a seat.

"How are you?" he asked.

The question sounded formulaic to her. She shrugged. "Confused and harried. So much is happening."

"You certainly have been busy," he commented.

Savannah frowned. "Not really. The script and the

contract all came about pretty fast. I had no particular thought or plan."

McCoy sat back in a relaxed position, his legs crossed at the knees. It was then that she noticed two things. He held in his hand, not the contract from Punch Wagoner but the copy of *Fade to Black*. The second thing was the tone of his voice. As he silently and thoughtfully scanned the first few pages of the script a third came to mind. Mac seemed to be avoiding meeting her gaze.

The revelations caught Savannah off guard and left her startled. He had not greeted her at all. Gone was any sign that they knew one another, that there had just recently been conversation, laughter and a kiss between them that was still open to interpretation.

"You wrote this?" McCoy finally asked.

"Why is everyone so surprised by that?" Savannah asked. "Yes, I did."

"I wasn't questioning the authenticity," McCoy said calmly. "Just expressing my admiration and my awareness that it's a good script."

"Thank you," Savannah said quietly, bewildered by his formality, and not even sure that he was actually paying her a compliment.

In that moment McCoy finally gazed into her eyes. His were clear, focused and coolly professional. Now he gave her his complete attention, and Savannah reasoned that he was doing exactly what she needed him to do—being serious in his appraisal and advice. She suddenly realized that it was she who had to make the adjustment and accept that she'd called him on a business matter, and that he was behaving in an appropriate businesslike way. But she found it unsettling.

Savannah realized she was looking for much more in his eyes. The something that would have reassured her, and that would not necessarily have been all about business, but also about…

About what? Their knowledge of each other? Growing camaraderie? Affection?

"I had to read it quickly, but I enjoyed it," McCoy said.

"I didn't mean to rush you," Savannah said.

"I'll read it again, when I can take my time, but I think what you've done is very good. The concept is fresh and daring, with a lot of heart and a lot to say."

"Thank you," Savannah said again, this time warmly and with relief. "I had no idea what I was doing. I was writing by the seat of my pants," she attempted to joke. It fell flat.

McCoy suddenly fastened a speculative searching look on her. "Why this story? Is it based on someone you know?"

"Why are you asking?" she countered.

"It's a painful story, Savannah. Very revealing, and very humiliating," McCoy said. "It airs some of our own dirty laundry from the history of black Americans. The story is filled with desperation, but it's also about someone who was undeniably brave. Who do you know who's like this character?"

Savannah was surprised by the sharpness of McCoy's question, but she knew she shouldn't have been. One of the reasons she'd thought to discuss her project and the contract with him at all was because she believed she could trust his opinion.

"Her name is Rae Marie Hilton. I don't know her, but I found a lot of information about her in my father's personal records. What I learned about her leads me to believe she was a black actress passing for white, and that my father was her friend and confidant. I've also seen some pictures of her. She was stunningly beautiful, and she did look white. That's about it. I don't know if she's still alive or, if she is, where she lives. I've found very little about her career as an actress and nothing about her personal life. It's as though she's vanished from the face of the earth."

McCoy was closely watching her as she spoke, but again, as with Punch Wagoner that morning, Savannah had the sense that he was studying her, appraising her as well. She didn't understand why he'd feel the need to. She'd allowed him to get closer to her than any man had in a long time.

He nodded in understanding when she'd finished what she knew about Rae Marie. "Is your script based entirely on her?"

"No, it's not. I only used her as the model for my heroine. I made up the story to suit my theme."

"And that is?"

"Be careful what you wish for."

"I see that," McCoy said.

He grew silent, once again giving his attention to the script, taking time to reread random pages. He pursed his lips and furrowed his brow and seemed to be considering much more than she was asking of him.

"Mac, I want you to be honest. You won't hurt my feelings, I promise. I don't want to make a fool of myself. Should I put it in a drawer and forget about it?"

"No, you definitely should not do that," he said, pulling his chair up to the desk and seeming to settle down to the business at hand. "Let me make something clear. I'm not an entertainment attorney."

"I know that."

"So you have to take what I tell you with a grain of salt."

"I trust what you'll tell me because I believe you'll be fair."

"I appreciate your faith in me," he said coolly, "But let me tell you what I see here."

Savannah was surprised by the thorough and thoughtful assessment he gave her script. Like Punch Wagoner, McCoy was honest about what he saw as her chances for selling her concept, the bottom line for any producer or director being whether there's an audience, or if a film will earn back the investment.

"I think Punch was being straight with you about that part. It's an excellent script and story, but Hollywood has been known to go for total nonsense to make money," he said dryly. "The first thing I want you to do is to register a copy of your script with the Writer's

Guild of America. It acts like a copyright office for the film industry. Do it tomorrow on your lunch break. And make sure you keep all your original notes and computer versions of the script. Just in case."

"Okay." Savannah quickly dug out a notebook from her bag and wrote a note to herself.

"I know Punch Wagoner socially," McCoy suddenly confessed. "He's got a good reputation in the business and I think he's a straight shooter. That said, I have some problems with his agreement."

Referring to the first page, and methodically continuing through the entire document, McCoy alerted Savannah to the terms, clauses and language that he felt she should be aware of and careful with. He suggested changes.

"Something else," he said, frowning over one page. "I don't like that Punch has put the title of producer for himself into the contract. It's not illegal, but I think there's a big conflict of interest. It looks like he's using your project as leverage to further his own interest in that area."

"What should I do? Will he take that out if I ask him to?"

"You won't have to. That's why you talk with a lawyer before signing anything. I'll call him and give him a heads-up, let him know that you and I are acquainted and I gave you my professional opinion of his agreement. But I'll give you the name of someone I know who'll work with you and Punch to make the contract more acceptable. He probably told you it's a boilerplate contract, but no contract is written to the benefit of the person who's to sign it. I'm glad you didn't sign this," McCoy said dryly.

"I never would have done that without talking to you first," she said.

McCoy glanced at her, and for a brief moment she saw that electric spark in his eyes that had first appeared once they began to learn more about each other. The same spark had signaled awareness and interest and burgeoning respect, and something more that had not even been defined between them. But it was quickly gone, and Savannah was left with the prowess of a professional whom she knew she could trust. Anything else did not come into play at that moment.

"I'll talk to Punch tomorrow. Expect to get a call from this attorney."

He flipped through a Rolodex and turned it to face her with a name and phone number displayed.

"Thanks," she murmured, busily writing down the information.

"Is this what you want?"

She looked up sharply, not so much at the question but at the change in his voice again. For the first time since she'd entered his office, McCoy's question seemed personal, and closer to touching on what he'd learned about her in the past few months. His whole demeanor now was not only questioning, but seemed to be waiting for an answer that Savannah was sure had little to do with the contract or the script.

"What do you mean?

"This could open a Pandora's box. Or it could be the start of the Yellow Brick Road for you. It could get you a lot of opportunities and a lot of attention. It could change you."

She had to smile at his use of fictional images and analogies, the sense of ominous drama. "To be honest, Mac, I wrote the script for myself. Whatever happens, happens. I want to be surprised."

"I think you can count on that. If there's anything more I can do, let me know."

A few things came spontaneously, and unbidden, to mind, but they had nothing to do with the contract or script or Punch Wagoner.

"You've already done more than you needed to," Savannah said, keeping to the unstated rules McCoy had laid out when she'd entered his office. This was business. But there was another awkward hurdle to get over. "Should I see your assistant about payment?"

He stared at her and his eyes clouded over. McCoy averted his expression and stood up. "You don't owe me anything. I'm glad you believed I could be of help. Consider this a consultation call. Or a conversation between friends."

She still didn't know what to make of his aloofness, but decided that now was not the time to confuse the issues.

"You've been very generous, as a consultant and a friend. I appreciate your honesty."

She stopped short of offering her hand in thanks. That would have been too cold. But, given the distance that remained between them, she also didn't feel comfortable with offering a friendly peck on the check as she said goodbye. McCoy walked her to the door.

She turned and faced him and they stood very close together. She didn't know what he was thinking, but she was overcome with an image of the two of them riding together in his car from L.A. to Long Beach. And sitting at a café laughing over conversation and drinks. Savannah could see none of that Mac she'd spent time with in the strict, impersonal demeanor of the man next to her now. But she smiled at him.

"Thank you for everything, McCoy. I mean it."

"I know you do."

To her relief he seemed to soften for a moment. He reached out and stroked her arm, a gesture that went a long way to alleviating her qualms. But she'd said as much as she was going to. The ball was in his court. He reached beyond her to open the office door. He was once more the lawyer.

"Someone will get back to you with a revised contract. Sign it and return it to Punch. And then, wait to see what happens. And don't forget to register that script as soon as you can."

"I will." Savannah swallowed and rushed on. "Are you free to join me for drinks or coffee?"

His smile didn't quite reach his eyes.

"Are you still trying to pay me back?"

"I thought it would be nice to get away from business. Just enjoy ourselves. Like last week."

He lowered his gaze, staring down at his shoes before looking at her again. "Thanks, but I can't. I have some catching up to do here before leaving tonight."

Savannah silently nodded and hid her disappointment. It took all of her willpower to appear as casual and calm as she could when something entirely different was happening inside.

"Then I'd better go." She waved briefly and turned away.

"Savannah?"

She looked over her shoulder and found that McCoy had followed her almost to the elevator. "Yes?"

"I hope this works out for you. But I hope you won't think me a spoilsport if I add a final caution."

"What is it?" she frowned.

"You can't always get what you want."

Chapter 10

McCoy took a sip of his drink and looked over the gathering. The setting was a restaurant in West Hollywood on a drizzly weeknight. The hostess was Kay, a friend of Savannah's whom he'd only met for the first time when he'd shown up as a guest. Kay's response to his introducing himself had been revealing.

"Oh, you're the guy that Vann said ran into her a couple of months back on the freeway. I thought your name looked familiar."

"What else did she tell you?" he'd asked, intrigued.

"Not a hell of a lot," Kay had chortled. "I only know you two made up, and she's been keeping you all to herself. Now I can see why." Kay frowned at him. "You didn't say anything to her about tonight, did you? It's a surprise."

It was easy enough for him to admit that he hadn't, but McCoy held back from saying that he also had not spoken with Savannah for almost two weeks. That might have required a further explanation, and he didn't have one.

The fact is, Savannah's sudden interest in, and her immediate success with, writing a film script touched too close to home. The same thing had happened with his ex-wife Paula and, he'd believed, had ultimately been the cause of their divorce. Unexpectedly, she'd become an instant hit after a record producer, a friend of his, had offered to listen to her demo tape. He'd always known that Paula had an above-average singing voice, but she'd never once expressed an interest in a professional career. That is, until nearly three years after they'd married and moved to L.A. for his practice.

He never saw it coming, and he still wondered if it had all been part of her game plan. Paula had never sought out singing engagements. At least, as far as he knew. But she enjoyed being asked to perform and had an alluring stage presence. When had the applause and attention taken hold and spawned bigger dreams? When had Paula decided that being married to a real-estate attorney might be holding her back?

Mac had thought he could handle her record deal. After all, not every singer registered with an audience, let alone hit the charts. But getting a chance to perform as a backup singer for a group that led off the concert tours of a few big names had really set the ball rolling. He'd found himself caught between wanting his wife to make singing and performing second place in her life, and knowing that if he had to ask that of her they were already in trouble.

Mac had never been able to decide what had disappointed and hurt him the most: that she'd made the decision in favor of a singing career, or that she'd only returned from touring long enough to move her things out of their home.

McCoy finished the rest of his drink and placed the glass on a nearby table. There was a wait staff circulating trays of sushi, spring rolls and spicy Buffalo wings. There were platters laid out in various places with cheese and fruits, and there was a stand for pasta dishes made to order. *Very nice,* Mac thought. He was impressed that Savannah's friends thought enough to surprise her not only on the accomplishment of writing a script, but on the recent news that Punch Wagoner had optioned it.

McCoy had felt all the warning signs go off inside when Savannah had called with the news. He'd gotten a voice-mail message from her. An unsettling feeling of déjà vu had immediately cropped up. He hadn't been very responsive to Savannah, and he knew full well that his behavior was confusing to her. He could have stayed away and yet here he was to help celebrate her good news. And it *was* good news. Savannah had still not arrived, so McCoy grabbed another drink from a passing waiter as he meandered through the slowly growing number of guests. He didn't recognize anyone until he spotted Punch Wagoner sitting at the bar, having an animated conversation with a young man.

"Punch. Good to see you," McCoy opened.

Punch Wagoner stopped in mid sentence and turned to him.

"Hey. McCoy Sutton himself. Good to see you, man."

They shook hands. The young man chatting with Punch stuck out a skinny arm to McCoy.

"Taj."

Punch looked to McCoy with an indulgent expression. "Aka Tyrone James Sparks. Grab a chair. Join us. Tyrone and I were just talking about Savannah Shelton. Tyrone is the one that found her, brought me her script to read."

McCoy arched a brow at Taj. "You *found* her? I didn't realize she was lost."

Punch laughed at the obvious humor. Taj stayed cool and went along with the joke. "Baby Girl wasn't lost, but she needed me to get her jump-started."

"Baby Girl?" McCoy questioned, not realizing the tone of objection he used.

"Yeah, that's what I call her," Taj admitted openly. "'Cause she's clueless about the business. She's not one to be impressed by actors and actresses, and all the Hollywood stuff. Savannah is *real* folks. That's why I thought her script was so off the charts. Right?" he said, turning to Punch for confirmation.

"I think you should know, Tyrone, that my man here is responsible in some ways for Savannah's success. He gave her good legal advice, and wouldn't let her sign my contract until I'd made changes."

McCoy watched as Taj nodded and looked at him with newfound respect.

"Cool. She sure ain't like every other black woman who comes to this town. She already had a career. Her father is a famous dude and she's not easily impressed, know what I mean? You gotta work to get her respect and trust. I was the first person she let read her script," Taj boasted nonchalantly.

McCoy was surprised at the tinge of envy he felt at that announcement. He wondered how he would have responded had Savannah shown the work to him first. Would it have made a difference in how he was feeling now?

"I'm sure she appreciates you being in her corner," McCoy said.

"Yeah, but it was like pulling teeth to get her to see Punch. The girl didn't even know who he is. Sorry, Punch."

Punch shrugged good-naturedly. "No offense taken. Savannah is clearly an excellent writer. Must have inherited some of her father's talents, but she sure don't come across as a dilettante. And she's very clear on what she will and won't do."

"What do you mean?" McCoy asked, interested.

"Well, she absolutely refuses to let me use her father's name to talk about her and her work. But she will take meetings with producers or even actors interested in the script. It's not like she's shy or anything."

McCoy looked into his wineglass, pursing his lips. "Maybe just private?"

"Yeah, that's it," Punch and Taj said almost together.

"How come you know Baby Girl?" Taj asked.

McCoy realized quickly that he didn't much like Taj's nickname for Savannah, even though he knew it was said affectionately. "We met by accident," he said wryly. The other two men stared blankly at him, waiting. "I'm serious. I rear-ended her on the highway one night about two and a half months ago. She made no bones about calling me a lousy driver."

Both men broke into laughter.

"Ah, man. My girl ranked on you," Taj chuckled.

McCoy turned to Punch who was silently watching him.

"Are you two dating? I'm just curious," Punch quickly added defensively.

"Sorry I can't satisfy your curiosity," McCoy said, and he knew he was being completely honest. Not that he would have willingly shared information he considered private. Yet, he knew that not only was he confused, but that Savannah had to wonder about his aloofness. He'd seen the question in her eyes when she'd first come to him with Punch's contract.

His ego had made assumptions that his feelings couldn't justify.

They all turned when the latest group of people

walked into the restaurant, and Kay suddenly made a bloodcurdling yell.

"*Surprise!* Gotcha, didn't I?"

There was a smattering of applause and whistling. McCoy moved away from Punch and Taj, who'd both remained seated at the bar, so that he would witness Savannah's arrival. Not only did she look totally surprised, she looked bewildered. An attractive woman, tall and slender, ushered her forward as Savannah blinked in silence at the people rushing forward to welcome and congratulate her. Slowly, a smile replaced the stunned look, and her eyes filled with warmth as she was hugged and kissed, and a glass of champagne was thrust into her hands. She nearly spilled it when Kay threw herself at Savannah, making everyone laugh when she said,

"I *know* you have a part for me in your script, right?"

McCoy stayed out of sight as Savannah's gaze scanned the small crowd, greeting everyone as she recognized them. She suddenly looked up and right at him. She froze for a moment, her expression unreadable, but her eyes large and bright. Found out, McCoy silently raised his wineglass to her in a private toast.

An elderly white man who held out his hand as he talked with her grabbed Savannah's attention. She looked surprised but pleased to see him, and gave him a brief hug. McCoy rejoined Taj and Punch, but Taj excused himself to go and say hello to Baby Girl.

"Tell me about the option," McCoy asked Punch as Taj walked away.

"It was pretty easy. I know this producer who has a three-picture deal with a cable network that does a lot of made-for-TV movies. He was blown away by Savannah's script and wanted it. I was able to get her a nice bit of change, but it came with a warning. He's already considering two other scripts, so it's not a done deal that he'll buy Savannah's outright and put it into production. We're still a long ways from that."

"What do you think her chances are?"

"As good as anyone else's in this business. It's all about timing and who you know, and whether or not the sun is shining on the second Tuesday of the month, and if the director got *any* the night before reading the script."

McCoy laughed at Punch's assessment, and knew that to a great extent he was right. It was a capricious process, at best.

"I want to get one thing straight, Mac. About that producer credit in the contract…"

McCoy put his glass down and wiped his damp hands together. "Don't even try that with me, Punch. You know full well you were hoping to get over. I don't blame you, but I wasn't going to let you use Savannah that way."

"She asked some sharp questions herself. Like, what do I get out of it moneywise if I become producer."

"And you said?"

"I was honest with her. I said, a lot of money. She's nobody's fool, and she understood that. I handled it badly with her." Punch studied him intently. "Do I detect a special interest in Ms. Savannah Shelton?"

McCoy hesitated for just a second. "Savannah can take care of herself. But I *will* have to hurt you if you try to take advantage again."

Punch burst out into a boisterous laugh.

"What's so funny?"

Punch came quickly to his feet and McCoy turned to Savannah, who stood gazing between them with an uncertain smile.

"Guy talk," Punch said. He picked up his glass. "Nice party. You looked genuinely surprised."

"I was," Savannah said, as Punch patted her shoulder. "There'll be many more, if everything works out."

"I'm ready." Savannah grinned, watching him walk away to greet someone else he recognized.

McCoy was glad that Punch and Savannah had had the exchange, giving him time to decide what he was going to do and say to her.

She looked wonderful and was dressed not in the way most people would expect of someone in Hollywood with a career about to break out. But then, what had attracted him to Savannah from the start was that she followed no one's dictates but her own. Her style was her own. And she seemed not to care what anyone's opinion of her was.

Many of the women in the restaurant were dressed fashionably in light, colorful, eye-catching attire, designed to reveal décolletage and/or belly buttons.

Savannah was wearing a simple black dress with a V-neckline, emphasizing her face, short brushed-out hair and slender neck, under a coral-colored V-neck cardigan with a single button closing. Her only jewelry was a pair of large pearl ear studs, and a wide mother-of-pearl bracelet. Her sandals were not Jimmy Choo or Blahnik, but espadrilles with ankle-ties.

"Hi. I'm surprised to see you," Savannah said bluntly, though without any rancor or emotion.

McCoy knew this might not be his finest moment, but he hoped he did a credible job of showing Savannah that she had every right to her skepticism.

"I consider myself lucky to be invited. I wouldn't have missed this for anything."

Savannah continued to study him. "Not for anything?" she questioned, taking a drink of her champagne.

"Only if I'd known you wouldn't want me here."

Savannah's gaze held his without flinching. "That's not fair."

McCoy blushed. "You're right, but that's not how I meant it. I think I've been behaving like an ass, and you don't even know why."

"I agree with both statements."

He grinned, remembering that she wasn't afraid to square off with him. "I'm sorry. I know it's a weak response, but I don't want to spoil your party. Your friends are honoring you, and you deserve it."

She finally lowered her gaze, accepting his remark, and McCoy felt relieved.

"It's very sweet and thoughtful, but embarrassing."

Someone passed by, took her now-empty glass, and thrust another into her hand.

"Why?"

"Mac, I haven't done anything great. And I know enough to know that an option doesn't mean that much. I mean, I'm glad about it, but that's not why I wrote the story."

"I know," he answered, wondering if he was finally "getting it" too late.

"Anyway," she began somewhat reluctantly, looking briefly over her shoulder at the gathered guests. "I guess I'm supposed to circulate and say hello to everyone. It's really nice that they all came tonight."

"I'm very glad I did, Savannah," McCoy said, and was deeply gratified when she smiled before turning away.

But he knew he wasn't out of the woods, yet. He'd made a great tactical error with Savannah and he wasn't sure he could easily make up for it.

McCoy spent another twenty minutes or so talking with the exuberant Taj and another few minutes with Punch before the agent left the party. He was introduced to Donna, Savannah's other girlfriend, who was responsible for getting Savannah to the party and making sure she didn't find out about it. McCoy learned that the elderly white man he'd seen earlier with Savannah was Simon Raskin, Will Shelton's agent.

He watched covertly, even while chatting with any number of people, as Savannah circulated around the room. She had a very quiet grace, and made sure she spoke to everyone, most of whom seemed to be co-workers from her studio. McCoy didn't attempt to approach her again, but was oddly content just to watch her.

A few hours into the party, just as several people were starting to leave, someone else arrived. It was a simple but elegantly dressed older woman who looked familiar, although he couldn't place where he'd seen her before. Unerringly she walked over to Kay and introduced herself. Kay then led the petite woman over to Savannah. When Savannah recognized her she showed genuine surprise and they embraced. Someone brought them each a glass of wine and for the next half hour the two woman chatted, occasionally laughing together. And just when McCoy was certain that the last guest had arrived, yet another woman came in. Young, white, very pretty with a mass of curly blond hair. She seemed to know both Donna and Kay and spent time with the two women.

McCoy was aware when the older woman finally stood to make her goodbyes. She and Savannah again embraced and Savannah escorted her from the restaurant and, he guessed, to the parking lot. When Savannah returned she joined her other women friends, and he watched as they toasted the occasion with another glass of wine.

He'd come to the party out of curiosity and mea culpa. He's spoken to Savannah and didn't catch any attitude from her, which he knew would have been justified given his recent behavior. And then someone recognized him, a former client who was a restaurant guest and not attached to Savannah's celebration, and cornered him to discuss a recent real-estate deal. By the time they parted company, McCoy realized that the party was pretty much over.

It was definitely time to leave. He went over to say good night, hoping for another minute alone with Savannah but accepting that it probably wouldn't happen.

"Oh, Mac," Savannah said, beckoning to him. "You're still here. I want you to meet my friend, Dominique Hamilton. This is McCoy Sutton. He crashed into my car. That's how we met."

It was said with calm straightforwardness, but it sent Donna and Kay into great peals of laughter.

McCoy saw the confusion on Dominique's face. He shook her hand.

"It was entirely my fault, but the story seems to have taken on a life of its own."

"I hope no one was hurt," Dominique commented, looking from one to the other.

"Oh, no," Savannah assured her with a benign smile. "But I think he did it on purpose so we could meet."

Touché.

Again Donna and Kay laughed. McCoy realized that while she was calm and alert, Savannah had been made a tad mellow by the wine.

"Time for the girl to go home," Kay declared ruefully. "I can't leave for another hour or so. I have to help close up tonight."

"I'm the one who brought her, and I'd better take her home," Donna lamented, drawing more laughter.

"I'd be happy to take Savannah with me, but I actually have a date in another twenty minutes," Dominique said.

"A date! At this time of night?" Savannah asked, grabbing onto the only part of the conversation she'd caught.

"Honey, this is L.A." Kay observed.

"I'll take her home," McCoy spoke up. All three women stared at him. It was Donna who recovered first.

"Are you sure? It would help me out. Savannah knows I love her, but I live on the other side of town."

"Don't worry about me. I can get myself home," Savannah said, as if that was a logical option.

Dominique responded by giving her a brief hug as she got up to leave. "You're the guest of honor. Let your friends take care of you, okay? It was a great party. Sorry I got here so late. And let me know how things go with your option."

"I will. By the way, are you still interested in reading it? I think you'll find it an interesting story."

"Absolutely," Dominique responded.

"Great. I'll send you a copy. Thanks for coming," Savannah said graciously.

"Are you sure you're okay with taking her home?" Donna asked him again.

McCoy realized that she wasn't trying to be coy or provocative, but just wanted to make sure that someone was watching out for Savannah.

"I'm totally fine with it. I live in Santa Monica so it's an easier drive for me."

"Santa Monica," Kay exclaimed.

"Ooohh," she and Donna chorused together, indicating their awareness of that upscale part of town.

McCoy grinned.

Dominique blew a kiss to all and left.

Savannah gave the rest of her girlfriends a hug, ending with Kay. "Thank you, Kay. This was a lot of work, but I really appreciate the thought. I'm very touched."

"I think it went well. I met some of your Hollywood contacts," Kay teased, and she and Donna again drawled, "Ooohh."

"And we met McCoy. That alone was worth the price of admission," Donna said.

"Don't pay her any attention," Savannah said seriously to McCoy.

He was amused that she thought he'd take offense.

Soon McCoy found himself escorting Savannah from the restaurant and to his car. In a million years he wouldn't have imagined that the evening would end this way. He felt the need to be careful with her as if he'd somehow, miraculously, been given a second chance. He kept an eye on her movements and a hand lightly on her elbow to guide her, but Savannah seemed in control. She walked slowly to the car and waited while he held the door for her.

Once he was out of the parking lot she seemed to snuggle down into her seat with her head back against the cushion. They'd gone several miles when Savannah spoke.

"Carrie Spencer came tonight. That's so amazing," she said in a tired but clear voice.

"Who's Carrie Spencer?"

"The lady we followed the day you took me to Long Beach."

"You met her?"

"I went back the next day. She was expecting me."

"I repeat. Who is Carrie Spencer?"

She didn't answer right away, and for a moment McCoy thought Savannah wasn't going to.

"Carrie was in love with my father," she said, as if she was simply describing the moon in the sky. "He was in love with her. Later I learned that Carrie knew about his friendship with Rae Marie Hilton, but the two of them never met. She understood totally why they were friends and told my father he should never give it up. She wasn't jealous. She told me so."

McCoy glanced at her. "How do you feel about that?"

She sighed audibly. "Sad. I think Carrie understood my father's dreams better than anyone. She loved him knowing that they might never be together as a couple. She misses him. Love is complicated, isn't it?"

He couldn't have agreed more.

The only thing to do was be cool. Just like the movies. That's what Savannah told herself as McCoy drove.

She still had no idea what had gone wrong between them, nor when it had turned around for him and gone right again. But this wasn't the time to ask questions.

All things in their time.

Savannah only knew she'd learned something significant when she'd looked up at the party and seen him standing across a crowded room.

She chuckled softly to herself and closed her eyes. Maybe she had had a little too much to drink, but there was nothing wrong with her senses. Let him wonder what she was thinking.

When they got to the house she wasn't sure she wanted to get out of McCoy's car. She'd gotten comfortable and warm. They were together in a closed confined space and it was only the two of them. There hadn't been much talk on the way home, and she hadn't felt the need for any. Sooner or later she'd find out what had happened with McCoy in the last few weeks. For now, it was enough that he was here.

When he'd turned off the engine, Savannah got out of the car and started up the driveway to the door, alone. Behind her she heard his driver's-side door close and knew he was following. She couldn't feel her feet; it was as if she was floating, but she could feel her own heart beat and was aware of everything that was happening.

Almost.

She and McCoy had talked at the party. What had he told her again about why he was there? He'd been invited. He'd been standing with a drink in his hand, talking to Punch. She'd felt sorry for him, seeing the big searching question in his eyes—was she going to toss him out on his ear? Good. Let him wonder.

She'd felt silly, she was so glad to see him.

Savannah frowned. She was standing in the doorway of her bedroom. How had she gotten there again? The light was on. McCoy was turning down the bed linens. She hung her purse over the doorknob and sat on the edge of the bed. Now she had to take off her shoes. She stared at her toes. That would mean bending down. *Not.*

Then she saw McCoy's shoes in front of her. He knelt and silently began to untie and remove her espadrilles.

"You have small feet," he commented.

"Thank you. That was a compliment, right?"

McCoy stood up when he was done. "Yes, that was a compliment. Lie down."

She did as she was told. The going backward part didn't seem so hard until she was halfway down. Then she seemed to have gotten very top-heavy and gravity took over. Her head hit the pillow. It felt like a fluffy cloud. A soft moan escaped.

"Mac? I feel like...like I'm rolling down a hill."

"It will stop in a minute. Go to sleep."

She lifted an arm and it flailed about. Something really warm and strong caught it and held on. Immediately the falling sensation stopped. Savannah sighed.

And went to sleep.

* * *

McCoy leaned over and looked into her face. It was peaceful and relaxed and beautiful. He looked down at their clasped fingers and smiled. Just the fact that her grip hadn't loosened at all, even in sleep, gave him an odd feeling. He didn't want to let go, either. They were connected for the moment, but he knew it was still tenuous. He got his shoes off and eased onto the bed next to Savannah, carefully stretching out.

He felt a little keyed up, but, in another way, sort of relaxed. The contradiction made him pensive and McCoy drifted into a thoughtful review of his relationship with Savannah. He had to go all the way back to when and how they'd met. A small ironic smile curved his mouth as he recalled her comment just hours ago at the party. The story of the accident was becoming a legend. He wondered, in amusement, what would the next version be?

McCoy's head rolled slightly to the side, and he suddenly jerked it upright. The movement pulled him out of sleep and back from a dream that was quickly fading. He forced his eyes open. The room was bright with sunlight and he could hear the quiet sounds of morning.

Savannah still seemed to be asleep, but she had moved and turned over, snuggled against his side with her head on his rib cage. He could only see the top of her head and watched it move with his breathing. He was also still holding her hand. As he was thinking about how to get off the bed without waking her, she suddenly spoke.

"You have to go."

"I should," he responded carefully.

"You didn't have to stay all night. I would have been fine."

"I couldn't leave."

Her head came up and she looked at him, almost fully alert, but her eyes soft and questioning. "Why?"

He squeezed her hand. "You had a death grip on my hand."

"Oh." She tried to pull free.

He held on.

She looked at him. "Was that the only thing keeping you here?"

He stared back. "No, it wasn't. To be honest, I think I was afraid to leave. You might not let me back in."

A vague smile played around her mouth, making her look incredibly sexy. "You didn't kiss me good night. I missed that."

McCoy's stomach roiled. He recognized it as instant desire. "I can rectify that."

But she continued to stare at him. "I want to know what happened, Mac. Because I thought…"

He touched his hand to her mouth and silently shushed her. Then he gently turned her face up as he bent to kiss her.

"You will. But not now."

He made no pretense when his lips pressed onto hers. He was ready and she was willing. Their mouths opened against one another and the response was mutual and charged. Savannah rolled closer to him, her slim body undulating against him with a sleepy sensuality that rushed heat and blood to his groin and made him erect.

Savannah's mouth was soft and giving, and the kiss alone sent a wave of dizzying need through his body. He wanted to get closer. He wanted to feel her breasts beneath him, her soft thighs around him and himself inside her. It was so primal that McCoy was shaken by the intensity.

Savannah slipped her hand beneath his shirt to play her fingers on his chest. The tiny tips of his nipples were hard. She helped him shrug the shirt off over his head. He did the same with her light sweater but didn't even try to get the dress off. Neither wanted to stop touching long enough. Savannah pulled the dress from her shoulders, wiggled it down her hips and legs and kicked it off. She rolled onto her back, arched upward and unsnapped her bra. McCoy pulled it free and dropped it to the floor.

He bent forward to suckle a breast, rolling his tongue over the sensitive nipple of one and then the other as Savannah's chest heaved against him, and she moaned deep in her throat. She arched her back and groaned when his hand dug inside her panties and his warm fingers found the liquid opening, rubbing along the tender folds with a slow exquisite movement that had Savannah rocking her pelvis rhythmically against the source of her pleasure.

"Ooohhh, Mac. Yes..."

With his free hand, McCoy awkwardly worked his slacks open, and managed to pull his legs free. He gave his full attention back to Savannah in time to know that she was about to break, her fingers gripping his arms and shoulders as the tension increased in the deepest part of her body. He kissed her again, deeply, their tongues dancing together. He absorbed the panting sounds of her release as he continued to use his fingers to stimulate her tumultuous ride.

Savannah was breathing hard, her body loose and soft. McCoy didn't give her time to completely come down. Knowing she was still sensitive and wet and open, he wanted to catch the waves that rolled within her. He removed her panties, kissing her chest, her belly, as he did so. He lifted his body over her, his knees forcing her legs farther apart, and slid smoothly inside. McCoy gritted his teeth and grunted at the wonderful silky feel of her closing tightly around his penis. Her walls were still pulsing faintly from her first climax, but he began a slow steady thrusting.

Savannah responded, wrapping her legs around his hips and slowly grinding their bodies together. McCoy's hands moved beneath her butt to hold her at the right angle, and they performed a syncopated movement that grew heated and damp and desperate.

Savannah suddenly freed her hands and held them both gently to the side of his face. She kissed his forehead, and stroked his jaw, and held his head against her breasts. McCoy felt like she was offering forgiveness and absolution and the kind of tender love he wasn't sure existed anymore, or that he would ever find. The sweet gesture so moved him that he surged to an explosive release, feeling Savannah's arms holding him close, as if he might otherwise fall into an abyss to his death.

He couldn't have felt more alive.

Chapter 11

Savannah sighed deeply, rolled over and opened her eyes. She was alone in the bed.

She blinked at the ceiling, trying to remember if Mac had really kissed her awake, drawing a sleepy response from her and whispering she was going to be late for work, or if she'd only dreamt it. She still had her watch on from the day before and glanced at the time. She was definitely going to be late if she didn't get out of bed right now.

As she headed for the shower she spotted his jacket and shoes in the living room, and caught a whiff of brewing coffee.

In record time she had showered, returning to the

bedroom to find that McCoy had left a cup of coffee on her bureau. She sipped it while she dressed.

He's a keeper, she thought, surprising herself with the quick assessment.

Back in the bathroom for the last of her preparations, Savannah used her damp towel to wipe away the condensation on the bathroom mirror. She caught her own reflection and thoughtfully studied it. Her eyes were clear and bright despite the celebration the night before and the early-morning bedroom tango with McCoy. That was the image, however, that made her smile—the two of them entwined and going at it with joy and abandon. She *looked* positively content and satisfied. The only thing missing was the purr.

There was no time for a mental replay of the early morning when she and Mac had come to a mostly nonverbal understanding. She could still feel, however, the lovely and physical message he'd left on her body. Her lips looked even fuller from having been kissed, and from having known the full taste of him. Her nipples were still sensitive, as were her inner thighs.

Savannah returned her empty cup to the kitchen. Mac's jacket was still in the living room, but his shoes were missing. She looked through the window and saw him sitting in one of the poolside lounge chairs. He was fully dressed now and seemed to be enjoying his coffee, the peace and quiet and his own thoughts.

Savannah watched him for a moment, suddenly

feeling a bit shy. Something had changed between them last night, but she wasn't completely sure what it meant, or where it would lead.

She went out to join him. McCoy glanced over his shoulder at her approach and smiled.

"Good morning." He held out a hand to her.

She returned the greeting as she took his hand. McCoy gently pulled her closer and slipped his arm around her waist. He not only hugged her that way, but pressed a kiss to her breasts through her linen top. It was such a tender unexpected gesture, and sweetly erotic.

McCoy deftly shifted her and Savannah found herself seated on his lap.

"I can't do that," she frowned.

"I'll let you know if you're too heavy."

She sat, gingerly. It wasn't that she doubted the strength of his thighs, or feared appearing coy, but there was something very intimate about the position. And, playful. His arms looped lightly around her waist.

"I'm impressed. You're actually up and dressed in decent time."

"*I'm* impressed. You're still here," Savannah chuckled boldly, and then added. "You look so comfortable, sitting out here."

"I am," he said quietly. "What time do you have to be at work?"

"Within the hour. I won't be late. And you?"

"I have an eleven o'clock appointment and a lunch meeting at one. I'll call my assistant to double-check."

"Maybe we should get going," Savannah said, a little uncertain about what to expect the morning after.

"In a minute. Look, about last night..."

"No explanations needed," she interrupted quickly, her heart somersaulting over the thought of what he *might* say. "The party was very nice. I owe Kay a big one. This morning here was—"

"Amazing," McCoy now interrupted.

"Yes, it was," Savannah agreed almost in a whisper.

"That's what I wanted to say, Vann." He squeezed her waist, stroked her arm, pecked a little kiss on the side of her neck. "I wanted to tell you how special it was to me."

Savannah slowly smiled, even though she felt alert and tried to read where McCoy was headed. She nudged her shoulder into his. "Is there something else?"

"God, no. Believe me, I thought of canceling all my appointments and maybe talking you into taking today off so we could spend it together."

"And what would we do the whole day?" she asked with mock puzzlement.

McCoy sighed and closed his eyes briefly. She thought she detected a soft moan.

"Let me put it this way. Clothing would not have been required."

He then slid his hand up her back to press against her head, moving in for a kiss. She'd never had a morning kiss quite like it. It was softly erotic, their lips and tongues teasing together. It was gentle foreplay, and she felt her body responding.

He caressed her moist lips with his thumb. "If we keep this up…" His voice was a husky growl, replete with longing.

"I know," She nodded, her forehead against his.

Savannah shifted to get off his lap, acutely aware of the hardness of McCoy's growing arousal against her thighs.

He held her in place. "Wait a minute. There's something else I wanted to say. I have to attend an event next week. I was looking forward to—"

That was as far as he got when they both became aware that someone was at the front door of the house. They could hear the faint opening and closing of it, heavy footsteps on the tile entrance, followed by a deep male voice calling out.

"Vann? Anybody home?"

Savannah quickly stood up, as did McCoy when the intruder finally reached the side door leading out to the pool area.

"Hey," the male visitor said, looking back and forth between Savannah and McCoy.

Savannah shook her head. "Hey, yourself. You're about two weeks late."

She knew that McCoy stood silently, watching. She knew that he was drawing his own conclusions. She opened her arms as she walked toward the new arrival, and he did the same. They embraced, the taller man lifting her off her feet.

"Uncle Sam owns me lock, stock and my future pension. I got here as soon as I could. I have to fly out day after tomorrow."

Savannah was about to make introductions when the two men naturally approached one another. The grinning stranger thrust out a hand to McCoy whose hesitation was imperceptible except to her.

"McCoy Sutton," he spoke first.

"Harris," the man responded.

Savannah touched Harris's arm, but she looked at McCoy. "He's my brother."

Savannah accepted the hand of the valet who attempted to help her out of her car. Her legs got momentarily tangled in the voluminous flow of silky fabric, and the high heel of her dress sandals snagged in the hem. She fought with the dress but still managed to exit with grace, grabbing her evening clutch purse and the shawl purchased from Domino Hagan. She took a moment to compose herself before heading into the ornate theater complex where the black awards ceremony was being held and taped, to be televised later on network TV. Somewhere inside, Punch Wagoner was waiting for her.

To be honest, she would rather have attended with McCoy.

Harris's sudden appearance the week before had delayed McCoy's explanation of why he couldn't invite her. His attendance was not mandatory, but it was all about business. Over a Moroccan dinner a few nights later, McCoy had told her why. She'd heard all about

Jeff Peterson and his sister, the would-be actress Cherise Kim Daly. McCoy was attending the awards with Cherise, a fact made more acceptable by his admission that he wished it could have been her instead.

While hearing firsthand Cherise's real place in McCoy's life, Savannah couldn't help being disappointed that business would take precedence over their private wishes. But, to be fair, Savannah had told McCoy with equal candor that Punch had already informed her that she would be going with him because the awards ceremony was a must-go-to event for her now that she was almost an insider in Hollywood.

All around her, what seemed like hundreds of formally dressed men and women were also headed into the theater. Savannah automatically searched for McCoy, but there were too many people and it would be easy to miss him. Punch had told her he would meet her in the foyer, since he had the tickets, and she was his guest. Donna had been unable to secure extra tickets to the event even though she was to perform, but Punch had called, excited about the prospect of introducing her to several producers and directors who would be in attendance.

She was still getting used to the idea of being an insider. And it made her uncomfortable. Savannah admitted that she loved the attention being given to *Fade to Black,* but it meant dressing up and being put on display. It meant possibly curbing her natural reticence and showing her enthusiasm when talking about her option. It would mean talking about her father, and she knew that maybe even a comparison would come up. The name *Will Shelton,* as she'd discovered in the last year, was a familiar name in the industry, especially among black professionals.

Savannah suddenly quaked at the thought that she might be compared to her father, or that others had raised their expectations of her because of who he was and his status in black Hollywood. But more than any of these considerations, Savannah was deathly afraid that she might, even inadvertently, embarrass herself or stain her father's reputation.

She was a little intimidated, but Punch Wagoner would accept no excuse from her not to attend. It was a golden opportunity, he'd said. Savannah knew he was right. Such moments were hard enough to come by and it would be foolish to ignore the one being offered to her. After all, she was representing more that herself and her work.

She stood near the ticket booth feeling alone and out of place, hoping for the remote possibility of spotting someone else she knew. Instead, Savannah found herself a one-person audience for a private show on Hollywood taste, fashion and industry functions.

She'd never seen so many skinny black women in her life.

Many of them were stunningly beautiful, but almost all had the carriage and presence of someone who wanted or needed to be seen, and who already counted themselves as a VIP. They smiled and postured, and posed with practiced ease in front of the cameras as they sashayed past the cordoned-off media photographers.

She'd also never seen so many black women with long flowing hair, thanks to the advanced technology of believable hair extensions and weaves.

The parade of women were a kaleidoscope of colorful sparkly gowns designed to flatter and reveal. Savannah glanced down at her own dress, purchased just the day before on a frantic search with Kay to find something smart, comfortable and affordable. She'd settled on a strapless gown by Donna Karan without any extra adornments or glitter. The design flattered her curves, and the color, a matte champagne hue, emphasized the honey tones of her skin. She'd even submitted to getting her hair professionally done, and a mousse of natural ingredients gave it body, shine and a funky spiked styling that she actually loved. Her jewelry consisted of a pair of diamond stud earrings that, ironically, her father had given her for her eighteenth birthday. She didn't bother with a necklace. Donna had pointed out that when the stars went out for the evening they hardly ever wore elaborate jewels. Less was better. None was more effective.

"You look fabulous."

Savannah turned to the voice and found Punch viewing her from head to toe. His black tux made him look oddly uncomfortable, as if the outfit didn't quite suit his body type.

"Thanks. Can I go home now?"

He laughed and put his arm around her shoulder. "Not until I have a chance to show you off and introduce you around. We need to start laying groundwork, and events like this one, where everyone comes out, are a good place to start."

"If this is all about *Fade to Black,* wouldn't it be better to let the work speak for itself? Nobody knows me here."

Punch was steering her toward the ticket taker and the entrance to the theater. "In answer to your first question, that's not how things work in Hollywood. In answer to your second question, that's about to change."

He looked at her again with satisfaction and nodded. "You do your father proud."

"I hope so. I feel like he's done a lot of ground work for me just being my father. I…I don't want to let him down," Savannah murmured.

In response, he took her hand and hooked it through his arm, patting it. "Just leave everything to me. I know what I'm doing."

Savannah had never imagined that the much-touted event would be so unexciting.

For all the buildup about the awards show from others, she'd thought the night would be far more magical than it actually was. Because it was being taped, announcements, musical starts and award acceptances sometimes had to have two or three takes. Even during the proceedings on stage, the audience got up at will to leave and return to the theater, no one standing on ceremony. She became fascinated with watching how often some of the women left, presumably to use the facilities. But it finally occurred to her that they might also have been making repeated grand entrances to be seen and to catch the attention of important people.

The one thing that did catch Savannah by surprise was the realization that there were actual celebrities in the audience. She saw Steven Spielberg, Whoopi Goldberg, Jay Leno and Jamie Foxx. Even she couldn't deny the thrill of seeing people whose work she had enjoyed over the years.

At one point Punch recognized someone across the aisle and got up for a brief discussion. Then, to her dismay, he brought the man over to be introduced to her. Savannah smiled and was pleased she said all the right things, as evidenced from Punch's approving smile, but she had no idea who the man was. Afterward, the lights went down and the program continued. She perked up when a dance number was introduced and Donna appeared with the troupe. Savannah had never seen Donna perform before, and was blown away by her obvious talent and energy. The routine was fast, with intricate athletic steps that had the audience cheering at the conclusion and the dancers' bodies glistening with sweat as they left the stage.

But Savannah found her attention drifting after that. The proceedings around her faded into the background as she settled into the more satisfying activity of reliving, in her memory, the last night she'd seen McCoy....

It had been the previous Saturday, and he'd suggested that they go to a Rollerblading exhibition on the

Venice Beach boardwalk. She'd been enthralled with the daring and talent of the amateur performers, some in their seventies, she found out to her amazement. She'd gotten a kick out of realizing how many people were flat-out exhibitionists, doing anything to get attention while wearing next to nothing.

She and McCoy had foregone lunch in favor of ice cream and strolling leisurely through the carnival-like atmosphere of the pier. They'd sat overlooking the ocean together, once again comparing their upbringing, discovering more similarities between them, openly confessing what they didn't like. The sun began to set, sending afternoon light across the ocean so that it sparkled jewel-like, with dazzling clarity.

"You know, I have a rain check you owe me," McCoy said, looking at her through his dark glasses.

"You do? For what?"

"I seem to remember being invited to use your pool. How about now?"

"Would you really like to?" she'd asked.

"It's a lot more private, and we won't get salty," he'd grinned.

It was only after they'd reached the house and Savannah had gathered towels and poured two glasses of wine that she realized McCoy didn't have a swimsuit on or with him.

"What do you want to do?" she asked. But as soon as the words left her mouth she already knew what his answer would be.

"How do you feel about skinny-dipping? Would it offend you if I got in butt naked?"

"I've never done it," she confessed.

McCoy had taken the towels and wineglasses out of her hands. "Go change. I'll wait outside."

In her bedroom Savannah dug out her bathing suit, a one-piece tank that was good for actually swimming. She hadn't done much of that since coming to L.A. She also found a bikini she hadn't worn in two years. When she put it on she discovered that it still fit. And she was surprised and pleased with how she looked. She kept it on.

When she'd returned to the backyard, the sun was very low in the western sky. There were no lights on around the pool, but the interior lights glowed, sending out a bluish watery wave of muted color. McCoy was already in the water, breaststroking laps from one end of the pool to the other, hardly making a sound. She could see his body, but the rippling water hid any details.

Savannah sat on the edge of the pool and dangled her legs in the water, enjoying watching McCoy's coordinated prowess.

"Want me to keep count?" she asked.

"I want you to come in and join me," he said before neatly executing a swimmer's turn and starting back toward her.

"I will."

But McCoy upped the ante when he suddenly turned on his back and did a dead man's float. She caught her breath as he was totally revealed to her. She wasn't embarrassed, but enthralled with his penis bobbing against his leg in the water.

Savannah knew that his actions were calculated, and didn't hold it against him. He was getting the effect he wanted from her. She was starting to feel warm and overdressed in her bikini, and a thickening heat and sensitivity was making her achy and aroused between her legs. She slid into the pool. The water was anything but cooling.

Savannah enjoyed just treading water, or gently sidestroking around McCoy as they played cat and mouse, her laughter breaking out often in the early-evening air. In that moment she felt deliriously happy just being in McCoy's company. She knew…hoped…that he was going to put the move on her. To his credit he was subtle and surprising about it.

After twenty minutes McCoy climbed out of the pool, dripping water as he reached for one of the fluffy towels. He dried his face, hair and chest, holding the towel out like a banner, waited for her to come out of the water as well. When Savannah finally did so, she turned her back and he wrapped the towel around her, drawing her against his body. Despite time spent in the pool, his skin was very warm. He bent to nuzzle her ear, and down the side of her neck. The juices of desire were already making her wet.

She closed her eyes as her tension grew, as did his arousal. It was completely dark in the yard now, except for the pool lights, so that when McCoy silently kissed her, took away the towel and removed her bikini top with a one-handed gesture, Savannah made no objection. She aided him in his goal by stepping out of her bikini bottom, and letting McCoy embrace her so that their bodies pressed together in all the important places. The dalliance in the pool had just been a warm-up, but already it was way beyond that.

She boldly reached between them and rubbed and stroked his erection. He rotated his hips against her hand. Savannah gently broke free and made to turn toward the house. He grabbed her hand, pulling her, instead, into the dark overhang of a tree, where a cushioned lounger had been left on another day.

She no longer cared where they were, as long as she could have McCoy's experienced lovemaking and the tender caring he brought with it. Besides, there was something highly stimulating about doing it under the open sky, at night, with the warm California air rushing over their bare skin. The lounger didn't allow for much creative positioning, and they were both too hot, too ready, to play around any longer. But it was McCoy who lay flat on the lounger, drawing Savannah down on top of him.

In a role reversal, she lay nestled between his legs while they kissed languidly, undulated together, their hands freely exploring wherever they could reach. Savannah definitely felt she had got the better end of the bargain, and wondered if McCoy had selflessly planned it this way. It didn't take long for her to want more. She wanted to know the full thrusting power of him as he skillfully brought her to a satisfaction that left her limp and breathless.

Just when she thought she could stand no more, McCoy, holding her tightly to him, flipped their positions. Without waiting, without warning, without any need for further stimulation, he slid into her body. Savannah arched her back, welcoming him and maneuvering him deeper.

Neither of them lasted very much longer, the urgency of the moment and the danger of exposure heightening the experience. They were both sweaty and panting when they collapsed together. She opened her eyes and looked up through the tree branches to a bright starlit sky. She smiled.

This is the stuff of romance, she remembered thinking. And of movies…

During yet another break in the presentation, after stifling a yawn, Savannah excused herself and left the theater. The foyer was mostly empty, although there were several people being individually interviewed and photographed, the bright strobe lights creating isolated bright spots in the open space. She had no real need to use the facilities, but opened the outside doors and enjoyed the feel of fresh air. Savannah stood for a few moments before making her way back into the theater to take her seat. She hadn't worn a watch. Donna had also told her it was déclassé to wear one to any social evening in L.A. Time was not important.

She was crossing the lobby, her gown swishing and billowing around her legs when a door opened and McCoy suddenly walked through. They were about twenty feet apart, both taken aback by unexpectedly encountering the other. But the surprise quickly faded. Wordlessly McCoy beckoned with a slight incline of his head, and Savannah followed his lead. He walked unhurriedly, uninterrupted by security and various personal bodyguards, until he reached a series of rooms all labeled VIP/Invited Guests Only. He opened one door and held it as Savannah entered ahead of him.

The greenroom, as she'd learned the preperformance waiting room was called, was elegant if simple. It was empty of anyone but laid out with refreshments and other amenities for the comfort of the guests. He turned to face her, slowly putting his arms around her.

"My God, you look beautiful," he said quietly.

"Why the surprise?" she teased, still delighted with his compliment.

He chortled silently, shaking his head as he carefully looked her over. "I'm not surprised, I'm pleased."

"Thanks, Mac," she whispered. "You look pretty hot yourself. You clean up good."

"It's almost over," he whispered, his hands restlessly holding her by the waist. He began kissing her. It was sweet and thorough, but brief, and seemed to serve the purpose of taking the edge off a much deeper need.

"What are you doing after this finishes?" she asked, enjoying the cuddling.

He sighed in resignation. "Escorting Cherise to a party. My job is mostly to make sure no one tries anything inappropriate. She makes it a lot harder when she flirts with male celebrities in an effort to be seen and photographed with them. And you?"

"Pretty much the same. Not that I'm going to flirt with anyone. Punch has this grand plan and I know he's going to make sure I get photographed with whomever he thinks will do me good to be seen with."

"I warned you," he said, not unkindly. "Hollywood is an alternative universe. The rules are different here."

"I know, but I'd rather…" she stopped, grimacing prettily.

"Me, too," he said, kissing her again. "Got any plans for the weekend?"

"I've invited Caroline Spencer to the house for dinner. I'd like to get to know her better. What do you have in mind?"

"I thought we'd drive down to Long Beach, stay at the house down there. A friend is playing at a jazz club Saturday night. We could do the beach…"

She grinned broadly at him, knowing his idea of beaching didn't necessarily involve the beach or swimsuits.

"…play the rest by ear."

"I'd like that very much."

"Good. I guess we should get back inside. Are you ready?" McCoy asked, releasing her and opening the door.

Again, there was no one around as they headed back

to their respective seats, McCoy peeling off to the left and covertly blowing her a kiss.

She was still smiling when she retook her seat. Getting through the rest of the evening was going to be a snap.

"You know," Taj said, chewing thoughtfully on his food. "This tastes so good 'cause I don't have to pay for it."

Savannah laughed, watching as he devoured a side of baby back ribs coated with a thick tangy sauce. She was working her way through a plate of mahimahi served with roasted vegetables. They were at a restaurant that she'd let him select. It was noisy, with the tables too close together, but it had a lovely atmosphere, a very decent band playing music, free wine with dinner. She knew it wasn't necessarily going to be great wine.

"I can see you're enjoying the food."

"This is one of my favorite places," Taj said, enthusiastically sucking the tender meat from a bone. "A lot of musicians hang here. Sometimes Hollywood biggies will show up for the food and the music."

"If I haven't already said so, thanks for all your help with *Fade to Black*."

"I should be thanking you," Taj said, attacking another rib. "I got a call from a friend of Punch's who has a record label. He wants to hear some of my stuff. Word got around that I produce and I have my ear to the ground on up-and-coming talent."

"I'm happy for you."

He looked at her pointedly over the top of his glasses. "This don't mean that I now owe you dinner. I ain't rich like you."

Savannah laughed. "I think we're even."

She heard a ringing tone and realized it was her cell phone. She hastily searched for it in her purse but it had stopped ringing by the time she found it. Checking the LCD she read that the call and text message was from Punch. It instructed her to call right away.

"Taj, I'm going to step outside to return this call. It's too loud in here."

"Take your time, Baby Girl. Can I order another side of the sweet-potato fries?"

"Of course. Order anything you want," she said, making her way through the tightly spaced tables to the front of the restaurant and outside to the street. There were several bistro tables, and she sat at an empty one, keying in Punch's cell-phone number.

"Hi," Savannah responded to his hello. "Sorry I missed the call a moment ago. I couldn't find my phone," she chuckled.

"I figured you were at dinner."

"I am, but the message said it was important. I thought I should call you back right away."

"Well, I have good news and bad news," Punch started.

Savannah grew focused on the tone of his voice. He sounded disappointed. "I think I'd like to have the good news first," she said, trying to keep it light.

"I got a call from the agent of the actress the studio was considering for your script. She loved the story but was concerned about the impact on her career if she played a black actress passing for white. I guess I should tell you that the actress herself is white. It seemed the only way to go, given the story line. She's a wonderful actress with a solid reputation. She asked if you'd written anything else. I told a little white lie and said you had something else in mind."

"And that's the good news?" Savannah asked, puzzled. "I'm afraid to ask what the bad news is."

Punch sighed from the other end of the line. "I'm really sorry Savannah. I tried my best, but the producer has decided to pass on the option. He's chosen one of the other two scripts to film."

Chapter 12

McCoy reached for the telephone even as he continued to review the closing documents for one of his clients.

"Yes?" he answered absently, turning a page.

"A messenger just arrived with something from Ben Damon. It's marked urgent and confidential."

McCoy grew alert and closed the report he was reading. "Bring it right in." He was standing when his assistant, Colin, entered the office, handed him the envelope and turned to leave.

McCoy was already breaking the seal on the package. "Thanks. Hold my calls, will you?"

He was so anxious to read the contents that he simply leaned back against the edge of his desk and quickly reviewed the information. He sat just like that for nearly half an hour. When he was done, he went around his desk and sat down again. He silently considered what he'd read, sometimes staring off into space, sometimes scribbling notes. He made a few phone calls, indirectly related to the delivery, and then called Colin to give him further instructions.

He responded to a few business calls, but prepared to leave an hour before he normally would. The last thing he did was to call Savannah at her office. She answered, sounding professional as she always did, her voice and tone light.

"Am I interrupting anything?"

"Hi, Mac. No, it's kind of quiet right now. What's up?"

"How are you doing?"

"I guess you mean since Punch called about the option. I'm fine, really. I admit the idea of having a movie made from my script had me going for a while, but I guess it wasn't meant to be. It's too bad. I even had an actress in mind for the part." She laughed lightly. "It's a good thing I didn't give up my day job."

On his end, McCoy silently grinned at her sense of humor. "Maybe something else will happen with the script. Punch told me he'll continue shopping it around. He has some ideas."

"It's nice of him. This whole thing has given me so much more pride and admiration for my father. To think about the constant rejection he faced every time he tried out for a part…I don't know how he kept going for twenty-five years."

"Because he was a good actor, and he believed in himself and he understood that you never take no for an answer. You're just like your father, Vann, whether you know it or not. You may not be part of the Hollywood thing, but you're talented and smart and level-headed."

"I bet you say that to all the girls," she accused lightly.

"No, I don't," McCoy answered in a dead-serious tone. "I say what I mean, especially to a *woman* I care about."

"Are you trying to make me cry?" she asked, her voice now quiet.

"No. I thought I was calling to cheer you up, but I'm doing a damned poor job so far. Look, no matter what you say, I know that having the producer turn down the script so fast after getting you all excited, must have bummed you out. Let me take you out to dinner. I have a surprise for you."

"You do?"

"I think it's something you've been wanting for a while now, whether or not you know it."

"Are you going to give me a hint?"

"Are you going to have dinner with me?"

"You know the answer to that, Mac. I'd love to."

"Good. Then go home. I'll pick you up there and we'll eat someplace local."

"Okay."

"Now for the surprise. I've located Rae Marie Hilton. She's alive and well and apparently living in paradise."

He was confused when there was total silence from the other end of the line. No exclamation or gasp, no shriek of surprise.

"Vann?"

"Are you serious?"

"Of course I am."

"But…how did you find her? How did you even know where to look?"

"I have my sources."

She sucked her teeth. "Mac, that's a line from a movie. It's a cliché."

"But it's true. I used a P.I. service. It's the first time, and I still can't believe that they actually found her."

"Where is she? What do you mean, she's living in paradise?"

"According to the file I received on her, she's been living on the island of Kauai for at least the last fifteen years."

"Kauai? Like…"

"Hawaiian island. The Garden Isle. Remote and quiet."

"Is she okay? Does she live alone? What else did you find out?"

"Quite a lot. I'll tell you all about it at dinner. But I have another idea you might like even more. A good friend of mine owns a house on the north shore of Kauai. I've already called and asked if I could use it for a weekend. He said yes. How do you feel about the two of us flying over to meet her? It might answer a lot of questions you have about Ms. Hilton and your father."

"I don't know, Mac. If she went there to get away from her bad experiences in Hollywood, our going over there to ask a lot of questions might bring them all back. Maybe she doesn't want to be reminded of that time in her life."

"Maybe. But what if she'd love to tell someone about it? What better person than you?"

"Why would she? Rae Marie Hilton shared a lot with my father. Maybe that's all she needed. What if she's, you know, still pretending to be something other than what she is? If I go nosing around in her business she might resent it. It sounds too much like using her."

"Okay, I understand that. But here's a suggestion."

"I'm listening."

"Why don't you call her and find out? I have her phone number right here."

Savannah had never been to Hawaii. It was on her short list of places to visit, but it somehow seemed like something to do once she retired. She knew only a few people who had ever been, and mostly they'd stayed on the popular tourist island of Oahu where Honolulu and Waikiki were located, along with the Pearl Harbor Memorial and the dormant volcano, Diamond Head… and they'd complained about the long brutal flight from the east coast. She'd often heard Oahu referred to as a big metropolitan city but with palm trees and coconuts.

It had taken her a week to get up the courage to call Rae Marie, as McCoy had suggested, and then she had been stunned into nonresponsiveness when the mysterious lady herself had answered the phone, in a soft but deep voice with a silky, brandy huskiness to it.

"Speak up or I'm hanging up," came back the blunt order.

Afraid that Rae Marie would be true to her word, Savannah had confirmed that she was talking to the right person, and then had rushed into an apology for interrupting her. Then it was Rae Marie's turn to be silent for a moment.

"How did you find me?" was her first question.

"A friend of mine did the legwork. He's an attorney in L.A."

"And just why was your friend looking for me? Am I supposed to know him? Am I being sued?"

"No, of course not. He was doing me a favor. I'd found out about you from papers my father kept. Your journals and letters."

There was a very soft intake of breath from Rae Marie's end. "Who was your father?"

"Will Shelton. I'm his daughter, Savannah."

There was another gasp.

"Will Shelton. Good Lord. I haven't heard that name...how is he?"

Savannah had immediately warmed to Rae Marie when the flurry of questions had been not about herself or about trying to find out what Savannah knew about her, but about Will Shelton. It had probably been a decade or more since they'd laid eyes on each other, but still her first thought was of her old confidant, fellow actor and friend.

"My father passed away about ten months ago. He'd been sick for a year before that."

"Oh, no. Oh, Will..." Rae Marie had tsked and moaned quietly to herself at the news.

Savannah heard pain, regret, even helplessness in the woman's reaction, and there was nothing she could say to soften the blow of her news.

"I'm sorry. I thought that somehow you'd know."

"No, no. I knew nothing. I've cut all of my old Hollywood ties. It was not a happy time in my life."

"Yes, I know."

"You do? Of course. You said you'd found my letters and journals."

"Yes. And I did read them, but I promise you, I haven't shown them to anyone else..."

"Then, you know?"

Savannah understood exactly what Rae Marie was referring to. It was at the center of her friendship with her father. It was, quite frankly, at the core of Rae Marie's life. Her identity. Who she was, or who she wanted to be.

"Yes, I know. Yours is an amazing story. It must have been so hard for you."

"It was. It was a terrible burden not to be found out." Her chuckle was hoarse. "I made fools out of a lot of Hollywood folks. I was estranged from my family for years because of what I was doing. Lord, if I didn't have Will... Tell me about Will. He was my only friend in those days. The one person who knew everything, and didn't hate me for what I did."

"Ms. Hilton, I have a lot of things I want to tell you. There are hundreds of questions I need to ask. I was wondering if it's possible for me to come over to Kauai to meet you? I already have a place to stay, and—"

"When can you come?"

Savannah and McCoy landed at Lihue Airport on Kauai late on a Thursday night after a six-hour flight from L.A. McCoy had taken care of everything: arranging for a rental car, getting directions to the house in Princeville and driving the two of them, in near-pitch-black darkness on one-lane roads, to the north side of Kauai. He'd done most of the talking and calming of nerves, reassuring her that the arranged meeting with Rae Marie would be a good thing. It would answer questions and perhaps provide closure for both of them.

But Savannah had not admitted to Mccoy that one of her greatest fears had been that the woman who was her father's friend had had her private history trolled for the benefit of a film script and might reject her if she knew. While it hadn't been completely self-serving, it had been an invasion. Savannah wasn't sure if Rae Marie would or could forgive her for that.

The split-level house belonging to McCoy's friend was set back about fifty yards from the road. In the dark, as they unpacked their luggage from the car, Savannah could hear the ocean breaking on the shore behind them in the night. They had to walk down one set of stairs from the parking area, and then up another to the front of the house. Inside, the common spaces were on the first level: the kitchen, dining alcove, living room and lanai or outside terrace. There were two bedrooms on the lower level, one with its own bathroom and walk-in closet. Savannah and McCoy chose this master suite to use during their stay.

They'd brought no food with them, as McCoy's friend had recommended, opting for the adventure of eating out locally. They finally settled down in the king-sized bed together, snuggling close under a lightweight comforter. With the lights out and the quiet outside wrapping them in a safe blanket of peace and comfort, Savannah listened to McCoy's resonant voice as he reminded her that she now had a chance to set the record straight by reaching out to Rae Marie. It was she who was now keeper of keys to the kingdom that was her father's rich history. She was the remaining conduit of his connections to Hollywood and of his loyal friendship to a woman who had needed it.

Savannah curled herself against McCoy, letting his voice lull her into a safe place where she could sleep—and dream.

With McCoy at the wheel of their Jeep, Savannah was free to sightsee and fill her eyes with the incredible color and lush landscape of Kauai. It was a very small island, dominated by Waimea Canyon in the middle and the nearly inaccessible Na Poli coast on the north. The towns and villages hugged the coast, connected by one main highway. But that continuous line was broken at the start of the Na Poli coastline, discouraging development of any kind.

She had a sense of why the island might have appeal to Rae Marie Hilton. In some ways, like L.A., it was possible to become anonymous here, to fade into the slow and easy lifestyle. She'd been told that people either fell in love with it or could only stay for a limited period of time before running back to what a larger community might offer. Those who stayed embraced the laid-back daily life of few demands and little stress.

The small towns seemed like a throwback to the slapdash hippy days of the sixties, and, indeed, there was plenty of evidence that the sixties sensibilities were alive and well here.

The next morning Savannah thought she was still dreaming when the distinctive crowing of a cock woke her up at dawn. It was such an unexpected sound that she got out of bed to peer out a window to see the majestic bird, feathered in red and black, strutting along the walkway next to the house.

But her amusement quickly gave way to nerves as she and McCoy prepared for their drive to meet with Rae Marie. She had given Savannah precise instructions on how to find her house, saying she was not easy to find, and that had been by design.

While McCoy maneuvered the winding narrow roads, Savannah sat with a box balanced on her lap. It was the one she'd found in her father's closet with all of Rae Marie's secrets.

"It's going to be all right, Vann," McCoy said, sensing her excitement and anxiety.

"I know. I just don't want to say the wrong thing to make her uncomfortable or bring back bad memories."

"Relax. She's probably a little scared of you, too. You know her secrets. She knows nothing of you, except that you're Will Shelton's daughter. I think you're going to find that Ms. Hilton is a tough survivor. She'd have to be to live the life she has."

They found Rae Marie's paradise hideaway near Ha'ena. The small cottage was off a dirt road, obscured by thick shrubbery and trees, bird-of-paradise, plumeria and hyacinth growing wild around it.

"Oh my God, it's beautiful," Savannah whispered, not realizing that she'd spoken at all.

The house was painted green and faded easily into its surroundings. It seemed almost magically tucked away.

There was an ancient Volvo parked under a tree on one side of the house. Three steps led to the front door, the landing of which was the start of what seemed to be a wraparound porch. Mac turned off the engine, and they just sat in the car staring through the windshield at the setting. The house gave the impression of being just a few hundred feet off the beach, but it was actually built on a plateau or shelflike flat rock about thirty feet above the rugged beach. The surf could be heard breaking against the shore.

Despite the roar of the ocean, it seemed a quiet setting. There were the sounds of the land and the woods and the beach, of birds and the incredible throaty crowing of another rooster. Savannah and McCoy got out of the car, feeling very much as if they had stepped back into the forest primeval. Savannah caught a movement from the corner of her eye and turned to find an older woman dressed in dark loose pants and a light tunic top with a mandarin collar, coming from the side of the house where the Volvo was parked. She carried a basket laden with fresh-cut flowers and greens. Accompanying her, the way the family dog might follow its owner about, was a black cat, its yellow eyes questioning their presence but showing no fear of them.

"Hello. You made it. I thought I heard a car come up. Sorry it took me so long to get here. Not as fast as I used to be," the woman said, calmly accepting her limitations brought on by age.

To Savannah, however, her movements appeared brisk and energetic and far more youthful than aged.

"I'll take that," McCoy said, jogging forward to relieve her of the large basket.

"Oh, it's not all that heavy, but thank you. You're McCoy." She stopped and stood glancing between them. "And you're Savannah, of course." Making her own assessment, she nodded finally in approval. "Come inside. I made some lemonade and shortbread cookies with macadamia nuts."

Despite all that she knew about her, Savannah was still taken aback by Rae Marie's appearance. If she didn't already have the knowledge she'd gained from reading the letters and journals, she could never have mistaken the woman for anything but white. The once-thick dark hair was cut bluntly at the nape, and was now almost all silvery gray. The texture was still wavy, as in her youth, and was now made even more so by the constant humidity of a small island with its own rain forest. Her eyes were an inquisitive green, clear and bright in a face that was still beautiful despite exposure to damaging sunlight, ocean air, wind and probably a lack of respect for any skin care regimen.

But one thing was clear, at least to Savannah. Whatever demons had once ruled Rae Marie's life had been banished. She saw only an aging woman who'd finally made peace and settled with grace into being exactly who and what she was.

"Out back I've been experimenting with growing some of the smaller orchids. The air is perfect up here for that. I also have some white ginger and frangipani. I know a young man from the Kauai Nursery and Landscaping on the west side who's been promising to build me a little greenhouse."

"So, when do you have time to sleep?" McCoy asked, making her laugh.

"Well, you know what they say. There's plenty of time to rest when you're dead."

She sat in a worn chair that was angled to take in the view out her window overlooking the ocean to her left, and her guests on the inside to her right. The cat jumped up on the arm of the overstuffed chair, not to sit in Rae Marie's lap, but to lie along the back of the chair just behind her shoulder.

"You seem happy here," Savannah observed.

"Oh, I am," Rae Marie said. "But it took a while, and it wasn't easy. I fought it tooth and nail, as if I didn't have a right to be happy. Believe it or not, things actually got easier after a local accused me of being another mainlander pretending to be a native. I got angry and said I *am* a native. I'm not Hawaiian but my existence is rooted in the culture of brown and black people. Of course I had to explain that, but it turned out to be true what we were taught—the truth *will* set you free."

Savannah exchanged a look with McCoy who, finally seeing Rae Marie, had an intuitive sense of how unsettling and confusing her life must have been. His gaze was filled with respect, as if he recognized just how her life had finally come full circle.

Rae Marie grew reflective, her eyes distant and wistful as she let her past creep back.

"I was the lightest one in a family of high-yellow

blacks. I think even my parents were shocked at how I looked. You could see all my family in my face, my eyes and mouth and laugh. But I was so *white.* Don't know how to explain that. I do know it made my life and the life of my family very stressful. We were accused of all kinds of things I still can't talk about. I guess I was fifteen when I decided what I was going to do to make it better."

Savannah could see the pain that still surfaced to haunt the older woman.

"If you read my letters and journals you understand what I'm talking about. But instead of coming to Hollywood and finding myself, I got lost there. Keeping a secret as big as the one I had was tiring and very dangerous. Will Shelton was the one who kept me on track so I wouldn't go out of my mind. He never judged me. He was just my friend. I don't know what I would have become without him during those years."

The black cat stretched and arched its back, and then jumped carefully into her lap, walked in a circle and settled down in a ball to sleep. Rae Marie stroked its glossy fur absently.

"I know a lot of people would have vilified you passing," McCoy spoke up. "But I think you were pretty gutsy to attempt what you did. In a way, it was a great feat of acting, pretending to be someone you're not, on and off the screen. It was a great performance that no one really saw except for Will Shelton," McCoy commented thoughtfully.

"I never looked at it that way. I just wanted to be accepted. I wanted to fit in. The whole time I was in Hollywood I kept thinking of that movie, *Pinkie*. A beautiful young Southern girl who is black passes for white. Then she comes back home to face the music and the humiliation from both blacks and whites in town. It was quite a movie for its time. Very daring. Very true.

"Where I fell into trouble, I think, was believing that Hollywood could validate me, make me real. I put too much store in the whole becoming-a-star dream. I was lucky to realize before it destroyed me that becoming a star wouldn't save me. That trying to be white wouldn't either." She squinted at Savannah. "Did your father ever marry Carrie?"

"You know about her?"

"Oh, yes. And I know she knew about me, but we never met. I also knew she and your father were in love. I told him to marry her."

"He never did," Savannah acknowledged.

"Fool," Rae Marie lamented, her voice quiet and sad. "He wanted to fix everything for everyone, but could never quite see how to fix his own life. He told me if I wanted to save my soul I better get out of town. Take up another career. I ended up here. No career, no husband or children, but hundreds of dear loving friends. I think now on how silly it all seems, to chase after those celluloid dreams. It took me all my life to learn I am responsible for my happiness. I can *choose* to be happy. Sounds simple, doesn't it?"

McCoy glanced at Savannah and she knew what his silent look meant. She lifted the box from the floor where she'd placed it after sitting down.

"I have something for you."

"Oh, no gifts, please," Rae Marie chuckled. "I don't have room for another thing in this house. Not if it needs to be dusted."

"No, it's nothing like that." She got up to carry the box to Rae Marie and held it out to her. "These belong to you. I thought you'd want them back."

Rae Marie lifted the box top and found inside all her letters and journals left in Will Shelton's keeping.

"Will kept all of this?" she asked Savannah. "I wonder why? I always thought that after I left California he would just throw it all away. Writing was a way for me to vent, since I had only your father to talk to. These letters and journals aren't important anymore."

"The thing is, I think they are," Savannah said.

"Me, too," McCoy added.

"Well, what do you think I should do with all of this?"

"I have a confession to make," Savannah began. She saw that she had Rae Marie's attention and rushed on. "When I first found the box I read through just about everything. Afterward, your life and what you went through in Hollywood as an actress gave me an idea for a story. I sat and wrote a film script."

"You wrote my life story?"

"No, not at all. I didn't know where you were, or if

you were even still alive. I didn't know if you'd approve of having your life exposed, so I wrote a story about a character who goes through some of the same things that you did when you came to Hollywood. Then, just when she's about to make a real breakthrough in a major project and will be promoted as the next big star, she's found out. She's pulled off one of the greatest acting feats there is, and no one sees it. The studio execs only see that she's not what she said she was, instead of seeing her true talents. Etc., etc."

Rae Marie stared at Savannah wide-eyed for a long time. "How clever. It sounds like a daring idea to me. What happened to your script?"

"Vann got an agent who got her an option deal that fell through just two weeks ago."

"My agent is still trying to sell the idea, but I think what I'd really like to do is write your life story. I could fictionalize it, if you like, or maybe interview you over a period of time and put together a biography. What do you think?"

"I don't think my life's interesting enough, but I'm flattered and honored that you'd want to take the time. Let me think about it." She replaced the top on the box and rested her hands there. "And thank you for returning this to me. I might read these letters and journals again."

"Vann and I would like to take you to dinner," McCoy said.

"That would be lovely. I know a nice little place in

Poipu if you don't mind the drive." She started to get up and suddenly settled back down in her chair. "Wait. I have some questions of my own to ask."

"Of course. Anything," Savannah offered.

"Do you know that your father has a theater named after him somewhere in L.A.? I forget where."

"Yes, McCoy took me to see it a few months back. I met some of the theater troupe."

"Good, good. And do you know that Will and I did a movie together that was never released? The movie hinted at a love story between the two of us that the press made a big thing out of. That's not what was happening in the story but a lot of people missed the bigger picture.

"Mac had a copy and we watched it together. I thought it was very good," Savannah said.

Rae Marie stared at McCoy, her gaze thoughtful. "What do you think of Savannah's film-script idea?" she asked him.

"It's surprisingly good. I'd only suggest one change."

"You would?" Savannah responded, surprised.

McCoy looked at her. "I think you should write into the script a role that's very like your father. It would be a nice way of honoring who and what he was."

"I like that idea. Would you mind if I see a copy?" Rae Marie questioned.

"There's one inside the box," Savannah said, pointing. "I'd love to hear what you think."

"Oh, I'll be honest with you," Rae Marie said dryly. "So, are you two an item?"

Savannah glanced quickly at McCoy, but she could tell that Rae Marie's question had caught him off guard as well.

"Savannah and I haven't talk—"

"Okay, here's a simple, straightforward question. Are you in love with her?"

McCoy gave his full attention to Rae Marie as if they were the only two in the room. But then he took so long to answer that Savannah felt disheartened. She knew what he had been going to say before he was interrupted: that the two of them had not discussed anything personal involving a future, let alone marriage. She'd never before seriously considered getting married, knowing she was perhaps overly influenced not only by her parents' failed relationship, but by her father's lack of action on his love for Carrie Spencer.

Her relationship with Mac was a surprise to her. It seemed to have evolved naturally, but in a way that had already led Savannah to the conclusion that she was falling in love with McCoy Sutton. It was happening, so what was there to talk about?

But Rae Marie's question had put the idea of marriage out there. Now, Savannah wondered, what if the love was all one-sided? That Mac liked her she had no doubt. But what kind of future did he have in mind if it was nothing more than "like"?

McCoy turned his attention directly to her. She was afraid to breathe, afraid to move or do anything that would disturb the delicate balance of the moment. He reached out his hand to her and she entwined her fingers with his. She could see the muscle working in his jaw.

"As it turns out, yes, I'm very much in love with her."

Savannah tried to say something, but there was a curious blockage in her throat. Still she couldn't pull her gaze away from his.

"Don't lose your way like I did," Rae Marie cautioned quietly. "There is nothing as important in life as loving and being loved. Nothing."

"Oh, it's pouring out," Savannah said disappointed, sliding closed the glass door to the lanai off the bedroom they were using. "I thought it never rained in paradise. Tomorrow's our last day here and I wanted to drive to Kee Beach. The guide book says it's mostly deserted."

The room was a little bit chilly and she quickly got into bed, pulling the comforter up around her neck. McCoy finished brushing his teeth and turned out the light in the bathroom. When he started across the carpeted floor he had a towel wrapped and secured around his waist. He pulled it free before climbing in next to Savannah.

She turned to him, seeking the warmth of his body.

"If you read that in the guide book I can guarantee it's no longer deserted. Every visitor to the island is going to find it because they think they'll be the only ones there. If it rains all day tomorrow I promise I'll bring you back for another visit, TBA."

"I haven't thanked you yet for this trip. Maybe I should start a running tab with you."

He laughed quietly. "No thanks needed, but I'm curious. What do you have in mind?" he asked.

"It wouldn't be a surprise if I told." She kissed his chest, playing idly with his nipple, letting her fingers trail seductively downward into the valley of his navel. "Mac, I want to know what happened between us weeks ago. Around the time I met with Punch Wagoner."

He sighed. "I was hoping you'd forgotten about that. I was behaving like a jealous kid."

"Over who? Who?" Savannah asked, her voice puzzled. "Mac, there wasn't anyone else I..."

"I know that. This was different. I thought I was being played."

"By me? I don't understand." Her fingers were still teasing along his skin. When she reached a little below the navel she felt the muscle contract. She lightly went back and forth with the same results. McCoy moved his hips restlessly, and she felt the head of his penis as it grew to nudge against her hand.

"Are you going to torture the answer out of me?" he asked, his voice suddenly deeper and strained.

"Why don't you just tell me?" When he lay with his eyes closed Savannah came up on one elbow and studied his features. "Mac, did you mean what you said to Rae Marie? When she asked if you're in love with me?"

He looked at her, his expression a cross between bewilderment and annoyance. "Of course I did. I wouldn't go around saying something so important if it wasn't true. And I knew that Ms. Hilton would probably not take kindly to me lying to her or Will Shelton's daughter."

"I agree. But it's just you and me now. I'd like to hear it firsthand."

Mac was looking at her, as if calculating the risk of being honest. Finally, he let out a deep breath.

"When you got the deal with Punch, I felt as if I'd been there before. It spooked me. I got married when I was in law school. We moved to L.A. together when I got a job with a law firm there, before I decided to specialize and open my own practice. In those days I didn't care that much for L.A., but you go where the work is. What I didn't know was that my wife, Paula, who I always knew had a very good voice, was quietly planning and building a voice career behind my back. Maybe she was afraid I wouldn't understand. To be honest, I probably wouldn't have."

As McCoy talked, Savannah once again snuggled next to him, once again went back to stroking his chest and stomach and listening.

"I can't decide what hurt more, that she wasn't open with me, or that she was ultimately successful. Of course, once she became successful, and I mean the whole nine yards—record deal, tour, concert opening—we were through. I couldn't compete with the kind of attention, money, opportunities that she was getting. Fast-forward, she's a big performance star in

Europe. She makes three or four appearances in the U.S. each year."

McCoy rolled his head to look steadily at Savannah. He suddenly reached out to caress her cheek, her neck and shoulder, urging her to lie against him as he hugged her gently to his side.

"When I was starting to know you, what first caught my attention was your strong sense of self. You seemed centered and not easily influenced by anything or anyone. I liked that you didn't look like every other woman in L.A. You stood out. Everything about you was different and attractive to me. You were not only not particularly interested in all things Hollywood, they didn't seem to impress you. It was surprising, to be honest, once I learned Will Shelton was your father. But I liked that you could hold your own, weren't afraid to speak your mind. You got points for making me laugh."

"Can I interrupt to say the feelings were entirely mutual?"

"I'm relieved to hear that," McCoy said quietly. "But I think I almost blew it when I realized you'd written a script, and I assumed you were about to go Hollywood on me. And I thought you might be trying to use whatever influence I had to get ahead. I was disappointed."

"You were being an ass," Savannah said just as quietly.

For a second McCoy was stunned by her response. Then he suddenly chortled and broke out into a full chest-and-belly laugh.

"I'm glad you find it funny now," Savannah said calmly. "At the time I couldn't figure out what was going on. Did I suddenly grow a horn in the middle of my head? Did I show a few extra pounds in the wrong place? Were you just not that into me? I was hurt, Mac, because like you, by then I was also very attracted. And it was for all the same reasons. Considering you tried to kill me at our first meeting, I loved that we actually had so much in common."

He was still laughing, but it had died down somewhat. He rolled toward her, gathering Savannah into a tight embrace, kissing her face and searching for her mouth and silencing both of them. *Enough talk, already.* But she was relieved. The facts, when revealed, were understandable and human. Much better than if he'd withdrawn suddenly because he'd decided she should get bigger boobs.

McCoy controlled the kiss, finally ending it and relaxing back into the bedding again.

"Maybe Ms. Hilton tipped my hand quicker than I would have thought to, but the message and meaning are the same, Vann. I do love you. It kind of snuck up on me. I finally realized how I felt just when I thought I'd lost you to La-La Land."

"You really confused me, too. When I saw you at that party Kay gave for me when I got the option, I didn't know what to think."

"I'm surprised you even remember the party."

"I remember everything, Mac. Especially the next morning." She sighed. "That was wonderful."

McCoy took her hand and led it inexorably down to his groin and his full erection. He placed her hand back on the thick stem to, once again, encourage the erotic stimulation she'd been teasing him with.

"There's more where that came from," he whispered.

Savannah followed through, playing with him to great effect while he kissed her and toyed with her nipples until her breasts seemed engorged and she was quietly panting.

She suddenly moved onto her back and McCoy rolled atop her body. He cupped her vagina, using his fingers to test her readiness, drawing a whispered sigh of longing from her. She trapped his hand between her thighs, urging him to continue his exploration, and making her moan in ecstasy.

"Now, now," she pleaded.

McCoy obliged, sliding deep inside with one smooth stroke.

She arched her back. "Mac, wait. There…there's something…I have to say."

He'd already begun to thrust between her legs, riding against her and drawing out the response they both wanted.

"Can't it…wait?" he growled, right on the edge.

"It's important. I love you, too," she said against his ear.

He climaxed.

Chapter 13

"Hi, Mr. Raskin. This is Savannah Shelton calling."

"Ah, Savannah. How nice to hear from you. As a matter of fact I had in mind to call you myself."

"Really?"

"Yes, but you first. What can I do for you?"

"Well, I've been thinking about doing something for my father. You know, like a memorial of some kind. When he was sick he didn't want a lot of people to know about it, and he didn't want a fuss when he died. But, now I'm feeling that something needs to be done to recognize his life and contribution."

"I agree, and that's exactly what I wanted to talk to you about. I understood Will's feelings about publicity and too much exposure. He was very careful not to let his personal life overlap with his work. That's not always an easy thing to do in a town that seems to thrive on gossip and scandal."

"It's taken me a while to see he was all about the work."

"In a way it was too bad," Raskin lamented. There are lots of people here and abroad who liked and admired your father. He was a real gentleman. He was a great mentor to other young black performers. He knew that Hollywood wasn't always a fair environment, but he managed to survive."

"That's kind of what I'd like to celebrate about him," Savannah said. "I didn't always understand the pull that Hollywood had on him, but I respect that he had the courage to go after a dream. I know that now," Savannah recalled her own recent adventures. "Anyway, I don't want my father's name to be forgotten."

"I agree with you.

"I'm planning on giving his scripts and papers to his alma mater, Morehouse College. I've also been in touch with the American Film Institute and they're interested in some materials."

"That's a great start. Now, for a memorial here's what I have in mind. I think we need a big name to MC the event. There should be testimonials and maybe even clips from Will's films shown throughout. Have you thought about establishing a scholarship fund for aspiring black talent?"

"No, I haven't, but it's a great idea."

"Good. How about sometime in the fall? Everyone's back from summer breaks, and the new season of films and TV is just starting up again…."

Savannah stood at the back of the small conference room holding a plastic cup of white wine. Crowded into the space were about fifty of her coworkers who, like her, were listening with amusement and pride to their former music coordinator, Tyrone James Sparks…aka Taj…as he thanked everyone for the great send off. The oval conference table was littered with the aftermath of the surprise party, and several balloons had drifted to the ceiling and hovered over the gathering.

"Yeah, I had a real good time here. My paycheck was a little skimpy—"

Everyone laughed.

"—but I think I'm about to make up for it."

Taj searched the room until he spotted her. Savannah shook her head slightly, not wanting him to single her out for anything, but she already knew that Taj was going to do his own thing, as he'd always done.

"I'd like to thank Savannah Shelton for the part she played in me getting this opportunity. No point in trying to hide, Baby Girl." Taj pointed in her direction. "This woman is on the money. I did her a favor, and she turned right around and did the same for me. Because of Savannah, I was put in touch with a record-label exec who listened to my demos, and asked me to produce the CD of a new group they have under contract."

Savannah grinned at Taj, thanking him for his acknowledgment while also signaling that thanks wasn't necessary. Everyone in the room turned as one to look at her, some breaking out in applause and whistles.

"Y'all better keep an eye on Baby Girl. She's about to break out. I'm tellin' you. Major writing talent right under your nose."

Savannah joined the chuckles at Taj's warning, knowing that it was due to her own tenaciousness that word had not gotten out about the failure of her option.

Pretty soon people began leaving to drift back to their own departments and offices, everyone wishing Taj well as he was about to head out on his great Hollywood adventure…just as he'd always predicted he would. Savannah remained where she was, watching Taj work the room as he made his way to her, shaking hands and accepting additional congratulations.

"See, this is what you get for not letting me do the music on your last hip-hop film," Taj said to one of the execs. "You could have had me for *life.*"

"I don't know if we could have handled that," she said dryly, drawing even more laughs as the room finally emptied out.

Taj, grinning, stood in front of Savannah. "Was I cool or what?"

"You are *way* cool," Savannah smiled. She kissed Taj lightly on his cheek. "And I'm so proud of you. Now don't do anything to embarrass yourself out there. You've just become a role model."

Taj groaned. "That's what my mama told me. But I want to tell you that it ain't over for you yet. I'm tellin' you, you wrote a good script and someone is going to notice."

"I'm now confident that something could happen—*will* happen with the story. Anyway, I have something else I'm working on. I'm thinking about doing a book about my father."

"There you go," Taj said approvingly. "Pretty soon I won't even be able to talk to you. You're going to be huge."

Savannah laughed at the often-used Hollywood term for someone about to make it big. She put down the cup of wine and together they headed out of the room.

"I better get back to work. While I'm waiting to be huge I still have to earn a living. I don't suppose you're hanging around until five o'clock?"

Taj looked at her as if she was out of her mind.

"*Hell,* no. I'm outta here soon as I finish packing up my tapes and CDs. The serious celebration happens later. You coming?"

"Thanks for the invitation, but I already have plans."

They began walking slowly down the corridor in the direction of their respective offices.

"I'll still keep in touch, Baby Girl. You're like my good-luck charm or something."

"I'm glad it's worked for you."

Taj suddenly turned to her, his eyes bright and triumphant. "The first thing is, don't give up. Remember your father. Will Shelton *never* let anybody see him sweat."

* * *

McCoy chuckled over the note he was reading. It was handwritten in a beautiful classic script with an old-fashioned fountain pen on handmade rag paper. The entire presentation was done in the way a certain generation had been taught, a way that, in the age of e-mails and text messaging, was fast becoming a lost art.

In the note Rae Marie Hilton was thanking him for being the catalyst for her meeting Savannah and himself. She'd thoroughly enjoyed them and hoped they'd be returning to Kauai soon, this time as her guests. But also, Rae Marie wanted to thank him for showing her that the world had changed. She wasn't going to be hung in effigy for transgressions in her youth against her race, and against herself.

There was a slight knock on the door, but before McCoy could react the door opened and Cherise stepped in. There was a postscript to the letter that he'd have to read later. Resigned to the young actress's lack of protocol, he carefully replaced the letter in its envelope and slipped it inside his leather portfolio.

"You're not busy, are you?" Cherise said charmingly.

Her gaze looked troubled by the possibility, but McCoy knew that whatever he answered would not deter her for a minute.

"What can I do for you?" he asked instead, having learned her methods for getting his attention. "You have to make it quick. I have plans and I have to leave soon."

Cherise stopped short of grimacing, merely looking bored. "Oh, what's-her-name?"

"Savannah," McCoy said without a trace of rancor. He half stood and politely indicated the chair Cherise was to sit in.

"Savannah. That's so decades ago. She sounds like somebody's grandmother."

"One day she will be," McCoy murmured.

Cherise shrugged. She reached into her Prada bag, a recent acquisition made possible by her contract to costar in a pilot for TV about three African-American sisters, and removed a script. She held it in front of her chest, the title page facing him.

"I want to do this story," Cherise announced.

McCoy's gaze went from her excited expression to the front page of the script. He stared at the title and author, not allowing his own features to register recognition.

The script was titled *Fade to Black.*

McCoy leaned forward to take the script from her hands. "Where'd you get this?"

"My agent, of course. Actually, he doesn't even know I've read it. It was on his desk and I didn't think he'd mind if I took a look at it. After all, I'm paying him to find projects for me, right?"

McCoy said nothing as he thumbed through the script that he himself had already read months earlier.

"I don't know who Vann Shelton is, do you? I thought maybe you could find out for me."

He was not at all surprised that Cherise had not

been able to connect the dots and recognize the name of the author.

"Ask your agent. You're paying him, remember?" McCoy said, not unkindly.

He'd learned that he had to be firm with Cherise and set boundaries. Even then there was no guarantee that she'd honor them.

He made a mental note to tell Jeff Peterson that they were now square. No more favors for a while. He handed the script back to Cherise, wondering how many other copies were circulating among agents. Had anyone bothered to tell Savannah?

"As a matter of fact, why aren't you talking to him about the script, if you're interested?"

"Because I want to make some changes. This is about some black woman who passes for white. We are so over that," Cherise said with a dismissive wave of her hand and a roll of her eyes. "But the story could still work. Want to hear my ideas?"

"Not particularly," McCoy said. "It does no good to tell me because I can't do anything about it, and I won't. You don't know who the screenwriter is, or his intentions, and you shouldn't have taken the script without your agent's permission."

"Well, I didn't want him to show it to anyone else."

"Did it ever occur to you that he didn't show you because the part wasn't right for you?"

"But I can make it right," Cherise persisted.

"Cherise," McCoy began patiently, sitting back in his

chair and covertly checking the time, "I know you feel you can do anything, and maybe you can. But you *can't* do everything. No one can. Give it a rest. You have three or four projects already lined up. You've been in L.A. less than a year and your career is off the hook. What else do you want?"

"This script," she said, once again holding it up.

McCoy slowly shook his head, shrugging lightly. "Can't help you with this one. Sorry."

Cherise sighed and replaced the script into her bag. "You're probably angry with me for just walking in unannounced. Let me make it up to you. Can I take you for a drink?"

McCoy didn't let his surprise reach his eyes. Cherise leaned forward just enough to let her silky Tse sheer blouse, with its deep V-neckline, swoop slightly open to reveal an enticing glimpse of swelling breast. In his recollection Cherise had yet to thank him for anything, so he was only amused by her strategy. And a little disturbed. He had never been interested in Jeff's baby sister in that way, but knew there were plenty in Hollywood who wouldn't hesitate to take her up on the offer. It might even be the subject of a future conversation. But not today.

"Like I said when you came in, I have plans. And I don't want to be late. Anything else?" He stood up.

Cherise mewed with her glossed lips and stood as well. "I guess not."

And then, McCoy had another idea. She would never consider doing anything that would put her in a bad light. He suddenly realized that all he had to do was find a legitimate reason why Cherise shouldn't consider the part in *Fade to Black.*

"Tell you what," McCoy began, his hand lightly on her shoulder as he steered her to the door. "Leave the script with me. I'll read it over tonight and get back to you tomorrow."

"Oh, Mac, that is so great! I know you're going to see I'm perfect for the part. With a few changes, of course." Cherise pulled the script out again, kissed the cover sheet for good luck, and gave it to him.

McCoy gave her an indulgent smile. "We'll see."

He studied Savannah closely while she read through the letter he'd received from Rae Marie Hilton. McCoy was sure that she wasn't aware of the gentle lift of her brows or the warm smile on her lips, indicating pleasure and high regard. At one point she gave him a covert silent glance, and he knew she'd gotten to the passage where Rae Marie mentioned her expectations for the future of their relationship. He gave nothing away when he met Savannah's gaze. They hadn't gotten that far, yet.

"What a lovely letter," Savannah sighed, folding the letter. Before handing it back she took a whiff of the delicate paper. "I think she sprayed it with perfume. That's so sweet. I think she likes you, Mac."

"I don't think I've ever received a perfumed letter before. Definitely a custom I like," he said, putting the letter away.

"I got a letter, too," Savannah said as she took a sip of her wine. They were sitting in the open-air garden of a restaurant that was buzzing with conversation and laughter from diners seated all around them.

"Are you going to let me read it?"

"I don't think so. It's a girl thing."

"That's not fair, Vann. I showed you mine," McCoy said, trying to sound aggrieved.

"I know, and thank you very much," she said in a soothing tone.

He chuckled. "I'm going to remember this." He reached for her hand, smoothing over the soft skin with the pad of his thumb. "I missed you today."

She grinned happily. "I'm here now. We spoke this morning."

He shook his head. "Not enough."

"We'll have to do something about that," she murmured playfully.

"I'm counting on it," Mac said, raising a brow. He cleared his throat. "Have you heard anything from Punch about your script?"

"Actually, I put him onto Dominique Hamilton. She's a black actress I think would be perfect for the movie. She's interestd. But I'm also excited about the biography Rae Marie has consented to me writing about her life. She's going to send me more materials."

"Do the one about your father first. It will be a great lead-in to the one about Rae Marie."

"That's a good idea," Savannah said, nodding. "I'm

looking forward to seeing her again. The next time I'll take a recorder. But I'd like to see more of the island."

"Did you like it there?"

"Very much," Savannah sighed. "It had a certain peace and quiet that's hard to find."

"I actually have to go back over to the islands myself, day after tomorrow. I need to check out some property for a client. And I'm about to close on an investment I'm going into with two other partners. We've been negotiating for almost a year."

"I know it's business, but I wish I could go with you," She sighed and looked around.

"You sound content."

"I am. It surprises me a little. I never thought I'd feel this away about L.A."

"Any particular reason?" McCoy asked nonchalantly.

She gave him a sly look, her eyes sparkling, turning him on so suddenly that he felt like a kid with a crush. The feeling was thrilling, and scary. It had been so long since he'd been willing to let his guard down and open his heart, that the thought of losing Savannah made his palms instantly sweaty. Encountering her now seemed like a small miracle. He didn't believe it could ever happen again.

"One or two," Savannah answered.

Not caring that they were in a public place, not even particularly noticing at that moment, McCoy leaned farther across the table and kissed her. He was gratified by the sultry longing he saw in her eyes.

"Mac," she said softly.

He wasn't sure exactly what Savannah was acknowledging, but suddenly he wanted to be alone with her. He signaled for the waiter.

"Are we leaving? We haven't had dessert yet," Savannah said.

He handed the waiter his credit card. "I have something at my place I think you'll like."

There was no need for him to tell her what and, fortunately, it seemed clear that she very much wanted the same thing.

He didn't bother turning on the lights. They got as far as the living room before he deftly spun Savannah half around and into the circle of his arms. She was waiting for him with parted lips and hurried breathing. The moist meshing of their lips and tongues made blood throb in his temples, his heart and groin. He rocked his arousal against Savannah, his stiff erection drawing a whispered moan from her.

McCoy ran his hands down her thighs, gathering the material of her jersey dress until he reached the hem. He broke the kiss just long enough to pull it over her head. She kicked out of her sandals, and he made room for her hands to work on his belt and fly. He helped by quickly unbuttoning the shirt and shrugging out of it.

"Am I going too fast?" McCoy growled against her mouth, their breaths rushing together in need and anticipation.

"Am I?" Savannah asked in return.

"I just feel like..." he started, and then struggled for words.

What was he trying to say?

Savannah looked up into his face with a knowing smile. She released her bra and circled him with her arms to press her chest against his, her nipples gently stabbing him. McCoy hugged her, burying his face against her neck.

What was he trying to say?

"Mac? I'm not going anywhere. I'll be here when you come back."

"I was just remembering what Rae Marie told us," McCoy said, restlessly caressing her back, kissing her and cupping her breasts.

"I know," Savannah nodded. She kissed his chest. "If she's right, if what she said was true, then we're pretty lucky, don't you think?" She began slowly walking backward, unerringly maneuvering them to his bedroom.

He'd never felt so vulnerable, so wary of loss. When Savannah reached the edge of his bed she lowered herself, pulling him with her. His hands slipped into the elastic band of her bikini panties, tugging them down her legs as she positioned herself on the bed, willing, ready and able to give him what he didn't even know he was looking for until meeting her. Until the magic of falling in love with Savannah.

Nothing else matters, Rae Marie had said.

McCoy knew she was right.

Savannah was whispering in his ear, her breath sending a sensual signal down his spine as he settled between her legs. He drew a pillow under her hips to deepen the angle of his entry. She contracted around him, the exquisite pressure urging him into a rhythmic thrusting.

As if sensing what he was going through, Savannah held him, encouraged him, with sudden tenderness.

"Mac, it's okay. Don't worry. I'll be here when you come back."

That's what he wanted to hear.

Chapter 14

Savannah carefully carried the tray of drinks through the back door and out to the pool area. A small table was set up as a sideboard, with a round platter of fruit, cheese and crackers. The sun was hot and melting, but there was also a slight late-spring breeze that cut the effects of the heat in half. It was not, however, enough to stop Donna and Kay from their sunbathing routine. They both sat on the steps leading in or out of the pool, half in and half out of the water.

They were in conversation with Carrie Spencer, who was seated in a lounge chair under the complete shade of a tree, a wide-brimmed straw hat and the kind of oversized dark glasses made popular decades earlier by the likes of Audrey Hepburn.

In a lounger, also protected from the sun under a tree, Domino Hagan lay stretched out on her stomach, totally engrossed in a copy of Savannah's script, *Fade to Black.* She was reading revisions suggested by Punch Wagoner and her own agent.

"Iced tea, lemonade and sangria. Take your pick," Savannah announced setting the tray down. "But you'll have to serve yourselves. I'm off the clock," she joked. Having said that, she selected a glass of tea and took it to Carrie.

"You don't have to treat me special," Carrie laughed. "I would have gotten up like everybody else."

"I don't mind," Savannah said. "I'm so glad you decided to join us after all. And I wanted to show you that your African violet was alive and well," she added, pointing to the potted plant that Carrie had left outside the yard months earlier. It had grown and blossomed, necessitating a bigger pot.

"Will loved African violets. I don't really know what made me leave it that day I came by. But I'm glad you've taken care of it."

"So, where is he?" Kay said, sipping her lemonade and pressing the cold glass against her cheeks.

"Where's who?" Savannah asked, leaving a frosty glass on the ground next to Domino's chair and walking away.

"McCoy Sutton. You think we don't know what's going on? You don't even like L.A. and you manage to find one of the few eligible men in this town without issues," Donna huffed.

Kay and Carrie laughed.

"Maybe you're looking in all the wrong places," Carrie suggested to Donna.

"Maybe you shouldn't work so hard at looking," Kay added.

Savannah glowed under all the implied compliments from her friends. "Maybe we should just leave McCoy out of this and enjoy each other."

"Where is he?" Kay asked.

"He had business in Hawaii. He was supposed to return yesterday but he called to say he'll be back tomorrow."

Donna and Kay exchanged looks and together responded. "Aaawww."

"That's so sweet," Donna said.

"He called to say he's going to be late," Kay piped up.

"Don't laugh," Carrie said serenely. "We should all be so lucky."

That caused an instant silence. Then, Donna and Kay sighed longingly.

"Savannah, I need to talk to you."

Savannah turned to find Domino sitting up on the edge of her lounger. Her eyes were hidden behind dark sunglasses, but her voice and facial expression were otherwise very serious.

"Sure. What about?"

"Your story…"

"Savannah, you forgot the napkins. Want me to get them?" Kay asked, standing and stepping out of the pool.

"No, I'll do it," Savannah answered, heading for the kitchen. "Give me a minute," she called out to Domino.

By the time she returned less than a minute later, Donna and Kay were filling their small plastic plates from the platter. Carrie handed Savannah her empty glass.

"I think I'm going to leave now. It's getting late, I've probably had too much sun, and I want to avoid some of the afternoon traffic."

"So soon?" Savannah said with regret.

She'd grown close to Carrie in the months since they'd finally met, finding the older woman strong, centered and filled with a kindness and wisdom that Savannah admired. It was not hard at all to see why her father had loved Carrie, and she was sorry that he had not seen his way clear to making her his wife. She now believed it would have been the absolute right thing for both of them.

"Savannah?" Domino said again.

"I'm sorry. Just another minute," Savannah apologized to Domino once more, as she prepared to walk Carrie to her car.

Farewells were exchanged, and Carrie thanked all the younger women for including her in their afternoon.

"It's hard to find this kind of friendship in L.A. Everyone always seem to have their own agenda," Carrie said.

"I'm so glad you came," Savannah said, watching as Carrie got into her car and turned over her engine.

"I'm so glad you invited me. Maybe you and your young man will join me for dinner soon? I'll call you."

Savannah waved as the older woman drove away.

She returned to the backyard and encountered Domino waiting for her, her glasses pushed to the top of her head, her eyes wide and anxious and excited.

"Sorry 'bout that," Savannah shook her head. "You wanted to tell me something?"

"It's about your script. It's even better now."

Savannah smiled. "Thanks. It's stronger, don't you think?"

"It's great. And I'm doing it."

Savannah blinked. "Seriously?"

"Yes," Domino said, "I love it. It's just the kind of challenging role I've been searching for since I got to L.A. I know this director who's interested in working with me. Can I option the story from you?"

Savannah tried to talk, but didn't know what to say, Domino's obvious excitement steamrolling over her in a rush of words and thoughts.

"I…I don't know. I should talk to Punch…"

"Okay, he probably doesn't know who I am. The thing is, I was born to play this part. I understand this character."

"What are you two talking about?" Donna asked, nibbling on a cheese-laden cracker as she wandered over to join the conversation.

Savannah smiled ruefully. "Domino wants to do the script I wrote."

"It's *fabulous.*"

"Is it a musical?" Donna asked. "I'm trying to get back into my dancing."

"Can I do the catering? I can cook for a cast of thousands," Kay shouted across the yard.

Savannah laughed even though she could tell that Domino was dead serious. "I don't know what to say."

"Say you'll take an option. I'll have my agent call yours."

"Does this mean I have to throw you another party?" Donna asked.

"If all goes well she'll be able to buy some very expensive champagne," Domino chuckled. "And a dress to wear to the Oscars."

McCoy disembarked and headed directly for the terminal exit. He had no checked luggage to wait for, having taken only a carry-on leather duffel and his laptop.

He maneuvered LAX with the ease of someone who had left and arrived at the international airport so many times that he knew it by rote. The trip had taken two days longer than originally planned. He was tired and just wanted to get home, his mission accomplished.

McCoy tuned out the public announcements of flights arriving and departing and the pages being made for individuals as he considered the satisfying results of his trip. There'd been no time to see Rae Marie Hilton again, but he had spoken to her. But most reassuring had been his late-night phone calls to Savannah. His longing, her words of love and their promises had been enough to convince him he'd done the right thing while on Kauai.

He sidestepped a youngster running across his path and into the arms of a waiting relative. In doing so, McCoy realized that his name was being paged. Heading for the nearest information desk, he identified himself to the woman behind the microphone.

"I heard my name. You have a message for me?"

"Yes," the woman said, leafing through several papers on her counter. She read from one. "There's a car waiting for you. The driver is outside baggage claim."

He frowned. "Are you sure? I gave instructions to be met on the departure level."

"That's the request I got. About five minutes before your flight landed."

Slightly confused, McCoy shrugged. "Okay. Thanks."

He walked to the escalator and took it down, heading right for the exit. But once outside he didn't see his normal car service or driver parked at the passenger pickup point designated by the terminal. Feeling impatient and tired after three days of intense negotiations, McCoy was not in the mood for guessing games or delays. He began pacing the sidewalk, looking for signs of the distinctive car he was used to taking.

"Mac! Over here!"

He stopped in his tracks at the familiar voice and turned around. He saw a pair of feminine arms waving in the air to get his attention, and focused on Savannah's smiling face. Slowly smiling in surprise, he walked to her car, its hazard lights blinking.

Savannah was watching as he approached, her eyes bright but uncertain as she searched his face.

"I know you didn't plan on me being here, but I thought I'd surprise you. I called your…"

That was as far as he'd let her get. McCoy stopped in front of Savannah, put his bags down and engulfed her in his arms. His mouth covering hers in a hard kiss cut off her explanation in midsentence.

"C'mon. Take it home, buddy," a terminal security officer complained loudly.

"I hope you don't mind. I called your office and told your assistant I was going to surprise you. I wanted to pick you up."

"Great," McCoy murmured, inches away from kissing her again when Savannah pulled out of his arms.

"We can't stay here. Put your bags in the car."

McCoy did as he was told, although his astonished gaze followed her every move.

"I know you weren't expecting to see me, but…"

"Vann, this is one of the nicest surprises I've had in a long time. I can't tell you how much I'd rather see you than my sixty-year-old, balding driver."

She laughed merrily.

"How've you been?" he asked, taking her hand and squeezing it. The answering squeeze told him everything he needed to know.

"I've missed you. I'm glad you're back."

"Me, too. Anything interested happen while I was away?"

McCoy thought her smile seemed sly and knowing. "A few things. I'll tell you about them in the car."

"Where are you taking me?" he asked.

Savannah grinned like a Cheshire cat. "That depends. Your place or mine?"

"Surprise me," he said quietly.

"Okay. How was your business trip? Did you get what you wanted?"

McCoy thought of the half-acre plot of land just north of the town of Hanalei, with a two-story house that needed a little work, but had amazing potential.

"Pretty much," he answered. "It's something I think you'll like."

She looked puzzled. "Is it something you want me to like?"

"Absolutely. What you think is important to me."

"Thank you," Savannah said, her eyes bright and warm. She hesitated, and held out her car keys to him. "I know how you feel about my road skills. Here. You can drive if you like."

McCoy kissed her briefly and, leaving her by the driver's side, walked around to get in the passenger-side door.

"You drive," he said calmly. "I trust you with my life."

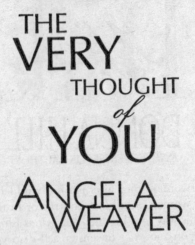